LIVE IT OUT
A SK8R BOI ROMANCE

JENN ALEXANDER

Bywater Books
2023

Bywater Books

Copyright © 2023 Jenn Alexander

Print ISBN: 978-1-61294-261-2

Bywater Books First Edition: April 2023

Printed in the United States of America on acid-free paper.

Cover designer: Ann McMan, TreeHouse Studio

Bywater Books
PO Box 3671
Ann Arbor MI 48106-3671

www.bywaterbooks.com

To Sandra, Addie, & Eloise.
You are who I want to live out all my adventures with.

Chapter One

Spencer Adams furiously strummed the high E string on her guitar, her pulse accelerating as she slid her finger along the neck, pulling the note higher and higher. The tension of the song coiled tightly inside of her, and then with an exhale, she stepped on the effects pedal that melted the note down into an electronic whirring, pulsing and filling the room. She locked eyes with Mari Tanaka, who held the final bass note grounding the static whir. The air vibrated with energy, and then they simultaneously stepped on their pedals to kill the sound.

A long, empty silence followed, as though the energy had been vacuumed up.

Then, the four band members erupted.

"That was fucking awesome!" Sienna O'Brien, their singer, sat at the very edge of her seat, the enthusiasm so tangible Spencer half expected her to jump up. "Wow."

"Hell yeah," Mari said.

"We nailed it," Wren Collins, their drummer, agreed.

Spencer had no words. She was still trying to catch her breath as she came down from the adrenaline high.

"I have a few new lyric ideas we can try out on our next run-through," Sienna continued, "but oh my God, that new ending. Chills."

Chills. That covered it. They all felt the power, and listeners would, as well. They dissolved into a wave of relief. The band had spent the better part of a month trying to find the magic needed to bring the song to life. What they'd started with had been good: a fun, energetic punk song. There had been nothing *wrong*, per se. But what they had now? This was a song the listeners would remember. They'd download

1

the album after hearing it on the radio. The energy could finally be *felt*, not simply heard.

"This is it," Spencer said. "*This* is what we've been trying to write. All that's left is to finalize the lyrics."

High-fives went around the room.

All four members of Shattered Ceiling acutely felt the pressure for the second album they were trying to write. After the breakout success of their first, they'd managed to acquire a huge record deal with their top-choice label, adding pressure for their songs to be not only good, but *perfect*. They shared an acute need to prove that their success was more than mere luck. In the whirlwind following the release of their first single, they'd been hit with tour bookings, television appearances, and three Juno award nominations. Now, the eyes of the nation were on them, waiting to see if their group of lesbians was the real deal, or whether their first album had been a stroke of luck.

Spencer was confident it hadn't been luck, but their first record had something their second didn't: *time*. What looked like instant success on the outside was the culmination of years of hard work. She and Mari had been playing together for over a decade, since they met in their high school music class. Wren had been with them for five years, and even Sienna, the newest member, had joined the band a full three years ago. They'd had years to write songs, rewrite songs, and write new songs—so many new songs. When they had finally sat down to record their music, they selected the best of the best. They didn't have that luxury anymore. If they didn't want to fade away, they needed to release a second album before the buzz from the first went silent.

"We could release this as our first single," Sienna said, as she scribbled ideas for lyrics into her notebook. "I think I can make the chorus really memorable. The weight of the lyrics will be in the verses, and the chorus can be something easy for listeners to pick up. If we get listeners singing along, even after the music has stopped, then we're golden."

Spencer was about to reply but Mari held up a single finger and looked upward, visibly thinking through something. Spencer killed her amp and began errantly plucking the strings of her guitar, giving Mari the space to listen through the piece in her mind in order to finish formulating her thought.

"What if we had some sort of repeating lyric during the breakdown?" Mari suggested, after a long minute had passed. "I think we could really grow the energy there, starting soft and moving into a chant. We already have a musical buildup. If we had a repeating lyric in that spot, then new listeners could catch on quickly and it would really amp up a live crowd."

"The drums come in a little later," Wren began. "When we play it live, I could get the crowd clapping along to that section."

"Yes!" Mari exclaimed, then closed her eyes and bobbed her head to the tempo. "I like that. I think we could—"

But she was interrupted by Sienna. "What are you playing?"

Spencer turned at the interruption and found Sienna's gaze focused solely on her. "What?"

"That song you're playing." Sienna pointed to her guitar. "It was pretty."

She hadn't even realized she'd been playing anything, but even so she knew what song Sienna had heard. She'd been working on it in private, playing in her downtime. She hadn't made a conscious decision on whether or not she wanted to bring it to the band, but now, with all eyes in the room on her, her subconscious had made a decision.

She sat a little straighter and adjusted the guitar in her lap. "It's one of the first songs I ever wrote, way back in high school. I was going through some old notebooks a couple weeks ago, found the lyrics for what started as a silly high school love song, and I've been playing around with it since. It's starting to take shape now that I can do more than just strum basic chords."

"Let's hear it," Sienna said.

Spencer pulled her guitar closer and began the opening riff, surprised at the sudden vulnerability she felt with each note she played. Guitar was one thing she *knew* she was good at. It was her one completely unapologetic form of self-expression. But this song differed from the aggressive punk songs she typically played with her band. It was quiet and gentle, and had been written during a particularly sensitive period of her life. She felt naked and had to close her eyes to shut out the faces of her friends and allow the music to take over.

When she finished, she opened her eyes and looked to each of her friends, seeing genuine interest and appreciation in each of their gazes.

"Wow," Wren said.

"It's really pretty," Mari added.

Spencer relaxed into the praise her fellow band members offered. It wasn't hollow praise. This band was a career for each of them, and they treated it as such. None of them ever hesitated to speak up when something wasn't working.

Sienna's eyes shone with interest and she leaned forward, really holding Spencer with her gaze. "I *love* it. You said there were lyrics?"

Spencer nodded. "I can send them to you, but keep in mind I was seventeen when I wrote this. They'll need some work, but if it's okay with you, I think I'd like to use them as a jumping-off point, at least."

"Absolutely," Sienna agreed.

"I know we don't typically play ballads," Spencer offered. "It's not really our style."

"I actually think it could fit perfectly on our next album," Wren said. "We have a lot of fast, heavy punk songs. A ballad would give it room to breathe and would potentially bring in new listeners who wouldn't immediately pick up our stuff."

She had a point.

"I think there would be a lot of room to push myself vocally," Sienna added.

Spencer hadn't realized how much a positive reception would mean to her, and she was surprised to feel her face warm at the all-around interest.

"We can play with it then," she agreed, her confidence building. "I have a few ideas for ways we can bring it to the next level. I was thinking it could start with just guitar and vocals for the first verse and chorus, and then the drums and bass can jump in with the second verse. The section at the end, just before the last verse, could really be expanded instrumentally."

"Play it again," Mari suggested, "but turn your amp on this time."

She did as instructed, this time, feeling nothing but excitement as she began the opening riff. When Wren and Mari jumped in at the start of the second verse, she felt her pulse quicken at the added layers.

Mari added a walking bass riff that transitioned them perfectly into a much bigger, fuller chorus than the first. The song took on a new life, as the musicians all added their own voices to the conversation.

Spencer loved this part of song writing—the moment when they just jammed out something new, each instrument falling in seamlessly with the others, allowing the song to grow and take shape.

Sienna sat back, eyes closed, listening to the three play. When they finished, she let out a breath and simply said, "Beautiful."

Pride welled within Spencer—a pride that reached down deep inside, through the years, to reach her insecure seventeen-year-old self.

They ran the piece a few more times with Wren and Mari both experimenting with different rhythms, notes, and textures. When they finished, it felt like a positive note to end their practice on.

"I'm so excited for these new songs," Sienna said, as she grabbed her bag and headed for the door. "Spencer, send me the lyrics for that last one. I'll see all of you on Monday."

Wren headed out along with Sienna, neither of them having much gear to pack up. With the excitement from their last song, the practice had gone on longer than they'd planned, so there wasn't the usual time spent hanging back and chatting afterward.

Mari and Spencer took a little longer to pack up, and Spencer was grateful for the chance to talk over the new song with her best friend.

"Honest opinion," she began, "what did you think of the ballad?"

"It's gorgeous, Spence." Mari emphasized the words as she spoke to make sure Spencer knew how genuinely she meant them. "Wren was right when she said it will be really accessible for listeners who might not have otherwise listened to our music."

"You were quiet when I brought it out."

"I was busy wracking my brain trying to figure out who you wrote a love ballad for."

Spencer rolled her eyes and laughed. "Mari, the song is ten years old."

"Was it for that girlfriend you had in high school?" Mari asked, her eyes and smile widening as the memory returned to her. "I forgot about her! What was her name again? Something pretentious."

"Faith," Spencer offered.

"Yeah." Mari drew out the word, nodding. "What made you bring out a song you wrote for her? Didn't she break your heart?"

"Into a million pieces," she confirmed with an overly dramatic sigh.

Mari laughed. "Ah, young love."

Spencer laughed as she tucked her folded guitar cables neatly on top of her pedal board in its case.

"I've felt a little reflective lately," she said, giving an honest answer to Mari's earlier question. "All of our success, the Juno nominations, after the struggles we went through, both as a band and individually, to get here... I was thinking about everything I went through in high school, and how music saved me. I ended up going through my old notebooks and found this song."

"It *has* been a long road."

Mari knew better than anyone what Spencer had gone through in high school. They'd become quick friends after bonding in their music class, and Mari had been the person beside her through it all.

"I'm going to volunteer with the youth at Sunrise House," Spencer admitted. "We've got some time now that we're home from touring to write new music. I have a meeting with the program coordinator tomorrow."

"Wow," Mari said. "How did that come about? Why didn't you say anything?"

She shrugged. It had seemed somehow too personal to share before things were actually in place. "I sent the director an email a few weeks ago. I had to finish getting my security clearance and all the other paperwork done. I'm going to run a music program for the teens there. I've been emailing back and forth with the program coordinator, and she seems really excited about the idea. We're going to meet to discuss the next steps."

"That's really cool of you," Mari said. "Those kids will be so stoked to have an actual guitarist come spend time with them."

Spencer waved off the comment, but the truth was, she recognized she was in a unique position to have an impact on teenagers struggling in the same way she had.

"Well, I have to meet my parents for dinner," Mari said, "but I love the new, old song of yours. And I want to hear all about your meeting tomorrow, okay?"

She smiled and slid her guitar into her guitar case. "I promise to call and tell you all about it."

Mari headed out of their rented rehearsal space and Spencer took her time packing up. When she'd first dusted off the song, the melody had immediately carried her back to her youth. She remembered how she'd stayed up late playing her guitar, the volume on max blasting through her headphones, just to drown out the sound of her parents fighting. She had played the happy ballad and remembered the lightness that bloomed in her chest when she'd written the song, and the way the music made her feel like she'd had a voice.

She hadn't thought about the girl the song had been written for, but rather the feeling the song always inspired in her. That feeling was what she wanted to capture for the new album, and what she hoped to offer to the youth she would be volunteering with.

It was why she played music in the first place.

"Would you pass the salt?"

Faith Siebert reached for the saltshaker but before she could pass it to her dad, her mom held out an arm to stop her.

"You don't need any salt. The salmon is just fine the way it is."

She pulled her hand back, picking up her fork to quietly eat her Brussels sprouts while the conversation unfolded. She'd sat through this same conversation countless times in recent months. She could save both her parents the trouble and recite each of their lines for them.

It's just a little seasoning, her dad, Bill, would say. *What do you have against flavour?*

And her mom, Peggy, would counter, *I have nothing against flavour. If you only added a* little *seasoning, we wouldn't be in this position. Your doctor made it very clear that you need to strictly reduce your sodium intake.*

They were dedicated to their stances, which Faith admired, but good lord was she ready for a different weekly conversation. Six months earlier, her dad had suffered a heart attack. It had been mild, as far as heart attacks go, but it had been a wake-up call for her parents. The problem was, her dad took the wake-up call as a warning that he needed to eat healthier and exercise more, both of which, to his credit, he'd done remarkably well. He'd cut out all fast food, now drank sparkling water in place of beer or pop, and had joined a couch-to-5K running club. But her mom had taken it all to mean his health was so dire any deviation from a strictly monitored diet would result in imminent death.

Faith took a bite of salmon and had to refrain from reaching for the salt herself. In her dad's defense, the fish was woefully bland. He'd been essentially living off of plain boiled or steamed foods for months.

"Tell him," her mom urged, pulling Faith from her errant thoughts and back to today's version of the tired argument.

"Pardon?" she asked. She could guess what her mom wanted her to relay to her dad, but she didn't want to guess wrong.

"Tell him he needs to take better care of himself so he can live long enough to see his grandchildren. I'm not trying to be unreasonable. I'm trying to keep him alive."

Faith had to suppress a sigh. Inevitably, any discussion of her parents' health eventually circled around to discussion of *her* life. Her mom had been on a grandchild kick ever since her friends started becoming grandparents, but Bill's health scare had put the fear in her that she would *never* get to enjoy being a grandma, and she'd doubled down on Faith to start working on a baby.

"Dad, we both want you to be healthy," Faith amended.

A brief flash of indignation passed across her mom's face at the correction, but it faded as quickly as it appeared. "See?" she said, turning her focus back toward her husband, "Faith agrees."

"And Mom," Faith continued, refusing to side with one parent over the other, "I don't think a tiny bit of salt will kill him. You've made a healthy dinner. He's not eating takeout. A pinch of salt is not a death wish."

Her mom's mouth became a tight, hard line, but she said nothing as Faith passed her dad the saltshaker.

"Just a little," she cautioned before she released the shaker to him. He winked at her and she had to stifle a smile.

"I talked to Sherry Brighton the other day," her mom said. "Her youngest daughter is pregnant. This is going to be her fourth grandchild."

Here we go. She'd hoped to avoid the detour toward this subject, but if she wasn't going to allow the conversation about her dad's health to continue, then her lack of children was the logical next topic for dinnertime discussion.

"That's exciting for her." Faith took another bite of salmon.

"I can't even begin to imagine how excited she is," her mom continued. "She just adores her grandchildren. They've brought so much joy and meaning to her life."

"I bet they have," Faith said, and then decided she didn't care about transitioning smoothly away from this subject, and simply turned the conversation 180 degrees by asking, "Dad, how's work been?"

"Oh, busy, of course," he answered. "I've had a couple of stressful cases lately-"

"Faith, I know children aren't in your immediate future," her mom interrupted, "but have you considered what your long-term plans might look like? None of us are getting any younger."

She meant *she* wasn't getting any younger. At twenty-seven Faith had plenty of time before she had to start thinking about children, and she was in no particular rush.

"I would like children one day," she said, dipping her toes into the conversation.

Her mom's smile broke wide across her face, the joy practically radiating from her.

"But I'm in no rush. I don't think I want kids anytime in the next couple years. Not even in the next five years."

Her mom's smile fell.

"Mom, you know as well as I do that this is hardly the time for me to think about having children. I'm finally back on my feet. Don't you think I should find a partner first, before I start thinking about babies?"

"Absolutely I do," her mom agreed. "In fact, I meant to ask you about that. I was talking with my friend, Cheryl, and she said her daughter met a really lovely man online through one of those dating sites."

Faith kicked herself. She had walked right into this conversation. *I never learn.*

"That's great." The exasperation was audible in her voice, but her mom either didn't pick up on it, or didn't care.

"Have you considered trying one of those? I had my reservations about them at first, but it sounds like they're actually a really great way to meet people these days."

She chose her words carefully. "I appreciate you looking out for me, Mom. You're my biggest cheerleader. But I'm not ready to date right now."

"The time is never right. It's been over a year."

"Mom, please," she begged. "I *promise* you, when I *am* ready to date again, I will. Right now, I'm really enjoying being single."

She could see the unsaid words written across her mom's face, frown lines marking her disappointment. Still, it was clear her mom knew she wasn't going to concede any more, so she nodded.

"I'm taking the lead on a new project at work next week," Faith said. "I don't know all of the details, but the director is planning to launch some sort of youth music program."

Disappointment melted off her mom's face. While Faith's personal life had been nothing short of a letdown to her parents over the past year and a half, they were proud of her career. They both talked openly about their daughter the social worker, and how she was making such a difference in people's lives through her work. She'd taken a job in a women's shelter providing support services for women and families fleeing domestic violence situations, and from the way her mom boasted to her friends, you'd have thought Faith single-handedly stepped in to stop abusers herself. Her parents had expected her to study law and work for her dad, but even he recognized the importance of her work, and the difference she made on a daily basis.

"What kind of music program?" her dad asked.

"I'm not really sure. Like I said, I don't know the details yet. Our program coordinator kept pretty quiet about it all. But it sounds like we'll be running some sort of teen music lessons."

"But you don't play any instruments?" her mom said, though the statement was more of a question.

"We have a volunteer coming in to lead that part of the group. My understanding is that my role is more to encourage participation and be available as a support, since our volunteer likely doesn't have a background in any sort of youth work."

"Well, that sounds really wonderful," her mom said. "I can't wait to hear more about it."

With the talk of her dad's health and her lack of children behind them, the rest of the evening remained much more amicable. Faith was grateful for her weekly dinner with her parents, but lately, the conversations seemed to be full of minefields that she was never quite sure how to navigate.

Her parents loved her, she knew, but she wished their involvement in her life wasn't so all-encompassing and demanding. She ached for breathing room.

Faith finished eating and helped clear the table and wash the dishes before politely making an early exit.

"Don't you want to stay for tea?" her mom asked.

Every week they had dinner together, and then her mom would put on the kettle and they'd have tea and play a game of Scrabble in the living room.

"It's been a really long week," she lied. "I have a bit of a headache. I really want to call it a night early."

Her mom's disappointment was visible, but she quickly masked it with concern for her daughter. "Make sure you call me in the morning to let me know you're all right, and if your headache gets worse, call us. We can be there in ten minutes."

"I'll be fine, Mom."

"I know you think I'm being overprotective, but you're my baby girl. My life would be meaningless without you."

Faith tried to let the words roll off her shoulders. She'd heard them enough times that she should've been numb to them by now, but still she felt as if the air around her was vacuumed out and it was hard to breathe. She wanted to open the door and get some fresh air.

"I love you, Mom," she said. "I love you too, Dad."

"See you next week, Faith-cakes," her dad called.

She went to her car and turned over the engine, steadying herself before pulling out of the drive.

They mean well, she told herself as she drove. Her irritation began to slip away, replaced with a slight sense of shame. Her parents only wanted the best for her. They could be a bit *much* at times, but everything they did came from a place of love.

She turned on the radio for the drive home, eager to push the dinner from her mind and unwind from the week. She flipped stations until she found one with a song she liked, and she drove, bobbing her head in time with the music.

The song ended, and the radio DJ quickly came on to introduce the next one.

"Next up, we have the newest band creating a buzz across the country, Shattered Ceiling, and their hit single, 'Bottle Rockets'."

The opening chords began, and she felt the familiar tightening in her chest, even while she reached to turn the volume up. She hadn't been surprised when she'd discovered Spencer was the guitarist in the new punk band making waves across Canada. Spencer had always had a passion and a gift when it came to guitar. Faith had always known Spencer would do big things with her life.

She hummed along, despite the pang of regret she always felt when the song came on the radio. In the ten years since high school, what had *she* done with her life? Spencer had gone on to great things, while she had the same conversation over the same Friday night dinners.

She drove the same road home, wondering how her life had grown so stagnant. She had imagined so much more for herself when she was younger. The song reached the outro just as she pulled up to her apartment.

She was glad Spencer was living the life she'd dreamed of. She only wished she could say the same for herself.

Chapter Two

Spencer stood before the trellised wall, trying to bring herself to press the call button on the intercom. From where she stood, there was nothing to see except a nondescript sidewalk a few blocks off the Vancouver core, but she was intimately familiar with the building on the other side. She'd been eight the first time she and her mom had stayed there. She'd stood right where she was now standing, with a tiny backpack holding her stuffed monkey, a toothbrush, and a single change of clothes. The ghost of her fear swirled in her stomach, and she reminded herself she wasn't a child anymore, and she didn't have a need to hide.

I'm here as a volunteer.

There were other children and teenagers staying in Sunrise House, though, whose fear wasn't a ghost but a very real and tangible presence. They all had unique stories and situations, but the fear was the same. And Spencer understood what it was like to live in fear of someone who was supposed to love you.

She pressed the button and waited, acutely aware of the security camera fixed on where she stood.

She didn't have to wait long.

"Spencer Adams in the flesh!" A middle-aged woman opened the gate and motioned for her to step into the yard on the other side. "It is *so* nice to meet you. I am elated you've offered to volunteer with us. Our teens are going to *love* this program."

The woman hardly stopped to take a breath.

"I'm Beverly Tate, but call me Taz, everyone around here does."

Spencer wondered at the nickname, but didn't ask, as Beverly—

Taz—was already showing her around the yard. This was the program coordinator she'd been communicating with through email? Their communication had always been brief and professional, and she had in no way expected this excitement or energy.

"We can house thirty women and families and we're always at capacity." Taz opened the door to the house. Here's our common area. We've got . . ."

The words faded into background noise as Spencer stepped inside. The old wooden floorboards groaned at her entrance—ten years of the same complaint—and the air had the same musty smell, which they attempted to mask with floral air freshener. Everything was exactly the same as she remembered: the same green couches, the same shelf filled with board games and books, the same painting of the ocean above the fireplace. She used to sit on that center couch and gaze at the portrait of the ocean, feeling acutely aware of the walls closing in around her. In those moments, she'd been safe, but it had felt as though it had come at the cost of her freedom.

"Spencer?"

The sound of her name pulled her from her memory.

"I'm sorry," she said, realizing Taz was waiting on an answer to a question. "Can you repeat that?"

"I asked if you have any questions."

She shook her head. "I've actually been here before. My mom and me. It's why I want to volunteer *here*. I want to give back."

Taz somehow became even *more* animated, her entire being lighting up. "Oh, it is so wonderful to hear this place was able to help your family, and that made such a profound impact, you've chosen to return to help others. That makes this music program even more special. When did you stay here?"

"It's been a long time," Spencer said. "We stayed here more than once, but the last time, wow, it's been nearly ten years already."

"That explains why we've never met. You were here just before me. I've been the program coordinator for going on nine years now." Taz hardly took a breath before shifting back to business. "Well, anyway, I guess you don't need a tour, do you? I'll introduce you to the group's co-facilitator. You'll be in charge of the music instruction, and we've got

14

one of our social workers paired with you to provide support should the need arise."

Spencer followed Taz down the hall. She wanted to listen to everything Taz said on the way, but Taz spoke so rapidly, and she got distracted looking at the rooms as they walked past.

Taz was wrong. She wasn't back because of how much she had valued her stay in Sunrise House. It had been a necessary means to an end, but she was fairly certain *nobody* valued their time there. She was volunteering because she empathized with the youth, not because she loved the shelter.

Sunrise House did important work. She had the utmost respect for the staff and their mission. But her personal connection made it hard to see past the pain of having to ever stay there in the first place.

Taz knocked on one of the office doors and led Spencer inside, and this time she *knew* she was back in a memory. Her right hand went to her left wrist where she used to anxiously pick at the sleeves of her worn-out hooded sweaters.

Faith sat at the desk and Spencer was seventeen again, sitting behind Faith in English class, tracing all of the folds and twists in Faith's French braid while wondering how soft her blond hair might be if she released it. Faith's hazel eyes landed on her, and the butterflies that had migrated so long ago returned to her stomach, fluttering as they first had when Faith's eyes had rested on her, awaiting her response, when the teacher had put her on the spot to answer some question about Shakespeare.

She blinked, expecting someone else to be sitting in front of her when she opened her eyes, but Faith remained, and Spencer felt just as put on the spot as she had that day in class.

"Spencer, this is Faith Matheson. She'll be working with you on the music project over the next fourteen weeks. Faith, this is Spencer Adams. She plays guitar for the band Shattered Ceiling." Taz laughed. "But judging from the awestruck look on your face, you've already heard of her."

Spencer now saw the evidence of age. The remnants of childhood had fallen away from Faith's face, replaced with an elegant maturity. Faith Siebert—*Matheson now*—wasn't seventeen anymore, but she *was* sitting across from her at the small desk.

Spencer's stomach dropped with the realization that the two of them would be working together.

"I've spoken with a number of local music stores," Taz continued, unaware of the tension coiled around the room. "We have a half dozen guitars being donated for this. I'll pick them up on Monday, so they'll be here when you start the group next week."

"Excellent," Spencer managed, forcing herself to remain professional and remember why she was there.

"The youth are going to be *so* excited. I've kept your involvement a surprise, and what a surprise it is! Look at Faith. She's starstruck. Oh, I can just *imagine* the expression on the teens' faces when they walk in and see you. It's going to be such a wonderful experience for them. They need joy, and you're going to bring them joy. But anyway, I have some phone calls to make, so I'll let you and Faith take it from here."

Taz took off as quickly and as purposefully as she'd done everything else, leaving Spencer and Faith alone together in the small office. Spencer had expected to face her past when returning to Sunrise House, but she hadn't expected *all* of her ghosts to be there ready to haunt her.

The silence stretched tight between them.

"Is she always so full of energy?" Spencer asked, cutting the elastic tension before it snapped.

Faith looked relieved that she had broken the tension, which caused anger to simmer in her stomach. She knew she had to be professional, but why should she have to be the one to make Faith comfortable? Her teenaged hurt and indignation rose within her.

"We call her Taz because she reminds us of the Tasmanian devil from the Looney Tunes cartoons," Faith said. "She's such a whirlwind. She never stops. Usually, she's blowing through about fifty things at once."

Faith sat at her desk with the same poise and perfect posture she'd always had. She'd been pretty as a teenager, but she was beautiful now, because *of course* she was.

"I'm exhausted after ten minutes with her."

Faith laughed, and Spencer fought down the fresh swell of

memories the sound inspired.

"She's exhausting, all right," Faith agreed. "But her energy drives this place. She's the backbone of the shelter."

Spencer fell silent again, looking at Faith, still half convinced her memories were blurring her reality.

"It's good to see you, Spencer," Faith said. Her words were warm and genuine and wrapped around Spencer like a hug.

Spencer shrugged them off. "It's been a long time."

Except with Faith there in front of her, it felt like there was no measure of time distancing them. What had been her distant past was now right in front of her, heartbreak included.

"You're living your dream," Faith said. "I always knew you were going to do big things."

"And you married Brett. You're Faith *Matheson* now." She hadn't meant for the sentence to slip out, and she felt bad for the bite in her words, especially when she saw the way Faith blanched.

"Siebert again. I haven't officially changed it back yet."

"Good," she said, not wanting to examine the relief she felt. "You were always too good for him."

"You're right about that," Faith said, the words heavy with regret. A small consolation.

"This is weird," Spencer admitted. "Seeing you."

"It doesn't have to be," Faith offered. Her voice was warm and kind and held a hopeful note. She'd always had a way of softening everyone around her.

"You're right," Spencer said, though she didn't know how it could possibly *not* feel weird. "We're here to work together. Let's do that."

Faith seemed to want to say more, but merely nodded. "So, here's how I envisioned the groups working," she began, and she launched into a detailed description of roles and structure and goals.

Spencer listened and tried to keep her attention focused on the planning. The project meant the world to her. She could lead the music lessons and process her feelings about her own past, her stay in the shelter, Faith, all of it, later.

Faith led them to the recreation room they would use for the group. It was a small room, and it was hard to imagine fitting a group

17

of teenagers with guitars into it, around the air hockey table, reading corner, and bean bag cushions.

"I'll have you come a little early each week for some setup," Faith said, as if reading her mind. "We will have to move most of this stuff into the staff office and bring in some folding chairs. It looks like a lot, but it really won't be."

"That all sounds good," Spencer said. "If I come for 6:30 that will give us half an hour to set up, does that work?"

"Perfect." Faith's gaze lingered on Spencer. She looked like she wanted to say more, but didn't, for which Spencer was grateful. Still, the intimacy in the gaze spoke of a familiarity Faith had long since lost her claim to, and anger bubbled up in response.

"I'll be here Thursdays at six-thirty. I'll bring my own guitar and be ready to teach some basics. Is there anything else we need to cover, or are we good to go?"

"That pretty much covers it," Faith said, her demeanor once again purely professional. "Hopefully we'll have a few youth join us, but we won't be able to guarantee attendance since we never really know who will be staying here on the dates that you come in."

"I understand." She knew all about attendance at the shelter. Then again, Faith already knew that.

"I'll see you Thursday, Faith," Spencer said, before turning to leave.

She had until Thursday to figure out a way to keep the memories of Faith neatly in their little box. She had no use for them anymore. They had dated. They had broken up. That was it.

She wished it felt that simple.

In the years since she had last seen Spencer, Faith had occasionally imagined what she might say if they ever saw each other again.

In her most vulnerable moments, she'd allowed herself to remember Spencer and think about how she might one day speak the words that echoed in those deep recesses of her heart.

You were the one truly good thing in my life.

Our time together meant the world to me.

I wish I hadn't ended it.

Sometimes, there was only one word she wished she could say. *Sorry.*

As it turned out, though, when she saw Spencer again, she had nothing to say of any consequence. Spencer walked into her office, and it was as though the floor had fallen out from under her. She would have never in a million years expected to see her standing there, and she had been completely caught off guard. The most she'd managed to say was *it's good to see you again.*

She'd gotten the impression that Spencer didn't agree.

Though she'd made it through, she was glad when their meeting ended, and even more glad when her shift ended. It had taken everything in her to mask her turbulent thoughts and maintain her put-together professionalism.

She left the shelter and drove as if on autopilot until she reached the dance studio a couple blocks over from her apartment. She parked her navy Volkswagen Jetta in the stall nearest the door and went around to her trunk to take out the duffel bag of dance clothes that she always carried with her. Then she pushed her way inside where she was immediately greeted.

"Faith, hi! I didn't know you were teaching tonight." Callie McMillan was the newest staff member at the studio, but her bright and energetic demeanor had already made her an important fixture.

Faith usually mirrored Callie's energy, but this time, she didn't have it in her. "Hey. No student. It's just me tonight. Are any of the studios available?"

If Callie noticed a dip in Faith's mood, she didn't let it show. She was still as bubbly as ever when she answered. "Studio D is empty right now, but I have my beginner's pointe class coming in at eight. The class in Studio B should be done in about ten minutes, though, if you want to wait and use that one."

"Perfect." Faith took her time changing into her white tank top and black tights. Even the simple act of changing made her feel better, as though she could strip off the day as well as her work clothes.

By the time she finished lacing her pointe shoes, the class had already filtered out of the studio, and she stepped inside, closing the door behind her. The airy room was made even more spacious with the floor to ceiling mirror covering the wall opposite the door. She exhaled as she moved toward the speaker system in the corner. Her thoughts felt less muddled just by being in the studio. She connected her phone to the Bluetooth on the speaker system and selected her music: a mournful ballad from an indie band that she had discovered recently: a duet between a man and a woman, a song about regrets and loss. It had spoken to her from the moment she heard it, but even more so now after seeing Spencer.

The opening notes expanded to fill the room, and she let herself move as the music compelled her, free of any choreographed routine, her body taking the shape of her feelings.

Spencer had grown up since high school, and the change was remarkable. Gone was the awkward teenager, hiding beneath thick hooded sweaters, short hair styled forward to fall over her eyes. The Spencer who had walked into her office had nothing to hide. She'd worn dark jeans, and a simple black t-shirt that clung to her as though it had been made for her. Her biceps were visible, even beneath the tattoo sleeve that decorated her left arm, a guitar and music notes extending up her forearm from her wrist. She still kept her auburn hair short, but now she styled it up, off of her face, and the ends had been dyed a soft lavender.

And the change wasn't only to her appearance. As a teenager, she'd exuded a tough exterior when she'd needed to, but more often than not, she sat in class folded in upon herself, as though she could physically tuck herself away. The Spencer who had walked into Faith's office today allowed herself to take up space in the room. No, she commanded it. There was a confidence visible in how she carried herself. She stood tall, with her shoulders back and her gaze up. She knew who she was, and there was no more hiding. Faith had watched videos of Spencer's band, and she'd seen the magnetism Spencer brought to the stage, but she was unprepared for how powerful Spencer's confidence was in person.

All of it only made Faith feel smaller.

She poured those feelings into her dance as she stretched and spun in the empty studio, while the sad notes from the piano filled the air.

And you married Brett—Faith Matheson now.

The name had never felt more wrong than when she'd heard Spencer say it. All her failures were highlighted by Spencer's successes. She'd never been able to live half as authentically as Spencer did.

You were the one truly good thing in my life.

Our time together meant the world to me.

I wish I hadn't ended it.

I'm sorry.

And yet, if she had everything to do all over again, would the ending have been any different?

The song ended, and the notes of the next one began playing over the speaker. She tried to push all of the regrets and insecurities from her mind as she danced and just lose herself in the movement. There was no point in wondering "what if". This was her life. The choices she'd made had never been without reason.

There would have been consequences to whatever choices she'd made.

Spencer got to their jam space early and set up her guitar; she wanted some time before the rest of the group got there to crank the amps and really play. She could play through her headphones in her apartment, but it wasn't the same. She wanted to be able to feel the music as it vibrated through the room. She wanted to stretch the notes with her effects pedals, bending the air with the sound. She wanted room to move with the music, as though she was on stage. She wanted to *feel* the music, not just hear it. And she could do that in the jam space.

She tuned her guitar and then turned on her effects board. She started with a warm-up, playing their song 'Bottle Rockets'. The fun, upbeat punk song, with its catchy riffs and a heavy power-chord chorus, always got her adrenaline racing, no matter how many times she played it. And now that they had a fan base to play live for, she could always feel the energy of the crowd, even when just practicing alone.

Then, once she finished playing through 'Bottle Rockets', she let the music just take over and take its own shape. She strung chords together with ease. She didn't have to sit down and think through what she wanted to play before she played it, she could simply pick up her guitar and let the music speak. Music was her language. At first, like learning a second language, she'd had to think about each component before she could string them together, but now she could converse fluently. It was her most natural form of self-expression. When she didn't have words, she could always find a chord formation to give voice to her feelings.

Going back to Sunrise House had been a mistake. She'd stepped in the door and stepped back in time to an age she'd never had any desire to revisit, not even in thoughts. The shelter... Faith... all of the hurt and confusion of her youth had flared to life inside of her once more. She strummed heavy power chords thick with distortion. Crunchy, loud, and raw music.

"It isn't you," Faith had told her in the end.

That was a lie. For all intents and purposes, the two of them should have never even been friends. She'd always known that. She'd wondered from the start what Faith had seen in her. They were so different. Faith was such a *good* girl. She had come from a *good* family, she got *good* grades, she had *good* friends. She was sweet and she was kind, and she was pretty and nobody had a single negative thing to say about her.

Of course, Spencer had fallen for her. *Everyone* fell for Faith.

The shocker had been that Faith had fallen for her back, the young punk boi, hanging out at the skate park instead of attending classes. The one everyone expected to drop out of high school. The fuckup. The *bad* kid. Her life had been a mess. She'd been in survival mode. But all anyone saw was her poor attendance and the chip on her shoulder.

The entire time they were together, she'd known things were too good to be true. It wasn't exactly a surprise when Faith started dating Brett. Popular, handsome, athletic... he checked all the boxes. Just as everyone fell for Faith, everyone fell for Brett. But she heard him whisper *dyke* when she walked through the hallways. And she overheard the demeaning way he and his buddies would talk about girls while they sat together in the back of the class, or gathered at lockers. The girls they thought were too fat, too tall, too plain—in their mind, girls served one purpose.

The thought that Faith had *married* that asshat burned at Spencer.

She could sense a song emerging from the hot coals in her chest: anger and injustice and shame and hurt. All of the emotions blended together into their appropriate chord combinations. A verse took shape, and she built the feelings toward a chorus.

She closed her eyes and felt the music, letting out her feelings in the only way she knew how.

Then, the bass joined in, a steady pulsing rhythm underlying the power chords.

While she had lost herself in her music, Mari had entered the studio, taken out her bass, and joined in. She watched Spencer's hands, picking up her chords and finding the right note to play along on bass.

Spencer kept going, nodding to Mari as she went. The bass added a new dimension. It filled out the song.

The magic of music. It was no longer her talking alone.

Eventually, she played around with an idea for a bridge. She chugged the guitar in a staccato rhythm with dead space in between. Mari found the rhythm and matched it on bass. Spencer imagined Wren hitting that same rhythm on drums.

Some songs took months to write.

Some, like this one, could be written almost entirely in one session. A simple jam taking form and molding itself into a fully realized song.

When they reached an ending, Spencer felt the catharsis of the music and she set down her guitar.

"What song is that?" Mari asked. "I dig it."

Spencer shrugged. "I was just messing around, but I think we should keep working on that."

"Definitely," Mari said. Then she changed the subject. "How was your volunteer thing at the shelter?"

Spencer stilled. She had expected Mari to ask her about that, but she still had not figured out how much she was ready to tell her friend.

She shrugged. "It was weird being back. I'm still processing it all, I guess."

"That's fair," Mari answered, thankfully not pressing for more details.

Just then, the door to the studio opened, and Wren stepped inside, checking her watch when she saw Spencer and Mari already inside with their instruments plugged in.

"Am I late?" Wren asked, hurriedly opening her backpack to take out her drumsticks.

"I got here an hour ago to play some music and unwind," Spencer said. "Mari just happened to be a bit early."

Wren visibly relaxed and eased herself onto the stool behind her drum kit. Her name fit her perfectly. She always reminded Spencer of a little bird, both in stature and personality. She was slender and soft-spoken, and her diminutive nature was only highlighted by the fact that she sat behind the largest and loudest instrument in the band.

She also looked the least like somebody who would play in a band. Spencer knew that she looked the part, with her full-sleeve tattoo and dyed hair. Mari's long black hair had a single blue streak down the front, she had the septum of her nose pierced, and she often wore bold makeup. Sienna had a trail of bright flowers tattooed over her shoulder, and her long, fiery red curls always hung wild. She often wore skirts that flowed just above her knees, and combat boots that came up to her mid-calf, giving her a look that was a duality between soft femininity and total kick ass.

Wren kept her dirty blond hair simple and unstyled. She wore plain jeans and t-shirts in solid, neutral colours.

But when she played, so much force burst out of her that there was no doubt that she belonged in a band. The entire group was talented, but Wren's playing held an unmatched raw power.

"How was your weekend?" Spencer asked.

"Good," Wren said. "My sister cane to stay with me for the week, so I took her to see the aquarium. You?"

Sienna blew in before Spencer could answer. Like Wren, she saw everyone already set up to play and assumed she was running late.

"Sorry. I thought I'd stop for coffee." She held up her take-out cup, no doubt filled with something over-sugared and overpriced. "I didn't realize the drive-through would be so slow, and once I was in it, it was too late to back out. I was committed!"

"All good," Wren said. "You're not late."

"Oh," Sienna said with a breath of surprise. "Excellent."

Sienna was often running a good fifteen to thirty minutes behind, so really, for Sienna-time, she was early.

"I read the lyrics you sent me," she said.

Spencer's stomach dropped. She'd forgotten that she'd emailed the lyrics for the song about Faith to Sienna following their last rehearsal. They'd been sent *before* she'd run into Faith again.

"The lyrics are *perfect*," Sienna continued. "I didn't tweak a thing. We may have to make a few minor changes here and there once we start to work on it musically, but the words are beautiful. I love them."

Spencer shifted her weight from foot to foot, uncomfortable with the praise. "Thanks."

"Can we start with that song?" Sienna asked. "I really want to try it out."

The room shrunk around her. She couldn't think of a way to get out of playing the piece without raising questions, but thankfully Mari spoke first.

"Actually, Spencer and I were just experimenting with something new. Can we work on that one today before we both forget it?"

The others agreed, and Spencer let out a breath of relief.

She could only put off playing Faith's song for so long, but maybe she only needed a little time for the shock of seeing Faith again to wear off. They'd broken up nearly ten years ago; the song didn't have to hold any power over her now.

She'd see Faith later that week at Sunrise House, and surely now that she was prepared, she would find no ghosts still lingering between them. Next week, the song would go back to being nothing more than something she'd written once upon a time in a different lifetime.

Chapter Three

"Oh my God, what a rough intake." Faith's colleague, Teresa, leaned against the doorframe to Faith's office, looking exhausted and sad and horrified, all equal parts. "I keep telling myself she's here and she's safe now, but some days, some stories, I just lose my faith in humanity, you know?"

Faith nodded, but then looked at the clock. It was 6:15. Almost time to start getting ready for the music group.

"Okay," Teresa said, and her no-nonsense tone forced Faith's attention. "What's going on with you? You've been super distracted all day."

"Nothing's going on. It's been a really busy day. Lots of paperwork."

Teresa didn't appear convinced. Faith had never been a good liar.

"Whatever it is," Teresa began, softer this time, "my door is always open. You can come talk to me any time."

"Thanks," she said, knowing she wouldn't take Teresa up on that offer. It sounded so stupid when she replayed it in her head. *My high school girlfriend is facilitating the music group with me, and I feel like my life has been uprooted.*

They'd dated for five months nearly ten years ago. It should have been no more than a funny coincidence.

Teresa didn't press, and she left Faith alone so they could each get back to their work.

Faith looked at the clock again. 6:18

After finding out she was going to be working with Spencer, she had considered speaking with Taz about withdrawing from the project.

She'd even gone as far as walking toward her office, with that very intention. She knew, though, that the shelter staff were stretched to capacity, just like every other aspect of the shelter, and the project had taken a lot of coordination to make happen—securing instruments, finding staff to cover her other roles for the duration of the group, waiting for Spencer to complete her background check, and finding an available room being just the tip of the iceberg. She could ask Teresa to facilitate the group, and Teresa would do it, but it hardly felt fair after she had campaigned to be the staff member in charge. It had seemed like such a great way to bring joy to the teenagers who were staying there. She'd wanted to be a part of that.

She checked the time once more. 6:24. Close enough.

She stood up from her desk and locked her office before heading to the small recreation room. She might as well start getting things ready. Spencer knew where to find her once she arrived.

She set to work bringing the folding chairs into the room from the storage closet, and then once she had a handful of those stacked against the wall, she began to clear the items from the center of the room. It was a hassle to have to move things every time, but the shelter was full to the brim, and they simply didn't have a space that could be dedicated to the music workshop.

"Hey."

She turned toward the sound, and saw Spencer standing in the doorway with her guitar case in one hand. She was dressed conservatively, in a gray, unpatterned shirt, and a black leather jacket covering her tattoos. The look was not quite dressy enough to be considered *professional,* but did demonstrate an effort to put her most polished self forward. Faith recognized the *intention* of the outfit choice, but the *effect* was somewhat different. Her mouth went dry, and she couldn't think of how to form words. Spencer wore confidence like a second skin, and the look made Faith feel that much more insecure. It was also sexy as hell.

Her teenage attraction to Spencer had started out more romantic than physical, and whenever she'd let herself imagine the "what ifs" a part of her had wondered if perhaps she was building up their relationship as being something more than it *had* been—a blurring of

27

friendship lines, perhaps. She'd let go of that thought over the years, and adult Spencer made the attraction impossible to deny.

"Should we start by moving the air hockey table?" Spencer asked, and Faith realized she still had not said a word.

"That would be great." Her cheeks burned with embarrassment. "You grab one end and I'll grab the other. It shouldn't be too hard to move."

Spencer set her guitar down and moved to the end of the air hockey table. The two of them shuffled it into the next room and then began setting up the chairs in a circle.

"Did you have a good week?" Faith asked, as she unfolded one of the chairs.

"I did." Spencer didn't offer any details. "You?"

"For the most part." She wanted to make conversation. She hated the chill between them. "I've been really busy with work, and teaching at the studio."

"You're still dancing?" Spencer asked.

"Not as intensely as before, but I teach a couple classes throughout the week."

"Good for you."

Spencer didn't ask any more follow-up questions, and it was clear she wasn't interested in furthering the conversation.

Faith set a guitar at each of the chairs and then took a seat.

"I'll have you sit across from me," she instructed. "It will be more comfortable for the teens that way, not having two adults sitting together and looking out at them."

Spencer nodded and took the seat across from Faith, opening her guitar case and pulling out her guitar.

She was so quiet. Faith hated the silence.

"Oh my God."

Faith looked to the door and saw a young girl she hadn't met yet staring, in awe, at Spencer.

"Spencer Adams?" the girl asked, almost vibrating with excitement. "You're Spencer Adams."

Spencer turned her entire energy toward the girl, lighting up bright and welcoming.

"Just Spencer. What's your name?"

The girl looked like she couldn't speak. In fact, she looked like she couldn't breathe. Her eyes went wide with awe, and then the words came tumbling out in an excited blur.

"Oh my God. I can't believe this! Am I dreaming? I must be dreaming."

Spencer was no doubt very used to fan reactions, and yet she held space for the girl's excitement, letting it bloom and fill the room. She didn't dismiss her or hurry her or seem bothered by the gushing. "You're wide awake. I promise."

"Come on in," Faith said, though she was fairly sure the girl didn't even register she was there. "Feel free to grab a seat and a guitar."

The girl chose the chair right next to Spencer and picked up the acoustic guitar that had been set in front, looking down at the instrument reverently.

"Do you play?" Spencer asked her.

The girl shook her head. "I *wish*. One day, I want to learn how to play all your songs. I listen to your band *constantly*. It's my favourite of *all time*."

Spencer's smile was kind. "Well, I'm flattered. I'll try to teach you the basics today to get you started. What's your name?"

"Haley," the girl said, her voice soft and shy.

"It's a pleasure to meet you, Haley."

If Faith had ever had any concerns about the music workshop, it was that they would be bringing in a musician who lacked the ability to properly engage with the youth. Spencer, though, didn't seem nervous or standoffish or vain. She came across as genuine and humble and kind.

It stood in contrast to the chilly distance Faith had been met with, and for a moment she felt a pang of jealousy for the way Spencer spoke with Haley.

Two teenage boys, brothers by the looks of it, stepped into the room. The older one sat in the chair nearest the door, slumped back with his arms across his chest and his feet out in front of him. He wore a flat-brimmed cap, pulled low, masking his face, but Faith saw the anger in the set of his jaw. The younger boy couldn't have been much older than thirteen. He immediately pulled a guitar from its case and began fiddling with the strings and tuning pegs. Neither of them seemed to recognize Spencer.

"Okay, first lesson." Spencer directed her attention toward the younger boy as he turned one of the pegs. "These little pegs at the end of the guitar are for tuning purposes. When you turn them, it tightens or loosens the string and changes the sound. I've already tuned the guitars, so we don't need to worry about them for today."

The boy kept fiddling with the tuning peg and his brother reached out to slug him in the arm. "She means stop."

Faith decided it was a good time to introduce the group. There likely wouldn't be any other teens joining them, but if anyone else showed up, they could be easily welcomed in.

"Let's get started, shall we?" she began. "My name is Faith. I'm one of the staff here. I'm going to help facilitate the group, but I don't know how to play the guitar, so I'll be learning, just like the rest of you. Spencer here is going to lead the lessons."

Spencer took over effortlessly, beginning with an introduction. "I'm Spencer Adams. I'm the guitarist for the band Shattered Ceiling. Our band has spent the past year touring, but we have a bit of a break while we write our second album. Since I'm home for a while, it means I get the opportunity to volunteer here, teaching you all how to play the guitar."

Faith watched the teens' reactions as Spencer spoke. Haley hung on her every word. It was clear the older boy's interest had been piqued, as he had looked up and pushed the brim of his hat up slightly, but he maintained his closed posture and slight scowl. The younger boy appeared impressed and when Spencer was finished speaking, he blurted, "So you're like a *real* musician?"

"Anybody who plays music is a *real* musician," Spencer said. "But if you're asking if that's my career, then yes."

"Cool." He nodded, and the way he drew out the word made it clear that he didn't really get the point.

"When did you start playing guitar?" Haley asked.

"I picked up a guitar for the first time when I was sixteen."

Faith saw a smile cross the girl's face as she looked at the guitar in front of her, visibly wondering what that possibly meant for her.

"I'm going to teach you the basics," Spencer said. "Consider this a jumping-off platform to learning how to play all your favourite songs. When I was younger, music really saved me, and I wanted to come share it with others who are in a situation similar to the one I was in."

The older boy snorted derisively, the first real indication he was actively listening. Faith foresaw the need to step in but wanted to give Spencer and the boy a chance to speak first.

"You sound bothered by that," Spencer said, her tone remarkably calm.

He shrugged but lifted his eyes to Spencer with fire in his eyes. "You don't know anything about our situation."

This time Faith opened her mouth to speak, but Spencer, who didn't hesitate for even a second, spoke first.

"You're right. I don't know what you're going through, and I shouldn't pretend to know. Whatever your story is, it is uniquely yours. What I will say instead, is that when I stayed here, I found music to be a good escape, and I wanted to share that escape with others who could maybe use one."

The boy said nothing, but he sat back, no longer coiled and ready for a fight. He nodded once and picked up the guitar.

"You stayed here?" Haley asked.

Faith could see the girl's adoration for Spencer grow. She'd just discovered one of her idols had survived a similar experience to hers, a realization that carried a profound impact.

"I did." Spencer didn't offer the girl any details. She'd shared enough to bridge the gap between her adult self and the teenagers, without over-sharing or making the moment about her in any way. It was a delicate balance to walk, and Faith was impressed with her natural ability to engage with the teens.

"Okay," Spencer said, transitioning them into less personal territory. "Who here has played the guitar before?"

Nobody raised their hands.

"Excellent," Spencer said. "You'll all be starting in the same place."

And she began the lesson with the very basics as she explained how to hold the guitar, labelled the various parts of the instrument, and then showed them how to form a few basic chords.

Faith only half followed along, concentrating more on how Spencer interacted with the youth. She was confident, compassionate, and patient. The older boy had come in with a chip on his shoulder, but his demeanor changed as he began asking Spencer for help forming chords. His younger brother was less enthused and easily distracted, but Spencer remained calm when the boy needed his guitar retuned, when he strummed as loud as possible and when he asked a million questions, seemingly to keep the attention on him, rather than out of a genuine curiosity.

Haley kept fairly quiet as she tried to absorb everything Spencer taught them, but Spencer didn't forget about her while dealing with the brothers. She made sure she checked in with her often, and complimented her as she picked up the chord formations. If Haley had been starstruck when she walked into the room, she was full-on in love, now.

Faith couldn't blame the girl. Spencer was impressive as hell. She always had been. As a teenager, she had lacked the confidence she now possessed, but she'd always had an uncanny ability to know the exact right words in any given moment. Faith used to wonder how others didn't see how brightly Spencer shone.

People were seeing it now.

"How do you move from one chord to the other so easily?" Haley asked, as she struggled to bend her fingers into the C chord, double-checking that each finger was on the correct string and fret.

Spencer could see her frustration, as her hand refused to form the right shape, but Haley was determined, and she had no doubt that the girl would learn to play the instrument. It was clear how badly she wanted it.

"It takes a lot of practice," Spencer said. "Eventually, though, your hand will know what to do. I don't have to look at my guitar when I play anymore."

Haley nodded with a steely resolve. She saw where she wanted to be, and she would work to make it happen. She reminded Spencer so much of herself that it hurt. The girl had her hair dyed black, and she wore a hot pink- and black-striped t-shirt over top of her skinny jeans, a bold shell for the shy, soft-spoken girl in front of her. Spencer remembered when she, too, had used clothes as armor, hiding her vulnerability beneath layers of fabric. Haley, however, also wore her heart on her sleeve—quite literally, with shallow cuts marking the skin across her forearm.

Spencer ached to hear Haley's story and then take that story from her and protect her from it, but she couldn't protect the girl from anything, a fact which overwhelmed her with feelings of helplessness.

However, she knew what a powerful weapon the guitar could be against all the darkness in the world. She had once wielded her guitar like a sword, and it had kept her alive through the hardest years of her life. She might not have been able to take away all the horrors Haley had experienced, or might still experience, but she could offer that layer of protection.

"My fingers hurt," the younger of the brothers complained.

Spencer looked at the clock and saw their hour was nearly up, although it had felt like ten minutes, maximum. She had spent the week worrying about the group once she'd found out she'd be co-facilitating it with Faith, but the minute the teens had shown up, she'd been in her element.

The youngest boy had not seemed enamored with the guitar, and she knew it wasn't going to be a beneficial outlet for him. His brother, on the other hand, sulked into the workshop expecting to hate every minute, and had shown a real affinity for the instrument once they'd started. He talked about wanting to learn how to play Tool, and Spencer had worried at first that he'd get frustrated once he realized how far off that goal was, but he worked hard for the entire hour, quiet and focused.

"All right," Faith said. "That's about all of the time that we have for today."

The youngest boy jumped up quickly, but the other two took their time, finishing the chord or chord combination they were working on before setting the guitars down.

Haley gave Spencer a hug and thanked her on her way out.

Spencer would be back in a week, but none of them knew if the teens would still be there. They could leave the shelter in the morning, or they could be there for the better part of a month.

Spencer remembered the uncertainty and the fear that came with not knowing whether they would go home, to her dad—who would be sorry at first and then angrier than ever because they'd dared to leave—or if they'd actually escape to that unknown *somewhere else* which could never promise safety either.

They should leave. Why do women stay to get treated like that?

How many times had Spencer heard that sentiment? If only people knew how impossible leaving often was.

The room cleared, and she quickly set to work gathering the guitars. It felt so minimal, the hour-long music lesson, so *not enough*. She hoped, though, it gave the kids *something* to hang onto throughout everything they had to endure.

"I think the group went well," Faith said.

"It did."

Why does it have to be Faith? She'd known the volunteer project would bring up old wounds and memories, but Faith's presence reopened *every* hurt she'd ever experienced. Her past shouted in surround sound.

"It's really good seeing you again, Spence," Faith said. The way she shortened her name, as though there was still a familiarity between them, set Spencer on edge.

"You too," she managed in response.

Once the guitars and chairs were put away, she and Faith went to pick up the air hockey table and move it back to its place. She carried one end, and Faith the other.

Her stomach knotted at the wistfulness that filled Faith's eyes, and she was forced to look away.

They set the air hockey table down, and she picked up her guitar to go home. She was eager to step out of the memories.

She turned at Faith's sigh.

"I don't want this tension between us," Faith said. "Can we grab a coffee and catch up?"

Spencer hated the uncertainty etched into Faith's delicate features, and she hated herself for causing it, but she needed to step back into the present. Her heart had reached its limit.

"I don't think that's a good idea," she said, as gently as possible. "I'll see you next Thursday. Have a good week."

She turned to leave, but not before catching the look of hurt on Faith's face. Guilt tugged at her, but anger pushed it away. Why should she worry about Faith's feelings, after the way Faith had played with hers so recklessly?

No, she didn't want to catch up.

That part of her past could stay in the past.

Chapter Four

"You're late."

Faith looked at her watch. "Barely. I'm like, five minutes late."

"Which is about twenty minutes later than you typically show up," Mandy pointed out.

Faith rolled her eyes and pulled out a chair to take a seat across from her best friend at the table.

Every Wednesday, she and Mandy met for cocktails and appetizers at their favourite seaside lounge. It started as a way to decompress after work and had quickly turned into a weekly ritual. No matter what was going on in their lives, they made time for their Wednesday friend night. This time, however, she had seriously considered texting Mandy to say she wasn't feeling well.

She picked up one of the menus and let her eyes travel across the page, but she found it hard to focus on the words.

"Split the bruschetta with me?" Mandy asked.

"Sure," she answered, not looking up from her menu.

"What are you getting to drink?"

She shrugged.

The server came by to take their order. Mandy put in an order for bruschetta and her drink, which Faith followed by asking for the same.

As soon as the server was out of earshot Mandy shifted her focus entirely onto Faith, and said, "Okay, spill."

"Spill what?"

Mandy sat back, arms crossed, and one eyebrow raised in a look that told Faith she wasn't going to be able to dodge the question. "First, you show up late, and I don't want to hear 'well, it was only five minutes,' you're Faith Siebert, you're never late. And then you have no opinion about our appetizer and order the exact same drink as me. Do you even know what you ordered?"

"I trust your choice," she said.

"I have excellent taste, but that's not the point. I know you well enough to know when you're distracted, and you've got something on your mind."

She sighed as she weighed how much she could tell Mandy. They'd been best friends since preschool, when they'd been enrolled in the same dance studio. They'd spent so much of their childhood together, between school, dance class, and dance competitions, they were practically sisters. But she had never told Mandy about her relationship with Spencer.

"It's been a long week. Work has been busy. I started that music workshop I was telling you about. And my mom has been on my case again about giving her grandbabies."

Faith buried the detail about the music workshop in the middle of her explanation, but Mandy didn't miss it.

"How's the music workshop going? I know you were really looking forward to that. Who did they end up getting to come in and teach the kids?"

"Spencer Adams." She tried to sound nonchalant.

Mandy's expression hardened for a moment so fleeting she would have missed it had she not been watching for it. Mandy had never cared for Spencer.

"I never would have expected her to grow up and be a role model for teens," Mandy scoffed. "Good for her. Her music's not my thing, but it seems like she's doing well for herself."

"She is," Faith answered, and then she felt compelled to add, "She's doing *really* well for herself."

Their server stepped up to the table with their drinks, and she was grateful for the interruption. She shouldn't have mentioned Spencer.

She looked at the Caesar which had been placed in front of her and took a drink of the complimentary water instead. Caesars were the one cocktail she couldn't stand. A fact which Mandy knew, and the smug smile visible behind the rim of her cocktail glass told her the order had been intentional.

Yeah, Faith should have stayed home. Mandy had been congenial enough, but she still felt her friend's derision toward Spencer. Whether she was picking up on her present feelings or an echo from the past hardly mattered. She didn't feel comfortable discussing Spencer with Mandy.

Even ten years later, she could still remember every detail about the last conversation they'd had about Spencer.

"People are starting to talk."

They'd been tying their pointe shoes, about to go on stage for a competition. No, not "a competition"—the biggest competition. The one they'd spent all season practicing for. Mandy had somehow decided that had been the best time to broach the subject.

"Why does it bother you so much that I'm friends with her?"

"She's weird," Mandy said. "And she's bad news. She hardly comes to class. She's probably at the skate park instead, getting high with Malcolm and his stoner buddies."

"She doesn't smoke pot," Faith said. She knew what people presumed about Spencer, but it wasn't true. She spent a lot of time at the skate park, sure, because she enjoyed skateboarding. But she didn't go there to get high, and she didn't go there when she was supposed to be in class. When she skipped class, it was usually because she was sleeping. She didn't get much sleep on nights when her dad came home drunk, which was most nights.

"Who cares if she does or not?" Mandy asked. "People think she does. They say she's a lesbian."

"What if she is? She's my friend."

She's kind and tender and she makes me feel okay with myself when I'm with her, *Faith had thought, but she'd said nothing, feeling the fear rise in her and choke out the words.*

"They're starting to say you're a lesbian," Mandy said.

She felt the fear edge into panic.

"So what?" she managed.

"So that impacts me," Mandy said. This time the hostility was clear in her voice. She didn't even try to mask it with concern for Faith. "If you're a lesbian, who are they going to speculate about next? We spend all of our time together. And do you think my parents will let me stay over at your place

anymore if they think you're gay? I get that Spencer is your friend, but I'm your best *friend. Is she really worth losing that?"*

Their conversation had been interrupted by their instructor calling the girls to get ready to go on stage. Faith had been distracted throughout the dance, and as a result cost their class a chance at even placing in the top of the competition.

But ultimately, the conversation had cost her far more than some silly ballet medal.

"Earth to Faith?" Mandy asked, waving her hand in front of Faith's face for a moment, bringing her back to the present. "Are you going to try the bruschetta?"

"Oh," she said, only then realizing their appetizer had been set in front of them. "Of course." She picked up a piece of bruschetta and took a bite.

"Are you sure you're okay?" Mandy asked.

"I'm just tired, is all."

She was exhausted. Guilt and regret piled onto her, and there was nobody she could even talk to, to help relieve some of the weight of those feelings.

"I want to start with the ballad this week," Sienna said as she blew into the studio.

Spencer had known it was coming. Sienna had demonstrated a clear enthusiasm for the song, and they'd already pushed it back a week. She couldn't avoid playing it forever. She'd hoped that after the initial shock of seeing Faith again had worn off, all of the old ghosts would have once again vanished, but the second visit to Sunrise House had felt just as disarming as the first. Short of telling her friends all of that, however, she could think of no other way to avoid playing it, so she nodded and tried to muster some enthusiasm in her voice as she said, "Let's do it."

She picked up her guitar and focused her attention on the technical aspects, the way the fingers of her left hand needed to bend to reach each note, and the smooth pull of the strings with her right. She tried not to listen to the notes as they spilled from her guitar into the studio. The thing she'd always loved about music, however, was the way in which it could be *felt* as well as heard, and despite her shift in focus, she was unable to stop the visceral reaction, the memory her body held.

"A spark of light flickers between us."

Sienna's voice was soft and smoky and thick with emotion, and Spencer was instantly transported back to the night she'd written the song.

She sat on her bed, tucked small into the far corner, her guitar in her lap. She wore headphones, but they weren't connected to anything. They served as a barrier against her dad's angry tirade, but fears for her mom's safety didn't let her blast her music to tune him out entirely.

"Let that spark become the sun."

She wanted to hold onto the happiness that bloomed in her chest when she thought of Faith.

Faith, who was light and hope and happiness.

"When you're around it feels like maybe this never-ending night is done."

Faith who had kissed her—*her*—of all people.

That kiss had been the start of things for them, and it was after that first kiss she'd written the song. She'd wrapped herself in the joy of that moment as if she could wear it as armor.

In her youthful naivete, she'd never thought to guard herself against Faith.

The music built to the chorus, and Spencer thought back to that last day. She had a change of clothes and a toothbrush in her backpack. She hadn't wanted to bother with school, but her mom had told her she had to go. If the school called home and reported her absent, her dad would come looking for her and would figure out something was going on.

"Faith? Can we talk?"

She'd caught Faith by her locker after first period. She should have known by the panicked way Faith looked around that something was off. She'd known Faith wasn't ready to be open about them, but she'd never seemed quite so *worried* to be seen with Spencer before.

"Um, I can't right now," Faith said. "I have to get to bio."

Faith agreed to meet her at lunch, in their spot out by the bleachers. Spencer was too busy worrying about everything happening at home to worry about the distance Faith kept when speaking with her, or the nervous edge to her voice. She watched the clock all morning, anxious and needing Faith to anchor her. She needed to tell Faith where she and her mom were going. She needed Faith to tell her she'd be okay, and they'd still manage to talk every day, and she wasn't alone.

Instead, Faith broke her heart.

"I have to talk to you about something," Spencer had said while nervously picking at the sleeves of her hooded sweater.

"I can't do this." Faith blurted.

The words didn't really register with Spencer at first. She had been busy planning how to tell Faith about what was going on.

"What?"

"Us," Faith said, and this time her voice broke. "I'm sorry Spencer. I can't."

She looked up and found tears glistening in Faith's hazel eyes, and the severity of the moment hit her like a truck.

"You're ending things," she said in a small, defeated voice. She couldn't even force the words into a question, because deep down, she'd never believed she was good enough for Faith.

"I'm sorry," Faith said, but the words offered no consolation. "I'm not brave like you. I wish I was, but I'm not."

Spencer sat there, numb. She wanted to argue, but the past week with her parents fighting had knocked all of the fight out of her.

Laughter echoed across the field, along with a chorus of familiar voices.

"I've got to go." Faith left too quickly for Spencer to protest.

She'd left her there feeling defeated and alone.

Sunrise house. Faith. Faith. Sunrise house. The two had always been intertwined. When school ended for the day, Spencer had met her mom by the bus stop, and never went home. She didn't know if she'd ever go back to the same school or if she'd ever see Faith again.

When she returned a few weeks later to see Faith kissing Brett Matheson by the lockers after class, she wished she'd never gone back. Faith had wanted to talk, but there'd been nothing left to say. Spencer had lost absolutely *everything* in her life, she didn't need to hear more reasons or excuses.

"Spencer?"

The sound of her name jarred her from her thoughts, and only then did she realize the music had stopped and her friends' eyes were all on her.

"Is everything okay?" Wren asked.

"Yeah." Spencer gave her head a shake. "All good. Just lost in thought for a minute."

"You didn't look lost in thought," Sienna said. "You looked like you saw a ghost."

Leave it to Sienna to state what everyone else might have been thinking but would be respectful enough not to voice.

She considered dismissing the concern, but these were her best friends; the band was practically family. Her go-to defense was to put up walls, and she'd long ago promised herself she wouldn't do that with her friends.

"I guess I did, in a sense," she answered. "I took on a volunteer project with the shelter my mom and I stayed at, and it turns out I'm working with Faith, the girl I wrote this song about."

For a long moment, it was clear none of her friends knew what to say; they all gaped at her and she shifted uncomfortably under their gazes.

"What is she doing there?" Mari asked.

Spencer shrugged. "I haven't seen her since high school. I didn't have the slightest idea what she was doing with her life these days."

"What do you think it means?" Sienna asked. She and Sienna had always gotten along really well, despite the fact that the two, in most ways, could not be more different. Spencer had always been pragmatic and cautious, while Sienna believed in fate and tended to throw caution to the secret workings of the universe.

"I think it means that she works at the shelter."

"Come on!" Sienna said. "You dust off an old love song that you wrote and then you run into the girl after not seeing her for ten years? You can't really believe it's just a coincidence."

"I wouldn't say it's *just* a coincidence," Spencer conceded. "I'd say it's one *hell* of a coincidence. The mother of all coincidences perhaps."

Sienna rolled her eyes but didn't push the matter.

"Tell me all the gossip," Mari said. "Has she aged terribly? Does she have like, five kids? Is she super sorry for breaking up with you now that you're a famous guitarist?"

Spencer considered the questions and decided to answer honestly. "She looks more or less the same, just ten years older. I don't know if she has kids. And we didn't talk about the band or my career or her feelings."

Sienna tossed her head back and let out a groan of frustration before interjecting, "You're *killing* me. What *did* you ask her?"

"I asked her what time she wanted me to show up to help set up for the volunteer music group."

Sienna shook her head with disappointment.

Spencer had to remind herself Sienna had never known Faith, and only knew the few details she'd been given during the current conversation. "We weren't thrown together by the universe. She broke my heart. I know it was ten years ago and shouldn't bother me anymore, and two weeks ago when I brought in this song the thought of Faith stirred nothing in me, but seeing her in person brought it all back."

Sienna softened. "That's fair. High school seems like a lifetime ago, but I guess it's not when you're face to face again, hey?"

"Exactly." Spencer hoped they could put the conversation to rest.

"Why don't we play something else for now?" Mari suggested.

She picked up her guitar, relief flooding through her. "Something loud."

Even as she prepared herself to disappear behind her guitar, she recognized the relief she felt at having her friends know about Faith. Maybe later she'd be ready to talk through her mess of thoughts. In the meantime, she hoped working together would allow her to finally take Faith down from the pedestal she'd set her on. She wasn't worth the heartache, especially not now, nearly a decade later.

She'd thought she'd moved on, but it was clear she still needed to let go of that piece of her past.

Chapter Five

"The feedback from your first workshop has been really positive," Taz said.

Spencer hadn't realized she'd been holding her breath, but she exhaled with relief at the news. Taz had emailed her and asked to meet prior to the start of their next session, and she had spent the days since running through the first session and imagining everything she'd possibly said and done wrong.

"I'm not surprised," Taz continued. "I think it is just a fantastic idea. I'm so pleased we have something positive to offer these kids while they're staying here. And to have someone whom they idolize, who has been through similar situations, is just invaluable."

"I'm glad to hear it was well received," Spencer said. "I really enjoyed getting to teach the teens. They all seemed really interested and were excellent students. I've been looking forward to tonight all week."

That was the truth. She had left the group feeling as though she was able to make a difference. Music and art could be impactful in their own right but being able to work with the teens and see their reactions made the impact that much more real and tangible to her.

"I spoke with Faith after the group and she told me that you were wonderful with the youth. She said you have a really natural way of being with them and you were able to connect even with the kid who came in with his walls up. That's a special skill to have."

"They were all good kids." Spencer waved off the compliment, but felt the pride settle warm within her chest. She tried not to wonder if any of that warmth came from the fact that the compliment had been passed on to her from Faith.

Taz looked at the clock. "I didn't mean to keep you for so long. I'd better let you go get everything set up. The project is off to a wonderful start. Keep doing what you're doing. We're so grateful to have you here."

"I'm really grateful for this opportunity." She hadn't anticipated she would end up seeing Faith again, and she had allowed that detail to overshadow how truly excited she was to volunteer with the youth at Sunrise House. She headed off to the activity room with the feedback from Taz having renewed her excitement.

Faith had already finished most of the setup by the time Spencer got there. She had cleared out the center of the room and was setting the chairs in a circle. Spencer paused in the entryway and watched as Faith moved with fluid grace. She had always felt so awkward next to Faith, who carried herself with an elegance honed through years of dance.

"Oh, hi." Faith noticed Spencer in the doorway, and a tentative but genuine smile pulled across her face, causing Spencer's stomach to do an annoying little flip.

She dumped you, Spencer reminded herself. *You were heartbroken.*

"Hey," was all she said in response. She ducked out from Faith's gaze and began setting up the rest of the chairs.

Once, things had been so easy between them. Now, they moved clumsily around each other, uncertain how to exist in the same space. Spencer knew she was the cause of the tension. Faith had been as warm and as kind as ever, while she remained distant and cold. She hated it, and yet it seemed safer than the alternative, which was to bridge that distance. She'd learned the hard way the danger of letting Faith get close.

Spencer went around the circle and tuned each guitar, then she took a seat and pulled her own guitar out of its case while she waited for participants.

Faith sat across from her, looking past her to the door.

A few minutes passed. Then, a few minutes more. She watched the clock on the wall, seeing their start time come and go. No youth came to join.

"We might not get any participants today," Faith said. "The three

45

from the other day have all left. There are a few teens staying here right now, but I don't know how interested they are. I let them all know, but..." she let the sentence trail off.

The disappointment was stronger than Spencer would have expected. She'd always known it would be a possibility, both that there would be no returning faces, and that there would potentially be times with no participants at all. The shelter was constantly in flux. She could only guarantee she would be there, once a week, offering an hour for youth to escape into music, should they want to.

Her job was simply to hold space, not to find participants to fill that space.

She picked up her guitar and began to pluck at the strings, eventually transitioning into a slow, soft melody.

"That's really pretty."

Spencer met Faith's soft gaze. "Thanks."

Faith had a guitar rested on the floor in front of her and held the neck of the guitar in her hands, rocking the instrument back and forth.

"Since we're here for this hour, would you teach me, at least?" Faith asked. "I enjoyed learning some of the basics last week."

Spencer hesitated but nodded. "Sure." They had to be there anyway.

Faith picked up her guitar and rested it in her lap. Spencer pulled her chair over, so she was sitting directly in front of Faith with her own guitar in her lap.

"Okay, show me what you remember from last week, and we'll go from there."

Faith began with the C chord, and Spencer watched her study each fret as she set her fingers down. When she strummed, the notes were all correct, but the sound was choked from the tense grip she had on the fretboard.

"You're going to want to relax your hand a little more," Spencer said. "Lift your fingers so they aren't muting any of the strings. Let the notes breathe."

Faith looked confused, and lifted her fingertips, as opposed to opening the curve of her hand.

Spencer reached out and guided Faith's hand with hers, pressing her fingertips into the ball of Faith's hand, to help open the arch more.

The correction had begun without thought, but Faith's hand was softer than she remembered, and she lingered just a breath longer than necessary before awareness hit and she pulled her hand back as though she'd been shocked.

"Try now."

Faith strummed again, and this time the notes were full and rich.

"Wow," Faith said. "What a difference."

Spencer met Faith's hazel eyes, finding Faith's gaze to be hopeful and pleading. She pushed her chair back a few feet, needing to distance herself.

"Keep going," Spencer said. "Work on the chords we practiced and try smoothing the transition between them."

But Faith didn't keep playing. Instead, she set her guitar down and leveled her gaze on Spencer.

"I'm sorry I hurt you, Spencer."

"Don't worry about it. That was years ago." She didn't want to talk about their past.

"It was, but this tension between us... I hate it."

Spencer stayed silent for a long time, as she tried to sort out all her swirling thoughts. So many things remained unsaid still between them: so many questions left unanswered and so much anger she had never been able to express.

"Why are you working here?" she asked, finally, her thoughts settling on her most pressing question.

Faith sat back, looking surprised at the question.

For a moment, Spencer wondered if she'd overstepped, but she needed to know. Faith had been one of only two people who had known about her stays at the shelter--well, besides her last stay. Mari knew the basics. Faith had been the one she'd shared all the intimate details with. All the fear and loneliness and hurt... she had confided in Faith. It burned at her to think Faith had rejected her but then held on to those intimate details of her life's story.

"Faith?" she pressed.

"I've been working here for about a year now, since separating from Brett." Faith let the sentence trail off, but her eyes spoke the words that should have followed, and when the realization hit Spencer, the burn of indignation morphed into a fire of white-hot rage. Brett had always been an asshole, but the thought of him ever doing anything to hurt Faith set her teeth on edge.

"I never stayed at the shelter." Faith held out a hand, clearly trying to tamp down Spencer's concerns. "It never came to that. I got connected with the agency through the community outreach center. The staff there were invaluable in helping me get a protective order filed."

The words hung heavy in the air, and Spencer's jaw clenched against the hate she felt toward Brett Matheson. "Faith," she struggled to find words. "I had no idea. I'm so sorry."

"It wasn't as bad as I can see you thinking. He only hit me once. When I left him, he was full of hot air and threats, but it never manifested into anything."

Her anger didn't ease in the slightest. She knew the qualifiers. Everyone *always* lessened their experience. *It was only ever verbal. He only hit me once. He just got a little rough when he was drinking.* There were others who always had it harder. Others who experienced worse abuse. Others who almost died. Others who did.

"He was very manipulative," Faith said. "Emotionally and financially. I got connected with a good lawyer, and he backed off fairly quickly once he realized he didn't have a chance of controlling me anymore."

Spencer swallowed her words, tasting the bitter bile of them. She wanted to say exactly what she thought of Brett Matheson, but it wasn't time for her feelings. This was Faith's space to tell her story.

"I'd wanted out of my relationship with Brett for a while at that point, but that was the first time I'd ever felt at all afraid of him. I knew then I wanted to use my social work degree to help women and families fleeing worse situations. I'd wanted to work with children in care, but this ended up being my passion."

Spencer understood that passion and shared Faith's desire to make a difference. She looked up and really met her eyes, seeing the depth of care and understanding she had for the women and families at the shelter, and also for what Spencer had gone through so many years earlier. Different paths had led them to their work at the shelter, but ultimately, they shared a connection and an understanding that Spencer shared with few others in her life.

She looked at Faith and suddenly no longer saw the teenager who'd broken her heart. Faith was a woman now, with a whole life lived since high school. She looked so much the same, and yet she was so unfamiliar all at once.

Spencer supposed the same was true for her. Time changed people.

She thought about Faith's invitation to go get coffee. She felt the invitation still hanging in the air between them. She knew if she reopened the offer, Faith would go with her. They could talk, catch up, and fill one another in on the lost years between them.

For the first time since seeing her in her office on that first day, she wanted to know more about Faith's life.

Instead, she looked at the clock. "I guess it's time to put the chairs away."

Faith nodded, and the two worked quietly, putting the room back to its original state.

"It was nice seeing you today," Spencer said, once they had finished. "Thanks for sharing. It was brave of you to open up."

And with that, she headed out.

Chapter Six

"You don't need any butter." Patti Siebert swatted her husband's hand away as he reached for the ceramic tray.

Here we go, Faith thought. *Tonight's dinner battle: Butter!*

"Why do you put it on the table if I'm not allowed to have any?" her dad challenged.

"Because the rest of us who *aren't* on our way to early graves might want some."

Faith had already added a small knob of butter to her mashed potatoes, which was a relief, because she'd have felt too guilty to reach for it in front of her dad after her mom's admonishment.

"I'm not about to add the whole damn stick. Just a little. I promise I'll go light."

Her mom didn't answer. She just leveled him with her stony glare.

Faith knew that glare well. Few people could stand up beneath its power, and she watched as the fight went out of her dad and his resolve shrunk.

"I might outlive you all, but at what cost?" He took a bite of his dry potatoes.

Faith caught the laugh that bubbled out of her, but not before some sound escaped. Her mom's hard glare turned to her.

"Do you want your dad to die before he has the chance to walk you down the aisle?"

"Yes mom," Faith said, her voice dripping with sarcasm. "I am actually hoping that he'll keel over any minute."

She wasn't about to point out the fact that her dad already *had* walked her down the aisle. From the minute her parents had learned of her divorce, both had acted as though her marriage to Brett had never existed. It was easier for them to believe that than it was for them to accept that her marriage had *failed*. They had never asked why she had ended her relationship with Brett, and she had never offered them any of the myriad of reasons.

"I know you think you're being funny," her mom said, "but I seem to be the only one concerned about keeping your dad alive."

"I appreciate your concern," her dad answered, and his response softened her mom, taking the fight out of her. "I'll make more of an effort. I want to stick around for a good long time. I'm making progress with my run club. I ran ten minutes straight this week, and I didn't feel like I was going to die after!"

"Congratulations, Dad," Faith said. "That's amazing." She knew how hard he had worked to get to that point. He'd barely been able to run to the end of the driveway when he'd started out.

"I went for coffee with my friend Wendy Blackwell this week," her mom said, changing the subject.

"Do I know Wendy?" her dad asked.

Her mom thought for a moment before shaking her head. "No, I suppose not. She's in my aqua Zumba class. We go for coffee after class some mornings. Anyway, we had a really nice chat. It was great to get to catch up. She told me that her son, Owen, just moved back to Vancouver. She's so excited to have him home. He studied medicine in Toronto for a number of years. He's back now and just got a job in a small family practice."

Faith knew where the conversation was headed, and she wished that there was some way to steer her mom off course.

"She showed me a picture of him. He's quite handsome. I guess medical school kept him busy, so he hasn't had much time to date. Wendy's hoping he'll find the right girl now that he's home."

"I'm sure she's out there," Faith said, an edge of snark to her words.

If her mom heard the snark, she didn't acknowledge it. Instead, her eyes widened as though she had been hit with a sudden idea and the conversation hadn't all been staged to get them to this grand plan of hers. "You should meet him! He sounds really lovely. He's smart, he has a good profession, he's attractive…"

"I don't—" she began, but her mom cut her off before she could politely decline.

"One dinner, Faith. If you don't like him, that's fine, but what's the harm in meeting him for dinner?"

She took a breath to quell the anger that simmered inside. Usually, she could handle her mom's persistence, but this topic—after seeing Spencer again—all she could think about was how her life might have been different had she not bent to other people's wills when she was younger, which only ratcheted up the pressure to stand her ground this time.

"When I'm ready to date again, I will," she said, and before her mom could say another word, Faith held up one finger to silence her. "And I will find my own date."

A long beat of silence passed, and she watched the emotions play across her mom's face: stony determination, then disappointment, and then what looked to be guilt.

"I already told Wendy you would be interested." Her mom at least had the good sense to sound ashamed. "She showed Owen your picture and apparently he's really eager to meet you. He made dinner reservations for the two of you next Saturday."

"You what?" This time, the anger burned white-hot. Faith pushed her chair back from the table. Her appetite was gone, and she wanted air.

"I knew you'd be hesitant, but Faith, he sounds like a really nice man. If not for yourself, then do it as a favour for me. He wants to meet you."

She pushed up from the table, took a few steps toward the door, then walked back toward the table, and opened her mouth to tell her mom exactly what she thought of her meddling.

"Sit down, Faith," her dad said, his voice stern.

She looked at him and she was ten years old again, wishing her feet would carry her out the front door, but not knowing how to blatantly disobey her parents. She sat back down at the table, hating herself as she did so. She felt pouty and petulant, her anger the anger of a child.

"It's one dinner," he said. "Your mother made a mistake in planning it without asking you first. Lesson learned. But it would reflect poorly on her if she were to cancel it now, so please consider meeting this Owen fellow for one dinner."

Faith felt trapped. Her mother hadn't made a mistake. Her mother had been very intentional about not asking her first. She was certain of it. Her parents wanted the best for her, but she wished they'd recognize it wasn't their place to *decide* what was best. She was an adult, even if she felt the furthest thing from it. She thought of Spencer, of how confident and self-assured she was. She wanted to be one-tenth as bold.

"I am not meeting him for dinner." She kept her voice as steady as she could manage.

"Faith," her mom said, eyes pleading.

Standing her ground meant disappointing her parents, and the thought of that felt like too much to bear. And yet, the thought of going on a forced date with this guy, Owen—she couldn't.

"I would like to be excused," she said. "I think it's best I go home now."

This time when she stood, for the first time in her life, she didn't sit back down.

Chapter Seven

"Can you *believe* her?" Faith asked. "She's so desperate for me to get remarried and give her grandbabies she doesn't even pause to think of what *I* want."

Not even the peach Bellini or the expansive view of the Pacific could temper her anger as she vented to Mandy about the disastrous dinner with her parents the night before. Mandy had noticed her mood while the two taught their Saturday morning ballet classes, and suggested they cancel their afternoon plans and head to their usual lounge for emergency cocktails and conversation.

"Who's the guy she's got picked out for you?" Mandy asked. She did *not* appear appropriately outraged.

"Owen Blackwell," Faith said. "The son of one of her Zumba friends. She's never even met Owen, but he sounds good to her on paper, so he *must* be Mr. Right."

Mandy said nothing, reaching instead for the phone she'd set on the table.

"What are you doing?" Faith asked.

"What do you think I'm doing? I want to get a look at this guy." Mandy tapped a couple of buttons on her phone and then turned the screen to face Faith. "Is this him?"

She took the phone and looked at the Facebook profile Mandy had found for Owen Blackwell. She took a moment to confirm a few key details: doctor, lived in Vancouver, went to school in Toronto. She nodded. "Yeah, that's him."

Mandy turned the screen back toward herself so that she could study Owen's profile. She nodded and murmured appreciatively a few times.

"So, what's wrong with this guy?" she asked at last.

"What do you mean?"

Mandy began listing all of Owen's top qualities on her fingers. "He's really attractive, he's a doctor, I can tell from his photos that he keeps active and likes to travel, he's got a really nice smile, he looks like a real family guy…" She ran out of fingers on her one hand. "What's wrong with him? Why *don't* you want to go out with him?"

She groaned. "Not you, too. For starters, my *mother* arranged the date."

"Mmm." Mandy nodded in exaggerated agreement, which told Faith it was clear she was still being judged.

She wanted to come up with more reasons, but she didn't have any good ones.

"Let me see his profile again," she said.

Mandy grinned in victory and passed her phone to Faith.

This time, she looked at the pictures. He appeared tall, with close-cropped blond hair and a clean-shaven face. He was smiling wide in his profile photo, taken somewhere in the mountains, with his arms wide and an incredible view behind him. He *was*, objectively, quite good looking, but she couldn't muster an ounce of interest.

"He's not my type." She handed the phone back to Mandy who looked at her as though she was crazy.

"This guy is *hot*," Mandy said, tapping the phone with her index finger. "If I wasn't married to Chad, I'd be asking your mom to set *me* up. You two would be totally cute together, and you'd have some beautiful blond babies."

"I'll pass," she said, and she looked out at the ocean, focusing on the waves in an attempt to quell her frustration.

"Seriously, Faith."

She turned to see Mandy leaning forward to study her.

"What *is* your type?"

The question hadn't been spoken with judgment, but rather a genuine curiosity. She thought about it for a long moment. She'd married Brett straight out of high school, and she hadn't looked for anyone since him. She knew, in retrospect, that Brett had never been her type. Not even in the beginning, before all the bad. At first, he'd said all of the right things, her family and friends all liked him, and it had felt like the relationship she was *supposed* to want. But her own excitement had always fallen flat.

Had Spencer been her type? They'd been so different. In high school, if she'd been shown a photo of Spencer, she would have passed the phone back then as well. At first, she'd seen what everyone else did: a bad attitude tucked inside of oversized black hooded sweaters. When she'd started to get to know Spencer was when she started noticing the crystal depths in her blue eyes, or the dimple in only her left cheek when she smiled, or the subtle ripple of muscle in her forearms when she played guitar.

"I like the creative type," she said at last, hoping to say something that would appease Mandy so they could change the subject.

Mandy's eyes lit up. "Like the brooding artist?"

She gave a noncommittal shrug.

Mandy was already nodding, her eyes looking upward indicating that she was deep in thought. "I can work with that."

"Please don't."

"Faith, *please*? I'll find you the perfect guy," Mandy begged. "Chad and I have no one to double-date with anymore now that you and Brett are over."

If Faith hadn't already been about to put her foot down, the mention of Brett ensured it. Mandy had pretty much hand-selected Faith's last relationship, and it had been a disaster. Not that Mandy knew the details. Chad and Brett had been best friends their entire lives, just like she and Mandy had, and so she had never divulged any of the details of her relationship with Brett to Mandy.

"Leave it," Faith insisted. "I'll date when I'm ready."

"Fine." Mandy held up both hands in concession. "I just want you to be happy."

But she *was* happy. She was happier single than she'd ever been.

The thought brought her up short and she flashed back to her time with Spencer. Okay, she was happier single than she'd ever been *with Brett*. There was one period of time that shone brighter than the others.

But that was in her past, their relationship long over. They were different people now, and there was no use thinking about what might have been.

And definitely no use entertaining the thought of anything that *could* be.

Chapter Eight

Spencer stepped into the small apartment without knocking and set the bags of Chinese food she'd brought with her on the counter.

"Mom, I'm here," she called, as she untied the bags of food and laid out the different containers: fried rice, chow mein, pineapple chicken, wonton soup, and ginger beef.

Her mom, Renee, came out of the bedroom dressed in a nice floral dress with a burgundy cardigan. She'd added some light curls to her graying brown hair, and had taken the time to apply makeup, which she rarely wore anymore. Every year she dressed up for this dinner.

She gave Spencer a quick hug then went to get plates from the cupboard.

"Year ten," she said as she set the table.

Spencer removed the lids from the takeout containers. "A whole decade."

And that was all they would say to acknowledge the fact that exactly one decade ago they'd finally left her dad for the last time.

Spencer spooned rice onto her plate and set some ginger beef atop the rice. Growing up, meals had never been anything fancy and Chinese takeout had become a treat reserved for all special occasions. When they'd come to the first anniversary of their new life, her mom had unceremoniously picked up their usual order. There had been no mention of the date, but the meal had been a quiet nod to the significance of the day. They'd done the same each year since. Her mom often dressed a little nicer than usual, and Spencer turned her cell phone off so she could be fully present, but otherwise, there was nothing special about their meal.

"How's the new album coming along?"

Renee took her plate to the table and sat down, while Spencer finished filling hers.

"Actually, really well." She took a seat across from her mom. "This past week, things have started to come together. The song writing is starting to click, you know?"

Renee nodded, even though she didn't know. "I can't wait to hear it."

Spencer knew her mom didn't understand her band's music— she thought punk music was loud and aggressive—but she always showed interest and enthusiasm regardless. While her appreciation of Shattered Ceiling's music may have been a little forced, her pride was never anything but genuine.

"You'll be the first to hear the album," Spencer said. "I promise."

She picked up some chow mein with her set of disposable chopsticks and took a bite, as she chewed over whether or not she should tell her mom about her volunteer project. She'd said nothing so far, uncertain about how her mom would react. They didn't ever talk about their stays in the shelter, but this seemed like the fitting night to finally do so, even if it was breaking their unspoken agreement to not discuss the reason for the anniversary dinner.

"I've, um, started volunteering at Sunrise House," Spencer said. "I'm teaching the teens there how to play guitar."

"Oh." Spencer saw the questions written in the frown lines that creased her mom's forehead, but her mom didn't ask more. "Good for you."

She let the conversation rest, but it remained on the table between them, nestled in with the Chinese food containers. She doubted either of them would pick it back up. She'd never been able to talk about how their past had impacted her. The pain of her mom's own hurt and regret had always eclipsed those conversations. What was important, was that she no longer felt she was volunteering at the shelter behind her mom's back. It was out in the open. They didn't have to discuss it further.

But her mom surprised her, picking the conversation up when she reached for the wonton soup.

"The first shelter stay should've been the last." She didn't look up to meet Spencer's eyes, instead opening the soup and ladling some into a bowl.

"Ten years," Spencer offered. "We got out. That's what matters."

But, quietly, she agreed with her mom. They should have been celebrating twenty. Time and again she'd watched her mom forgive her dad, and inevitably he would hurt them more the next time. She'd often thought of Maya Angelou's words: *When someone shows you who they are, believe them the first time.*

Her dad had showed them early on that he was bitter and angry and volatile. Her entire youth had been wasted on forgiveness and promises of change. People didn't change.

Her thoughts flashed to Faith, not for the first time that week. She'd found it hard to take her mind off of the tender way Faith's eyes held her and how soft Faith's hand had felt when she'd adjusted Faith's grip on the guitar. But Faith had shown Spencer who she was: somebody who put her image first, at the expense of herself and at the expense of someone she'd claimed she loved.

"I called and booked you a service appointment for your car," Spencer said, changing the subject. "If it's okay with you, I'll swing by tomorrow to take it in."

"I can book my own service appointments," her mom said, but Spencer heard the relief in her voice. For the better part of a month, her mom had been complaining about her car making a weird rattling sound, and yet every time Spencer asked if she'd taken it in, she said she'd forgotten and she'd call as soon as the office opened the next day.

"I know, Mom, but you've been really busy. I thought I could help out."

"You're the best," her mom said. "I don't know what I'd do without you."

Spencer finished her meal and then cleared the dishes. She'd grown up learning how to protect and take care of her mom, as well as protect and take care of herself. She'd seen where forgiveness got them.

When someone shows you who they are, believe them the first time.

Chapter Nine

Watching Spencer interact with the youth quickly became one of Faith's favourite parts of the week. She had a natural way of being with the teens that Faith envied. With her dyed hair and tattoos, she was approachable in a way most adults weren't. She didn't look like someone who would scold them for breaking curfew or for listening to the wrong type of music or for getting a bad grade on an assignment. But Spencer's impression on the youth went deeper than a simple bridge of the generational divide. The teens came into session wearing their hearts and identities on their sleeves, Spencer didn't make them feel like they needed to hide themselves because *she* didn't hide herself.

Faith had always admired that about Spencer: how unapologetically *her* she was.

Meanwhile, Faith had been molded and shaped into the perfect student, the perfect daughter, the perfect girl. She didn't even know what being unapologetically herself would look like.

"Good," Spencer said, as the girl adjusted her fingers on the strings of the guitar. "That's good. Now strum."

The girl strummed once, a single downward stroke, and a small smile formed on her face as the chord rang out, full and harmonious, no longer containing the dissonant note that had marred the sound.

They had two participants this week, both fourteen-year-old girls. One had been at the shelter for a little over a week and had attended the workshop the week before, and the other had just arrived. Both girls were enthusiastic about the workshop, and the new girl, who Spencer was helping, had been over the moon to find Spencer Adams leading the group.

Faith glanced up at the clock, surprised to see how quickly their time had evaporated. It seemed like each week the session grew shorter.

"I hate to interrupt," she said. "I just want to give you all a heads-up that we have about five minutes left."

The disappointment was evident on both girls' faces, and Faith felt the same, wishing she could extend the session another fifteen minutes.

"Can you play us something?" one of the girls asked Spencer, who sat back and looked to each girl.

"Please?" the other one asked.

Faith found herself leaning forward with the same interest as the girls. None of the other groups had asked Spencer to play for them, and as such, the workshops had focused on the teens' learning.

But both girls appeared equally enthusiastic about the request, and Spencer sat back, nodded, and pulled her guitar into her lap.

"What do you want to hear?" she asked.

"'Bottle Rockets!'" they answered simultaneously.

Spencer laughed. "Of course."

It was the song that *everyone* knew them for. Faith wouldn't have been surprised if it was the *only* Shattered Ceiling song either of these girls were familiar with. But Spencer didn't seem at all bothered by that fact.

"Sienna isn't here to sing," Spencer said, "so you'll have to bear with me."

And with that brief disclaimer, she began to play.

From the first notes, Faith was riveted. Spencer played through the opening riff, but she slowed it down, allowing the notes of the acoustic guitar room to breathe. The version Faith was familiar with was typically electric and heavy-charged. It pulled the listener in with the fast-paced energy that it ramped up and up until the final note. This version, stripped of the other instruments, amp, and effects, had an entirely different feel to it.

We're building bottle rockets in our basement.

Spencer began to sing the lyrics, and the rest of the room fell away. She might not have been the singer in the band, but Faith decided she *could* have been. Her voice held a soft, smoky quality that added gravity to the lyrics.

Just kids setting them off on the pavement.

The stripped-down version of the song had a wistful, nostalgic quality to it. Faith knew the words. She'd sung along with the lyrics while driving. It had never before been more than a catchy pop-punk youth anthem.

Light it, ignite it, this spark, you shouldn't fight it.

Spencer's gaze caught hers and Faith felt her breath catch at the wave of memories that hit her. She'd lived unapologetically once, but only briefly.

We only live once.

The regret that flooded her was so all-encompassing it deafened her to the rest of the song. Her youth hadn't been reckless and impassioned. She had gone from school and ballet to work and marriage without ever pausing to *live.* She'd done *one* thing truly for herself in life when she'd dated Spencer, and in the end, she'd given in to all the voices that told her who she *should* be.

She'd married Brett, the boy everyone expected her to marry—popular, attractive, from a "good" family.

From a wealthy *family,* Faith amended.

She had come to find the two traits were often conflated, even though one had nothing to do with the other. If anything, it seemed to her more often than not the two had an *inverse* relationship.

Brett had been popular, attractive, and wealthy, and he'd also been manipulative, controlling, and cruel. She'd withered in that relationship. After leaving Brett, it had taken months before she felt even a little bit like herself again, and she was still trying to rediscover her identity and passions.

Maybe rediscover wasn't the right word. Maybe she'd never discovered them in the first place.

"Faith?"

She looked up and saw Spencer's blue eyes, darkened with concern, fixed on her. She quickly realized Spencer had stopped singing, and everyone in the group was looking at her.

She blinked and then straightened in her chair. "Sorry, I got lost in thought for a moment there." Inwardly, she kicked herself. She had a group to help facilitate. She was expected to be present and attuned to the group, not lost in her own regret and bad life choices.

She checked the clock. "It looks like that's all the time we have for today."

The teens both thanked Spencer for the lesson and left, talking excitedly to each other as they headed off.

Faith quietly stood and began to fold up the chairs.

"Hey." Spencer rested a hand on her shoulder and warmth radiated down her back and arm.

She turned and met Spencer's worried gaze.

"What happened?"

"Just lost in thought." She picked up another chair to put away, but Spencer didn't move.

"About what?" Spencer asked.

She could feel Spencer's eyes following her.

"Probably my grocery list," she lied.

Spencer moved closer to her. Faith set the chair she had folded with the others and turned to face her.

"Do you still want to get that coffee?" Spencer asked.

The question surprised her. "I thought you'd taken that offer off the table entirely."

"So did I."

Faith studied Spencer for a moment. She couldn't decipher the look etched across her features. She *did* want to get coffee with her, she hated the distance between them, but she couldn't make sense of the invitation.

"What changed?" she asked.

Spencer lifted one shoulder and dropped it lazily. "I guess I realized that there's a lot about you I don't know."

Faith saw her try to make the statement sound casual, but there was an intimacy that added weight to the words.

"And you want to know me?" she pressed, her stomach tightening nervously against the hope that tried to bubble up inside of her.

Again, Spencer gave a one-shoulder shrug. "I'm curious."

"I'll take that." The tension fell away with gratitude and relief. Spencer was opening the door to her, even if only a crack. "Name your coffee spot."

Spencer parked in front of Black Soul Coffee and stepped through the doors to the delightful smell of roasting beans and the sound of punk music coming over the stereo. The little hole-in-the-wall coffee shop catered to a niche crowd, with its punk and metal music focus, but the staff's commitment to building relationships with their customers gave them a fiercely loyal customer base. It was her favourite coffee shop, and one of her favourite places in the city. She'd picked it as the place to have coffee with Faith not just because of its relative proximity to the shelter, but because it felt like home, which would keep her grounded.

And you want to know me?

Faith's question had echoed in her mind for the entirety of the short drive. She *didn't* particularly want to know her. She *had* known her once. She'd known the way Faith made people feel special by giving them her complete attention, and the deep and powerful way she cared about others. When they'd been paired together on their Shakespeare assignment, Spencer had known that she'd been Faith's absolute last choice for a partner, and yet she'd never once *felt* like a last choice. Faith had been patient and kind, and she'd made her feel valued for the first time in her memory. She'd known Faith's heart, and she'd fallen in love.

But ultimately, those good traits weren't all she knew. She'd come to know that while Faith might have made her *feel* valued, she was never truly valued. In the end, Faith had allowed all of the others in her life to show her who they thought she was.

Spencer knew enough.

But there had been a sadness in Faith's eyes, and she hadn't seemed able to let that be.

"Hey, Spence." Nikolai, the owner of the shop, greeted her with a smile, and she was instantly comforted by her friend's welcoming grin.

She stepped over to the counter to chat with him while she waited for Faith to find parking and join her. "Hey, Nik. How're things?"

"They've been good. We just got our new roaster in. It's a seven-kilo roaster, so we'll be able to roast larger batches of beans now."

"That's excellent," Spencer said, and Nikolai beamed with excitement.

Nikolai roasted all of Black Soul's beans, and often paired with local bands to release special blends alongside the bands' album releases. Their "Bottle Rocket Blond" roast had been a top seller, and the shop had struggled to keep up with the demand once the song took off.

"How's the new album coming along?" he asked.

This time, it was her turn for excitement to shine through. "It's really starting to come together. We've got a few songs that I think you'll really like."

"I can't wait to hear it. And keep us posted. We'd love to do another custom roast for you."

"For sure," she agreed.

The chime of the door opening interrupted their conversation. She turned to see Faith step inside and look around the small building. The place had a sleek interior: black tables and chairs, hardwood floors, and gray walls, clean and simple. But the walls were adorned with horror- and sci-fi-themed posters that had been created by various Canadian artists: bold images with bright colours.

"This place is neat," Faith said, stepping over to the counter where Spencer stood. "I didn't even know it existed."

No, she didn't suppose Faith would have heard of the place. It wasn't exactly the type of coffee shop she and her friends were likely to frequent.

"The coffee here is incredible. Trust me."

"I'll take your word."

Faith's smile softened Spencer despite her defenses, and she had to turn away, stepping up to the counter before Faith could pull her in further. She ordered a black coffee, while Faith chose a vanilla latte. Spencer paid for both drinks and took the hot mug of coffee Nikolai handed her, as he promised the latte would only take a moment. The warm mug was grounding, and she focused on the feel of it in her hands.

"There's some really neat art here," Faith said.

Spencer led her over to the far wall and swung her gaze toward a large, detailed picture of a sea monster. "This one is my favourite."

She watched as Faith studied the image, her brows furrowing as she took in all of the aching details before reading aloud the little title tag on the bottom. "*Grief* by Lisa Whelan."

"She's one of my favourite artists. I've followed her work for years. She illustrated a graphic novel series I love, but over the past few years, she's branched out and has started selling images individually. Her art is incredibly evocative."

"I see that." Faith continued to gaze at the framed print.

In the image on the wall, a small boat sat on top of a turbulent ocean. A sea monster had coiled around the ship, its tentacles crushing the frame of the boat. The captain was visible in his quarters, trying to steer the ship. Desperate. Helpless. How often had Spencer felt that same helplessness? She had followed Lisa's career closely enough to know the story behind Lisa's art, but the image was so universally powerful that she saw all of her own pain reflected in the sea captain's eyes.

"My band is hoping she'll design the cover art and t-shirts for our next album." She shifted away from the vulnerability she felt as Faith looked upon the piece of art. "We've been in talks with her and she seems pretty excited, but until we're finished with the song writing we can't give her too much guidance on theme or images that we want used."

Nikolai called Faith's name and she left to pick up her vanilla latte, while Spencer found a table for the two of them.

"I'm glad you decided to have coffee with me." Faith took her seat across from Spencer, who took a sip of her coffee before responding, thinking through how to answer. She didn't want to hang onto the hurt of the past, but she didn't want to open the door to connection with Faith only to get hurt again, either.

She decided to answer with a question. "What was going through your head earlier, in the group, when you spaced out?"

She'd seen the look on Faith's face. She hadn't been lost in thought about her grocery list, or the errands she had to run, or the friends she wanted to catch up with over the weekend. She'd looked far away and a little sad.

Faith studied Spencer, as though deciding how honestly to answer.

"I'd never heard 'Bottle Rockets' like that before."

She had so many follow-up questions and didn't know which one she wanted to pose first. She decided to start with the one that leapt into her mind first. "You're familiar with it?"

"I own a radio," Faith said.

That earned a laugh. Their song had become more popular than they'd have ever imagined, but still, she was surprised to hear *Faith* knew it. Their music didn't exactly seem the type that she would listen to.

"I really like your album," Faith said, as though she'd heard her thoughts. "There are a lot of really catchy songs on it. I wasn't at all surprised when it started getting so much radio play."

"Wait. You listened to our music even before we were on the radio?"

Faith's face flushed. "Maybe a little. I didn't know you were in a band, and when I found out…" She paused and trailed off.

"What?" Spencer pressed.

Faith met her gaze, her voice soft and sincere when she spoke. "I was really proud of you. We'd lost touch, but still, it made me really happy to know you were living your dream."

The words, and the way Faith said them, hit Spencer low in the gut. She hated the effect Faith still had on her, ten years later.

"So you heard 'Bottle Rockets' today and what?" she asked.

Faith suddenly seemed to take interest in the art on the walls, and she studied the various pictures as she sipped her vanilla latte. It was a long moment before she answered, and Spencer felt guilt sink in at the edge to her words.

"I'm *not* living my dream," Faith said at last. "When you played 'Bottle Rockets' tonight, without the rest of your band, I really *listened* to the lyrics. You sang about being young and in love and *alive*, and it made me regret the choices that I've made. I missed out on so much in my life. I've spent so much time simply existing."

Spencer hadn't expected that level of honesty, and she wasn't sure how to react. The ache of regret in Faith's voice tugged at her, and yet, at the same time, a very human part of her couldn't help but feel vindicated. Those 'mistakes' Faith had made had hurt her deeply.

"What is your dream?" she asked.

"I want to travel," Faith said without hesitation. "The world is so big, and I feel like the corner that I live in is so small. I would love to visit every continent. Maybe take a year to teach English in South America or go on a safari in Africa."

"So, do it. Why not? What's holding you back?"

"I'm just getting myself back on my feet after the divorce," Faith answered. "Both mentally and financially."

"Get a work visa," Spencer suggested. "Teach English or get a job in a cafe. *Something*."

"It's not the right time," Faith said, all the excitement extinguished from her voice. "My dad's health hasn't been the greatest, and my mom, she worries. If I took a year to work abroad, even six months, I'd never hear the end of it. And if something happened to my dad while I'm off travelling the world, I'd never forgive myself."

Spencer heard a lot of excuses. She tried to understand Faith's perspective, but ultimately, if she didn't want to live her life, then that was her choice. She would still have the same regrets another ten years down the line.

"You think I'm a coward," Faith said, as though she could see Spencer's thoughts written across her face.

"I don't." She would have never used a word so harsh, but their relationship had fallen victim to Faith's fear of living her own life, and so the assessment wasn't far off.

"It's all right," Faith said, her voice sad again. "It's probably true."

Spencer could see the regret and longing in Faith's eyes, and yet, Faith would do nothing to fight for what she wanted. It shouldn't have mattered to her, but she felt anger simmer within her at the thought. Life was so incredibly short, and Faith was letting it slip right through her fingers.

"So then, what else do you dream of doing?" she pressed. She knew she should let it go, but she wanted to see some fire in Faith's eyes. She hated the defeated look that lived there instead. "Maybe you can't take off and live in Costa Rica for a year, but what are some of your other dreams?"

She worried she was out of line and pushing too far, but Faith sat back and considered the question. "I don't know. Nothing specific. I just don't want life to pass me by, you know? I don't want to be the person who gets old saying 'I always wanted to try skydiving, but it just never happened.' I want to be the person who takes the risk and jumps out of the plane."

"Let's go then."

Faith blinked, as Spencer's words hit both of them. "That was a figure of speech. I don't *actually* want to jump out of a plane."

Spencer's suggestion had tumbled past her lips without thought but she felt her resolve strengthen around the suggestion as she asked, "Why not?"

"Why not?" Faith echoed. "Because I could fall from the sky to a horrible death."

Spencer didn't waver as she countered, "Or you could *live*."

Conflict played across Faith's face: fear, longing, regret, and desire. Had it only been fear in Faith's eyes, she would have backed down, but she could see how badly Faith wanted to take the leap and she hated the thought of Faith letting that fear oppress her. She tamped down her own fear of spending time with the woman who'd broken her heart and waited while Faith considered the offer.

Faith studied her latte, brow furrowed, until her jaw set with resolve, the rest of her features softened, and she looked up at Spencer. "Okay. Let's do it."

Chapter Ten

Faith tried to steady her heart, which beat like a hammer, as she drove to the drop zone. The sky yawned overhead, a clear blue that did nothing to calm her nerves, taunting her instead with the stillness. She tried to focus on the road, but she kept envisioning herself falling through that vast empty air. Fear kept her in its icy grip, but even as the knot in her stomach swelled, a very real undercurrent of excitement kept her foot on the gas.

She had lied when she'd told Spencer that jumping out of a plane had just been a figure of speech. Skydiving had always been on her bucket list. When she felt trapped in life—in her marriage, in her parents' expectations, in the pressure to look or act or *be* a certain way—she allowed herself to envision the free fall, imagining that it felt like flying. And yet, it had always been a "one day" activity, always just a pleasant vision she'd held onto through hard times.

Until Spencer had sent her a text message with the details of their skydiving appointment—then suddenly the whole spontaneous and foolish decision had become real.

She pulled into the drop zone's small gravel parking lot. Spencer had booked them the first slot of the morning, so the lot was mostly empty with only a handful of cars, but still she parked in one of the far corners, wanting the space and privacy to take a minute to breathe before getting out to meet Spencer. She'd read every fact and statistic about skydiving that she could find, and she reminded herself the drive to the drop zone was the most dangerous part of the morning, but knowledge did little to quell the instinctual panic of falling to her death.

"I can do this," she told herself, before taking one deep breath and stepping out of her car and into the warm morning.

A small building sat surrounded by open field, and she spotted Spencer leaning casually against its door, appearing unfairly relaxed.

"You're here," Spencer said, surprise evident in her voice.

That surprise rubbed at Faith like sandpaper, even if it *was* warranted. "Sorry. If you're hoping to get out of this, it's going to have to be you who backs out."

Spencer laughed and the sound was so warm and uninhibited that Faith momentarily forgot the fear that gripped her.

"I guess we're doing this then." Spencer squared her shoulders at the challenge.

Faith's boldness was not entirely authentic, but she refused to back down, even as she noted Spencer's eyes were the same soft blue as the clear and cloudless sky, and a new fear welled within her as she thought of falling into that tender gaze.

"Are you ready then?" she asked, bringing them back to the moment.

"Let's do this."

She followed Spencer inside and they were greeted at the sign-in counter by a young woman who handed each of them a thick stack of papers.

"Here's your waiver. I need you to read it carefully and initial each item. Once you're finished, bring it back here and we will get you started."

Faith's mouth went dry as she took the waiver, the physical weight of the document adding to the metaphorical weight of the moment. She sat at one of the small, round tables and began to read the waiver, which outlined all the ways in which she might end up dead or maimed. Her pulse quickened with each item.

It's not too late to back out, she reminded herself as she initialed the last item on the first page and flipped to the second page, but a quick glance over at Spencer showed her initialing items down the page, and Faith kept moving through the waiver as well.

She couldn't help but consider what Spencer might think of her if she decided she *couldn't* skydive. Spencer already thought she was a coward and backing out would only prove that. But that knowledge was only a very small part of what kept her going as she read through the waiver. More than what Spencer thought of her, she considered what she would think of herself. She was so tired of sitting on the sidelines watching life pass her by. She didn't want this to turn into another missed opportunity. If she went home *without* jumping out of the plane, she'd have one more item to add to her long list of regrets, and she'd no longer be able to imagine the exhilaration of the free fall without knowing how she'd let herself down. Again. Her fear of getting in the plane and being unable to jump out at least equaled, if not exceeded, her fear of plummeting to her death.

She finished signing her waiver and watched as Spencer signed the final page of hers. Slight fear echoed in Spencer's eyes as she read the final items, but when she stood to take the waiver back to the sign-in counter, she exuded her usual confidence.

Faith got up and tried to stand with the same solid certainty as she turned in her own waiver.

"All right! I hear we've got some first-time skydivers here!" An energetic man about the same age as Spencer and Faith approached them with a wide smile on his face, alongside a demure middle-aged woman, who looked like she belonged in a parent-teacher association or a knitting club, not jumping out of planes as a profession.

"That's us," Spencer said.

Was that a slight shake in her voice?

"Excellent!" the man said. "I'm Dale and this is Cathy and we're going to be your tandem instructors this morning. I can tell you already that today is going to be a ton of fun. It's a beautiful morning, there are no clouds and no winds, and it'll be an incredible jump with spectacular views."

Somehow his enthusiasm didn't rub off on Faith as she realized just *how* real this skydiving deal was about to become. She glanced toward Spencer and couldn't help but note her skin was a shade paler than usual and she was picking errantly at the skin around her fingernails.

It helped steady Faith to know she was not the only one nervous over what they were about to do.

"What are your names?" Dale asked.

Spencer introduced herself, and then Faith did too. When she said her name, she heard her voice as though from outside of herself.

"All right, Spencer, you'll be with me, and Faith, we'll pair you with Cathy. Let's head over there and get you suited up." He pointed to where a rack of bodysuits hung.

Cathy helped select a size for Faith and handed her a bright blue jumpsuit.

"I've been skydiving for fifteen years and have completed just over seven thousand jumps," Cathy said. While Dale radiated enthusiasm and energy, Cathy projected calm and certainty. Her voice was soft and reassuring.

"So, you're going to get me back onto the ground alive?" she asked, letting some of her fear come through.

"I never make any promises, but I certainly intend to."

Faith would have preferred a promise, but she stepped into the jumpsuit and pulled it on.

She watched Spencer finish zipping up her bodysuit. She felt certain the garment looked ridiculous on her, but on Spencer it somehow fit just right, highlighting her lean and strong physique, the bright blue cloth bringing out her eyes. It was unfair how good she looked even in a bright blue full-body zip-up suit.

Spencer turned and caught Faith watching her, and the smile she offered didn't hide her nerves.

"We're doing this," Faith said.

Spencer's smile widened as she nodded. "We are."

"All suited up and ready?" Dale asked as he zipped up his own bodysuit.

Faith nodded, though she felt anything *but* ready.

"Excellent. This is going to be a fun morning. We're going to take you up to fifteen thousand feet. Once we get up there, we'll level out and then we'll open the door. You'll be strapped to your tandem instructor and those straps will be tightened on the way up. You and your instructor will scoot to the door together. You'll sit on the ledge and we will have you both look up and count to three. On three we will rock out of the plane."

Faith's stomach leapt into her throat as Dale explained what was about to happen.

"We'll free fall for about a minute," he continued. "You'll reach terminal velocity of two hundred kilometers per hour."

The room fell away and a wave of nausea hit her.

This is ridiculous. What am I thinking?

But Cathy began to explain the flight position—chin up, arms out—and Faith forced herself to pay attention, grounding herself with the details of the things she could control.

Two younger women in flight suits walked over to where they were standing and introduced themselves as the photographers that would be making the jumps with them.

"I didn't pay for photos," she began, but Spencer stopped her by resting a hand on her arm.

"You're about to jump out of an airplane," she said. "You deserve a photo of that moment. On me."

Spencer's voice held a hint of admiration and there was a tender reverence in her gaze that warmed Faith.

"Thank you," she said, wanting more than anything to be worth that admiration.

"Let's do this!" Dale exclaimed, waving for Spencer and Faith to follow him outside.

It's not too late to back out, she thought, but her feet still carried her forward. She stood between Spencer and Cathy as they watched the rickety little Cessna taxi over to where they stood next to the tarmac.

"You don't have to do this you know," Spencer said, as though reading Faith's thoughts. "You don't have anything to prove."

"I know. I'm doing this because I *want* to."

Spencer was wrong, though; she did have something to prove. Maybe not to Spencer, but certainly to herself. She'd be damned if she turned and walked away.

But when Dale pulled open the plane door and motioned for them to climb in, any bravery she'd felt evaporated.

Getting in felt almost as dangerous as jumping out. The rickety metal aircraft looked like a tin can with wings.

Spencer followed Dale, climbing in first, as Faith's heart tried to jackhammer its way out of her chest.

"Ready?" Cathy asked.

She shook her head, but she took a step forward. And another. Until she had climbed in and took a seat on the metal bench with Cathy sitting behind her, clipping them together so they were secured for the fall.

I'm really doing this.

She looked to the bench on the other side where Dale was ensuring that Spencer was strapped securely to him, and it was no longer slight nerves she found in Spencer's eyes. All the fear and panic and excitement she felt were reflected back as Spencer smiled at her and flashed two thumbs up.

Their photographers climbed in last and closed the door behind them, and then the little tin can with wings began shambling along the runway, bumping and rattling as it gained speed.

I'm going to die.

But as the plane lifted off the ground some of the terror fell away and elation took its place.

She watched out the window as the cars and buildings in the distance became smaller, gradually disappearing from sight. She took in the view of the Pacific Ocean stretching out beneath her. The fear subsided as she relaxed into the ascent and allowed herself to enjoy the view.

And then, all too soon, the plane began to level out, and she watched with a fresh surge of panic as one of the photographers pulled open the door.

WHOOOOOOOSH.

The air was deafening as it roared past the open door. The earth was so incomprehensibly far away that Faith's brain seemed to short-circuit, unable to process the height. Every cell in her body screamed at the reality of being in an airplane with the door open. The tin can that had felt so rickety on the ground had somehow become a safe bubble during the ascent, but the minute the door opened to the rush of wind and wide-open sky, that safety bubble popped.

Cathy tapped her shoulder.

"We're up first," she shouted over the roaring wind. She used her hips to urge Faith to begin sliding forward.

It still isn't too late to back out.

But she inched forward along the length of the bench, and then scooted across the floor until she was sitting in the window, her photographer beside her, and Cathy behind her.

She cast a quick glance down at the earth, marveling at the curve of ocean and land so impossibly far away, and then Cathy shouted for her to tilt her head back.

She did as instructed, looking up and seeing nothing but blue.

"Here we go. On three."

Her heart thundered in her stomach.

"One."

I'm really doing this.

"Two."

Her lungs constricted and choked the air from her chest.

"Three."

And then she was upside down, spinning, aware of only one thought: *I did it.*

Cathy's hands tapped on her arms, forcing her brain into action, reminding her of the flight position, arms stretched overhead. She did as she was told, and the two of them stopped spinning, settling flat onto their stomachs, with the earth so far below that it didn't seem to be growing any closer. She didn't seem to be moving through the air, but rather she felt the air rush up to support her. She was stretched out in that open sky, completely free.

She no longer felt even an ounce of fear. Only exhilaration and adrenaline.

She blinked and the minute of free fall ended as the parachute opened. Her fall decelerated with such jarring speed she felt as though she were tugged upward.

And then she was floating, still and peaceful. She felt suddenly dizzy from the rush of endorphins spilling out of her, but her heart rate slowed, her breath returned to normal, and she watched in awe as the world grew closer. It was the same world that she'd taken off from less than an hour earlier, but everything felt different, and she realized that she was landing a different person.

She felt more alive than she'd ever felt in her life, and she knew immediately she wanted more of that feeling in her life.

Holy fuck. What did I get myself into?

Spencer's blood ran cold as Dale urged her down the bench toward the open door. She made no move to slide forward; she simply froze in place.

She had never thought that Faith would *actually* go skydiving. The suggestion had been blurted recklessly, but she'd held to it because she'd wanted to hold a light up to all of the excuses Faith was putting forth to show her how paper thin they really were. Even after Faith agreed to go, Spencer had felt certain she would back out at some point. Her own fear had not begun to simmer until she watched Faith walk toward the drop zone, and it had heightened steadily with each action that brought them closer to this moment: the open plane door she was expected to jump through. Now, panic had her in an icy grip.

A moment earlier, Faith had been sitting on that open ledge, and then before Spencer could even blink, she'd been gone. Sucked out into the endless sky.

"Take a breath," Dale shouted in her ear.

Spencer hadn't realized she *wasn't* breathing until that moment, and her lungs expanded greedily to take in oxygen.

It was too late to back out. She knew that. Riding down in the plane would make her a huge-ass hypocrite. But the fear had drained the blood from her limbs, paralyzing her with terror.

She closed her eyes against that fear, and was met with the image of Faith, sliding down the bench and edging her way toward the open door. Her hair had been tied back neatly in a French braid, and a pair of flight goggles had been pulled over her eyes, looking ridiculously cute. She'd seen the fear in Faith's eyes, but that fear had been outshone by excitement. She was almost certain Faith hadn't even been aware of the grin stretched across her face from ear to ear as she'd moved to sit on the edge of the vast open air.

She felt Dale urge her forward again, and she clutched that image of Faith while willing her body forward an inch at a time.

"You've got this," Dale shouted as Spencer let her legs hang out the open door. The wind rushed past and she fought the urge to claw her way back up onto the bench and hug tight to it until they were safely on the ground.

"Look up."

Spencer did as commanded, sucking in shaky breaths and picturing the bravery she'd seen from Faith as she made the jump.

Dale began counting, and she shut out the numbers, focusing instead on the warmth in Faith's hazel eyes when she'd first met Spencer outside the building that morning. She pictured Faith's gentle smile, so filled with both fear and excitement, and she imagined the smile she might see on Faith's face once she reached the ground.

And then she was falling through the empty sky, squeezing her eyes shut and praying to every god she could think of that if they were real, they'd somehow let her live. In the back of her mind, she was aware of the flight position, and she extended her arms to balance her body in the wind, but those actions were on some distant autopilot. She chanced opening her eyes only briefly, but she felt dizzy with the magnitude of the moment when she saw the earth large and looming beneath her, the ocean and the city and the stretches of land beyond the city, and she had to close them again.

It wasn't until her parachute opened and she felt the rush of wind slow, and her heart rate began to return to normal, that she dared open her eyes again. She was much closer to the earth this time, and she saw the field of the drop zone and the red of Faith's parachute drifting to a gentle landing below her.

I'm alive. I did it. I'm alive.

The words repeated themselves the entire way down, until the ground rushed toward her and Dale shouted at her to bend her knees and lift her feet for landing.

The earth caught her, and a relief bigger than anything she'd ever known flooded her as she set her feet on the ground, stumbling forward from the momentum. Dale immediately set to work releasing the parachute and detaching the two of them, and she wished he'd hurry the hell up because she wanted to kiss the grass.

Instead, by the time Dale got the last latch free, Faith was there, and her arms wrapped around Spencer in a hug. She was on the ground alive, feeling Faith's heartbeat match hers in speed and intensity.

"That was incredible," Faith said, and the joy burst out of her, radiant and warm as the sun.

Spencer tried to catch her breath and steady her own heart rate enough to answer.

"You did it," she said at last, admiration slowly seeping in to replace the adrenaline.

"*We* did it," Faith amended.

She grounded herself by taking in all of the details of Faith in that moment. Wisps of blond hair had been pulled loose from her French braid and they stuck out errantly around her face, wind-whipped and erratic. She had pulled off her goggles, but they'd pressed red circles into her typically flawless skin. For all intents and purposes, she looked a mess, but her hazel eyes shone brighter than any Spencer had ever seen.

A wave of admiration swept through her, as she thought of the bravery and confidence Faith had displayed when she'd jumped from the plane. She'd been far braver than Spencer, who barely managed to move, and could still hardly process what had happened.

In that moment, their past was the *furthest* thing from her mind. Nothing existed between them other than that moment and the incredible leap they'd taken together.

She shifted her weight, bringing the two of them closer together. It had been a subtle shift, but they'd already been standing close. Now, she could feel the hum of the electricity in the air between them as she breathed in Faith's soft floral scent.

Faith swallowed hard and pulled her bottom lip between her teeth. Just a hair closer, and Spencer could capture that lip in her own lips.

Was it just her imagination, or did Faith shift closer, too?

"All right," Dale said, with the same enthusiasm he'd exhibited as they readied themselves to skydive. "You two did it!"

"Smile!" One of the photographers stood there with a camera in hand.

Spencer blinked as she tried to process the words.

Faith was a little quicker on the uptake and she stepped beside

Spencer and put an arm around her back. Spencer tried to convince herself that her elevated heart rate was entirely from skydiving as she slung her arm over Faith's shoulder and smiled for the camera.

She'd just fallen fifteen thousand feet. What she was feeling was adrenaline. Nothing else.

"Why don't we go in, get these flight suits off?" Dale said a moment later. "We can get you all of your photos from today's jump."

Faith followed Dale, and despite Spencer's rationalization, she felt the loss when Faith walked away.

That night, Faith lay in bed, looking at the photo on her phone, still unable to believe it was actually her. In the picture, she had just tumbled over the edge of the airplane. Her eyes were squeezed shut, but that was the only indication of the fear she'd felt. It was the elation really shining through the photo, in the smile that was stretched wide across her face. She'd never seen herself smile so big.

Her body was still buzzing with the adrenaline of the day, even twelve hours later, but the high was from more than that rush of chemicals. She felt a boldness take root within her. For the first time in her life, she felt capable, unstoppable, *brave*.

All her once distant dreams suddenly seemed within reach. They felt truly *possible* for the first time ever. She wasn't going to jump online and book a flight to Argentina, but she *would* get there in her life. It was no longer a matter of *if*, but a matter of *when*.

She looked at the picture for another moment and then closed her eyes to relive the free fall in her memory.

I jumped out of a freaking airplane.

Even Spencer had been scared. When Faith had first arrived at the drop zone, she'd looked disarmingly calm, and Faith had felt the burn of embarrassment as she'd been unable to hide her shaky nerves. But she hadn't been surprised. Of the two of them, Spencer had always been the brave one. Once they'd climbed into the plane, however, she'd seen Spencer mirror her fear, and when they'd landed, Spencer visibly struggled to process the enormity of what they'd done. Faith didn't need to be told that skydiving was universally terrifying, but still, seeing Spencer's fear reassured her that she didn't have to be unafraid to be brave. Her bravery came from being afraid and taking the leap anyway.

She wasn't a coward; she was a bad ass.

She closed her eyes and smiled, hit with the sudden image of Spencer in her blue bodysuit and goggles, flashing her an overconfident smile and a thumbs-up to mask her fear. The memory of that goofy exaggerated grin made her stomach do a little flip.

She pulled out her phone and sent Spencer a text message before she could rethink doing so. *Today was incredible. I'm still on a high.*

Spencer's response was immediate. *Me too. I can't believe we did that.*

Her memory flashed to the moment after they'd landed, when, in that haze of disbelief and relief, she'd seen Spencer's gaze drop to her mouth, and for a long heartbeat the world around them had paused. Kissing Spencer would have destroyed the tenuous connection they were building, but still, she'd been disappointed when Dale interrupted.

Thank you. For everything, she typed. *It was the time of my life.*

There was a long pause before Spencer typed back, *Mine too.*

She set her phone down, lying back on her bed with a smile. Then she once again picked up the photo of her free-falling. The elation on her face, the total serenity she'd felt—Spencer had given her that.

She vowed to herself that she'd find a way to do something equally special for Spencer.

Chapter Eleven

Spencer stepped into Black Soul Coffee and took a deep inhale of the rich aroma of coffee. In her opinion, there were few smells in life better than coffee. She didn't even need to drink it to feel more awake. All she had to do was breathe in the scent and some of the fog would be lifted from her mind.

Not that there was a fog that needed to be lifted today. She was unusually energized for a Monday, still buzzing with the high from her skydive. She was fairly certain she hadn't slept more than five hours the night before, but she'd woke up feeling energized and ready to take on the day.

The energy had paid off, because she'd had a long day of rehearsal with the band after signing up for a last-minute gig coming up on Friday. Mari had spoken with the owner of one of their favourite local venues, and they'd needed someone to fill the headline slot after the out-of-town band they'd booked had needed to cancel. The venue regularly booked queer artists and stood for inclusivity and diversity in the local music scene. If there was ever a venue they wanted to help out, this was it, but it meant they had very little time to throw together a tight set. They'd played their old stuff live enough times that they would be more than okay playing those songs, but they all agreed that despite it being last minute, the gig would be a good opportunity to test their new material. They picked two of their fast-paced songs and spent the day fine-tuning them, figuring out which other songs they paired well with, and adding extended intros that would allow for some banter and give Sienna a chance to introduce the material.

"Hey Spencer," Nikolai called, interrupting her thoughts as

he stepped toward the counter from the roasting room with a large container of beans that he set in the display case. "Want to taste test the new Ethiopian roast I'm trying out?" He nodded toward the beans he'd just set out on display.

"Absolutely. I do," she said, even though she definitely did not need the caffeine.

He scooped some of the beans into the commercial grinder and set it to grind the perfect amount.

"I actually came by to talk to you," Spencer said.

Nikolai paused and turned to her with one eyebrow raised. "Me?"

She nodded. "Our band got asked to play a last-minute gig at The Lighthouse on Friday. I thought I'd see if you wanted to come by and sell some Bottle Rocket Blond Roast at our merch table."

A wide smile spread across his face. "You folks are the absolute best. You know that, right?"

Spencer waved off the compliment. They didn't take a cut of the coffee sales, but the partnership with Black Soul Coffee was mutually beneficial. Each bag of beans came with a download code for 'Bottle Rockets', and she could easily trace the number of people who went on to pay for the full album after redeeming the single download code. Black Soul Coffee may not have been a huge mainstream coffee shop, but it catered to a niche market that was already primed for liking the music Shattered Ceiling put out. Maintaining a partnership with Nikolai and his coffee shop was a good way to continue generating local interest for their little indie band.

"So, you'll be there?" she asked.

"I wouldn't miss it. You guys have my coffee flying off the shelves. In fact, I'd better make sure I start roasting extra this afternoon."

She laughed and Nikolai handed her the warm cup of the Ethiopian roast he'd been working on.

"Tell me what you think." He waited eagerly, clearly bursting with pride over the new roast.

Spencer took a small sip, careful not to burn her mouth. The coffee was bright and acidic, with fruity undertones. She had no doubt about the quality, but personally preferred the more mellow, nuttier roasts. She didn't have the heart to tell Nikolai that, though, so she said, "Why do you do this to me, Nik? Now I need a bag of this to go, as well."

"Tell you what," Nikolai began, beaming at her reaction, "I'll get you a bag on the house. You go grab a table."

She did as she was told, adding a little cream to her coffee to temper some of the acidic kick, and then took a seat in the far corner where she could decompress from the roller coaster that had been the past couple days.

She took another sip of the coffee. It was much better with the cream.

She gave a long exhale and relaxed into the comfortable chair. Band practice, skydiving, Faith… All of it had her head spinning. The image of Faith at the drop zone, after they'd landed safely on the ground, came immediately to her mind. Faith, with her soft blond hair highlighted in a sepia morning glow. Faith with her hazel eyes shining gold in the morning light, and a smile so bright and genuine it warmed her more than the sun had. Faith, who had jumped out of an airplane and proven a level of bravery she hadn't expected.

She still heard the distant warning echoing in the chambers of her heart, but maybe Faith deserved the benefit of the doubt.

She pulled out her phone and began crafting a message.

Hey. I hope you're having a good week so far. My band is playing a spur-of-the-moment gig on Friday night and I thought I'd see if you maybe wanted to come? No pressure.

Her stomach tightened with nerves, but she hit send before she could rethink the invitation. Then, she set her phone down, forcing herself to drink her coffee instead of staring at the screen and waiting for a reply.

Not that she would have had to wait long. The reply was almost immediate.

I have dinner with my parents on Friday.

The disappointment settled heavy inside of her, and she inwardly chastised herself for caring so much.

Another text followed. *We usually have dinner at five, so I could be out of there by six and meet you by seven?*

The happiness that bubbled up in her was so bright and immediate she again chastised herself, but she didn't tamp the happiness down.

That's more than enough time, she typed. *The show starts at nine. Doors are at eight. We'll be there by six, though, for sound check and setup. You're welcome to join us whenever you can. Just shoot me a text when you get there.*

Is this like a backstage invitation? Faith asked, followed by a winking emoji which caused Spencer's stomach to do a little flip.

Well, the place doesn't exactly have a backstage, but yeah, you're getting the real VIP insider access.

Lucky me.

She smiled and set her phone down on the table. She was the lucky one. She'd always felt that way around Faith.

"One bag of our brand-new Ethiopian beans." Nikolai grinned as he set the bag on the table pulling her from her thoughts.

"I'm going to bust these out for our next band practice," she said.

"Is it just about time to start working on our new pairing?"

"Just about. We're going to test run a couple of the new songs on Friday."

"I can't wait," he said. "I'll bring a notepad and I can start writing down pairings I think might work."

The enthusiasm radiated off of Nikolai.

"I can't wait either," she said. Except her excitement had nothing to do with coffee or even the band. The excitement had everything to do with seeing Faith.

Chapter Twelve

Faith felt an uncharacteristic confidence as she walked up the steps to her parents' house.

She had never considered herself brave. There were many positive qualities she valued in herself. She was generous, and caring, and empathetic, for instance. She prided herself on her ability to make sure those around her always felt special. However, she never would have used *brave* as a descriptor. She'd excelled in school and dance not because she took risks, but because she did as she was told and had a good deal of inherent natural ability. She'd gone through all of her life that way—doing as she was told, not rocking the boat, and staying on the path laid out for her.

And then she'd jumped out of a plane.

Nearly a week later, she still felt the effects of her big, bold leap into the unknown, and as cheesy as it might have sounded, she knew she was changed by the experience. For the rest of her life, she'd always be someone who'd had the courage to jump. A little ember of bravery would forever burn inside her.

That little ember sparked as she reached the door to her parents' home. She loved her parents, but she'd never been able to meet their expectations, especially not since leaving Brett. It seemed every week, lately, she left their Friday night dinners feeling small and broken. This time, she resolved not to entertain their pressures or expectations. She would enjoy the meal with her parents and ignore any unenjoyable aspects. She didn't need to indulge her parents' demands or wishes. It was *her* life.

Afterward, she had an easy and honest out: to go see Spencer and watch her band perform, and the thought put an extra spring in her step. They hadn't had much of a chance to talk with one another the other night when they'd facilitated the music group together. Faith had been slammed with work right up until time for the group to start, and Spencer had needed to leave after, but things between them had been noticeably different. Warmer. Less tense. She was really looking forward to seeing Spencer again outside of work. She tried not to examine those feelings too closely, but she also didn't deny herself the pleasure of them.

She stepped into the house and breathed in the welcome aroma of sauteed vegetables and roast chicken.

"Dinner smells amazing," she said, finding her mom pulling the chicken out of the oven.

Her mom looked up in surprise, and then quickly found work for her. "Can you grab those vegetables off the stove and set them into a serving tray? No, not that tray, the big round one."

She followed her mom's instructions, falling neatly into line. If the scene hadn't become so normal, she might have found it funny. Her mom bustled around the kitchen with a cutesy apron on, making sure each dish was presented perfectly. Her dad was likely still in his study, finishing with client case files before dinner. Her mom had made such an identity out of being the perfect housewife, cooking and cleaning dishes while her dad worked. Faith had grown up expecting her life to be the same. She'd never thought to question any of it.

And yet, she couldn't say for certain that her parents were happy. She had the impression true connection between the two of them was scant. They loved each other, sure, but each of them was so busy performing a role—housewife, parent, lawyer, husband—they never seemed to take the time to just be themselves with one another.

"How was your week?" Faith asked, as she stole a potato from the tray.

Her mom slapped her hand away from the dish. "Oh, you know, the same as any other week."

She thought of the free fall, the way the entire world had ceased to exist as anything more than distant topography miles below her. She had been so far removed from this endless Groundhog Day existence.

"How was *your* week?" her mom asked.

She stole another potato and then picked up the vegetable platter to carry it to the dining room. "It was good."

She wanted to say her week had been beyond good, that it had been incredible, that she'd felt what it was like to *fly*, but she held her tongue, suspecting the news might cause an aneurysm.

Her mom followed her to the dining room with the roast chicken, and set it in the center of the table, which had already been set for their Friday dinner. It was just the three of them, but they still used the fine china on Fridays. Everything was a presentation.

"So much paperwork," her dad said, taking a seat at the table to enjoy the meal he hadn't help prepare in the slightest.

Faith didn't know why her parents' arrangement suddenly bothered her so much. It wasn't any different from any other dinner, but the action grated on her.

"Let me tell you," he continued, "it's not the stress of my cases that puts a strain on my heart, it's all the bloody paperwork."

As a social worker, Faith could empathize, but she kept quiet, able to think of few things to talk about that interested her *less* than paperwork.

"Did you manage to get it all done?" her mom asked.

"I did. Now I get to relax and enjoy my weekend. I was hoping I could maybe sneak in some dessert tonight, since I have my first 5k race this weekend?"

"Finish the race without keeling over, and then we'll talk," her mom said.

The conversation continued on the same low plateau, never really hitting any peaks. It was dull and mundane. Her parents were sweet, but boring.

Did people say the same about her? Probably.

"Faith, are you okay?"

The sound of her name pulled her back to the present, and she startled to find both of her parents gazing at her with concern on their faces.

She shook herself back into the conversation. "Sorry. My mind drifted for a bit."

"You were just staring at the chicken," her dad said, and he gave a soft chuckle. "I wasn't sure if you were feeling sick, or if you were just really, really hungry."

She forced a little chuckle as well. "I guess I got lost in thought."

"About what?" Her mom still had an edge of concern to her expression.

"It was a long week. Just thinking about work." She felt the ember of bravery dim at the white lie.

But it didn't go out.

She had jumped out of an airplane. She wasn't boring and cowardly. At least not all the time.

The ember may have dimmed, but it was still there, flickering inside of her.

From the outside, The Lighthouse didn't look much like a live music venue or a lighthouse. It was a nondescript brick building just off the harbour on the outskirts of downtown Vancouver, tucked away between industrial buildings. The brick walls were heavily graffitied, primarily with names and crude words, not any actual street art. Inside, however, was the perfect balance of cozy and spacious. A stage sat in the back corner, and there was a large open space where people could press close, form mosh pits, and immerse themselves in the music. The place also had stairs on either side and an elevator leading to an upper balcony running the perimeter, so those who didn't like the hot press of bodies could watch in relative comfort. The front had a large bar with stools around the edges, as well as a few tables and lounge chairs, so people could sit back with drinks, if they chose.

It was a small venue, but it utilized the space well. Empty, it appeared sparse, but once the people packed in, it would be crowded and intimate. Spencer had missed playing at The Lighthouse. There was something extra special about the feel of the audience, pressed right up close around the stage, barely elevated, allowing them to play right amongst the crowd.

When their album debuted, they'd begun getting radio play, and suddenly they'd been thrust into the spotlight, filling larger venues: buildings with green rooms and a separation between them and the crowd. They loaded gear in and out through back doors, and security staff caught crowd surfers from behind metal barriers. The large venues were big spaces with big energy, but she missed the intimacy of the small-scale performances where she could see the faces of the audience as they sang along.

"This is going to be a fun night," Spencer said from the passenger seat as Mari pulled their van into the loading zone by the venue doors.

"I'm actually so excited," Mari agreed.

Wren tapped on her knees with her palms. Sienna was running late, and so she'd agreed to meet the band there.

Mari parked and killed the engine, and Spencer took a moment to check her phone for any messages from Faith. There were none, she noted with disappointment, but it was only six.

She got out and went around to the back, where Wren and Mari were already collecting gear to carry in. The majority of it was Wren's: drums, cymbals, and stands that all needed to be assembled. Spencer had three guitars she'd brought with her, as well as her pedal board. Mari had one bass and a pedal board. Sienna just brought herself. The venue provided all the amps and microphones they would need.

When they'd done their cross-Canada tour the previous fall, they'd been lucky enough to have a road crew for the first time ever, but Spencer didn't mind hauling her own gear. It felt refreshing to get back to their roots, even if only for one show. There was something very rock-and-roll about pulling up in a small, beat-up personal van and carrying in instruments and pedal boards and cables.

She waited as Wren pulled out the largest drum first: her big, round bass drum. She was small, but mighty. Spencer always admired her steadfast ability to simply go in and get things done. She never hesitated and she never complained.

Once Wren passed her with the drum, Spencer reached in and took two of her guitars. She'd take her stuff in and then help with the rest of the drum kit. The process felt like an old choreographed dance: easy and familiar. They'd done the set-up and take-downs so many times that it had become a well-choreographed routine.

None of their stuff had to be assembled just yet, as they would be the last band to play, so they moved their gear to the small corner that had been cordoned off beside the stage area.

"I'm so glad you folks were able to fill the bill on such short notice," Luci, the owner of The Lighthouse, said as she stepped over to where the group was standing. "I'm so excited to have you back here for a show."

Shattered Ceiling had played The Lighthouse a *lot* while establishing themselves around the city, and Luci was, and always would be, one of their favourite bar owners.

"We're excited to be back," Spencer said.

One of the other bands on the bill filtered in with their gear, and Luci began the work of introductions.

"This is the band Asterism. Have you all met before?"

"We haven't," Mari exclaimed, excitedly stepping in first to introduce herself to the other band. "I've heard really good things about you guys, though."

"And I imagine you folks are familiar with Shattered Ceiling," Luci said. Her attention was drawn to the bar where her bartender was waving her over, and she excused herself to go help her staff.

Spencer turned her attention back to the members of Asterism to introduce herself and the rest of the band.

A woman with blond, shaggy hair; heavy, black eyeliner, and a tattered black tank top extended her hand. "I'm Nova. Singer and guitarist."

The rest of the group introduced themselves: Beth on bass, Sam on drums. Handshakes went around the circle. Wren and Sam quickly started talking gear and Mari began her networking magic, asking Beth and Nova about their band and their music. Mari genuinely wanted to know about the other bands that they played with, and her extroverted nature and interest in others had served the band well in finding groups to play with and setting up gigs.

Spencer checked her phone. Still no message.

The third band on the bill brought their gear in and began setting up so that they could get the sound check underway. It was a small bar, not a large concert hall, so the sound check wouldn't be anything too elaborate. They'd test the levels with the first band's gear and hope that they more or less held true for the later bands.

The band set up and began playing a verse of one of their loud, aggressive screamo songs. Spencer had a feeling the sound tech would be making a lot of adjustments after they left the stage.

Sienna blew in just as sound check was finishing. "Sorry I'm so late."

As the introductions began for a second time, Spencer's phone buzzed in her pocket, pulling her attention away. She reached for it faster than she should have and hoped nobody noticed the overeager way she checked her messages, or the stupid smile on her face when Faith's name appeared across her screen.

Hey, I think I'm here? I'm in an alley next to a big gray door. Is this the front of the venue or the back?

Spencer suppressed a chuckle and typed; *I'll be right out to meet you.*

"I'll be right back," she said. "I'm stepping out for a minute to meet a friend."

A question flashed across Mari's face, but Spencer left before she had to answer. She hadn't told any of her friends Faith was coming. She hadn't known what to say. None of them knew about their coffee chat, or skydiving, or the daily text messages they'd exchanged since. Where did she start explaining the shift between them when she didn't even understand the change?

There would be questions later, but that was a future-Spencer problem.

She stepped outside and saw Faith standing in the alley, studying her cell phone, dressed in a soft white sweater and jeans, hair loose in soft waves and a small purse slung over her shoulder, entirely out of place outside of the grungy punk-rock venue. Spencer warmed at the sight.

"Hey," she said, and Faith looked up from her phone, a smile slowly spreading across her face.

"Oh my God," Faith said with mock awe. "Are you Spencer Adams? *The* Spencer Adams?"

Spencer played along with a little bow of her head. "In the flesh."

Faith tipped her head back and fanned herself. "I'm your *biggest* fan. I can't believe I'm meeting you. Will you sign my arm?"

A completely unbidden laugh was pulled from Spencer. "You're a nut. You know that? Come inside. I'll introduce you to the rest of the band."

Mari recognized Faith immediately, and Spencer was met with an intense questioning gaze, which she ignored, quickly breaking the eye contact to introduce Faith to the others.

"This is Faith," she said, and both Sienna and Wren's eyes widened with the same question. She hoped that Faith didn't notice. If she did, she'd know Spencer had mentioned her before, and likely guess Spencer hadn't exactly had glowing things to say. Spencer kept going, offering added information to cue her friends to the fact that they weren't to ask more right then. "She's a friend of mine. She's working with me on the youth project I'm doing on Thursday evenings."

"It's nice to meet you. I'm Wren."

Faith shook the offered hand while Spencer avoided Mari's gaze, which burned into her.

Sienna introduced herself and then it was Mari's turn.

Please don't say anything, Spencer begged inwardly.

"It's good to see you again," Mari said. "We never got much of a chance to get to know one another in high school. I'm Mari."

Spencer exhaled her relief. She'd have a million questions to answer later, but she didn't want to worry about that for the time being. The truth was, she didn't have any answers. She didn't know what she was doing with Faith Siebert. It felt a little like she was playing with fire, and yet she was *enjoying* her time around Faith.

She watched as Faith spoke to the members of the other bands. She leaned in with genuine interest as she asked about their music, and listened intently, even though Spencer was fairly certain Faith didn't generally listen to punk bands. Other than her band. Faith listened to Shattered Ceiling.

Yeah, Spencer hoped the warmth she felt wasn't from flames that would later burn her.

The minute Spencer had stepped over to her in the alley to greet her, Faith realized she was completely unprepared for seeing her play live. She'd been excited for the show. She'd left the dinner at her parents' house a few minutes early so she had some time to swing by her apartment, refresh her makeup, and change (she spent more time selecting an outfit than she cared to admit), and she had been eager to get to the venue and see Spencer. But then, Spencer stepped through the gray industrial door and Faith's mouth went dry. She wore dark skinny jeans that looked like they were custom-made for her body, with a large tear over the left thigh, teasing at the soft skin beneath. Her baggy black tank top revealed her well-muscled arms, as well as the full display of her tattoo sleeve, with the music notes that emanated from the guitar on her forearm transforming into colourful butterflies which flew up her shoulder. The magnetism she exuded in her day-to-day attire was amplified tenfold, and Faith felt the air rush from her lungs at the sight.

She feigned fangirl to hide the flush creeping up her neck.

The truth was, it wouldn't be hard to fangirl over Spencer Adams.

Spencer had led Faith inside to introduce her to the rest of the band, and it had taken a conscious effort to keep focused and engaged with the others. She found herself stealing quick glances at Spencer, and she was very aware of the fact that more often than not those glances were returned. It was both comforting and terrifying to know that whatever was building between them, it went both ways.

"Can I get you a drink?" Spencer asked once finished with setup, the first band ready to take the stage.

"I'd love one." She followed Spencer through the forming crowd to the bar. The Lighthouse wasn't packed yet, but people had begun to filter in for the show, and she had no doubt the place would be bursting at the seams by the time Shattered Ceiling took the stage. This venue was definitely too small for a band of their status, but Faith didn't mind, as it meant she would get to see Shattered Ceiling perform up close and personal. Still, even with the sparse crowd, they got stopped on the way to the bar no less than seven times by people who wanted to tell Spencer how much they loved her band, or ask for an autograph, or request a favourite song be played during Shattered Ceiling's set. Spencer was gracious and kind to each of her fans, and then apologized to Faith every time. Faith, however, didn't mind in the slightest. She couldn't have been prouder of the woman Spencer had grown into. In high school, she had walked through the halls with her head down, hiding inside of hooded sweaters as though she could make herself invisible. As an adult, she walked through the crowd like the rock star she was. She radiated confidence and handled herself with grace, answering questions humbly and taking the time to actually connect with each person who approached her.

"I'm sorry about all of that," Spencer said when they reached the bar, but Faith waved off the apology.

"You're a kick-ass guitarist in a kick-ass band. You have nothing to apologize for. These people are all here to see *you*."

Even dressed to kill, with the confidence to match, colour rose to Spencer's cheeks.

"The good thing about playing at a venue like this is that there's no backstage area," Spencer said. "So, I was thinking we could hang out and watch the first two bands together. I'll have to duck out to set up all of our gear after the second band, but we should be able to spend a decent amount of time together before our set."

Faith set her hand on Spencer's forearm to stop her. "You don't have to worry about me. I'm here to see your show. You're allowed to have fans, and you're allowed to leave me by myself while you play. I'll be fine."

Spencer smiled, and Faith was suddenly very aware that her hand was still on her arm. She pulled her hand back, a little too quickly, and shoved it into the pocket of her jeans.

"I've never brought anyone to one of my shows before," Spencer admitted. "I'm not exactly sure what to do with myself."

"What? None of the other girls in your life have had the honour of getting to see you play live?" She'd blurted the question without thought and regretted it instantly. She hadn't meant to imply she was of any importance. And she certainly hadn't meant to inquire about the company Spencer kept. She braced herself against the answer, sure she didn't want to know who Spencer dated.

She was met with a gaze so tender and serious she physically shifted under the sudden vulnerability.

"It's only ever been you." The admission was spoken low and quiet.

She met the honesty in Spencer's eyes and let the words sink in, a lightness expanding through her body.

Had the same not been true for her? In the years since their brief time together, she had made a concerted effort to *not* think about Spencer, and even so, the thoughts had often come to her unbidden over the aching stretch of years. Her mind had flashed to Spencer on the nights when she'd suffered through Brett's touch wondering how she could feel so lonely while being intimate with her husband. She'd always tried to let those thoughts pass fleetingly, never really giving them any weight, but suddenly Spencer was standing in front of her again and those thoughts were all she could think.

Faith opened her mouth to respond but was interrupted by the dimming of the lights and the sudden blast of loud, aggressive music.

Well, "music" seemed too generous a term.

On stage, a young man screamed into the microphone with a high-pitched, throaty rasp. The guitarist spun in frantic circles while his fingers flew over the strings in a seemingly haphazard string of notes. The drummer beat an obnoxious cacophony. All the while, the thin crowd pressed enthusiastically closer to the stage, giving her and Spencer more breathing room by the back of the bar.

Faith had no desire to move any nearer to the noise.

Spencer watched the band with interest, nodding along with a beat, though Faith wasn't sure there even was an underlying beat to pick up.

When the first song ended, cheers broke out in the room, and Faith wondered what the hell she was listening to, because it appeared she was hearing something entirely different from everyone else in the building.

"These guys are really good!" Spencer's eyes shone as she turned to Faith with excitement.

Faith managed a smile, though she wasn't sure how much

enthusiasm she actually managed to convey.

The next band was miles better. Their singer had a soulful, throaty voice as she sang, rather than screamed, the lyrics. The songs were ambient and melodic. They were heavy and loud, but they had structure. They didn't leave Faith feeling dizzy and disoriented. They all had a distinct political bent to them, with lyrics about colonization and indigenous rights, the trials faced by immigrants and refugees, women's rights, and transgender rights. Spencer shouted her agreement at multiple lyrics. Faith's heart warmed at the passion she felt from Spencer throughout the set. She kept sneaking glances at her, watching the show with eyes wide, and she thrilled at the little expressions of joy that passed over Spencer's face each time the band did something that excited her.

"The tones she's getting out of her guitar!" Spencer shouted over the music at one point. "Wow."

Faith didn't know about the intricacies of the music, but as a casual listener she found the second band enjoyable.

When they finished their set, Spencer could hardly contain her enthusiasm. "They were incredible. I can't believe they're not the headliners. I need to talk with my bandmates about booking tours with them."

She loved watching the excitement pour from Spencer, who was usually so cool and composed, closed off, even, at times. Spencer's joy after watching the two bands perform at *least* matched her joy after skydiving. It was so clear music was more than just Spencer's livelihood. It was her life's passion.

A pang of jealousy hit. She couldn't even imagine what it would feel like to have a passion so all-encompassing. She enjoyed her career and found it meaningful, but she didn't live and breathe social work. Maybe, once upon a time, dance had been her passion, but over the years, her love of dance had been eroded by all the pressures of competition and unspoken expectations to look a certain way or fit a certain mold. She still went to the studio to dance just for herself, but she didn't find the total joy that Spencer's face displayed.

The crowd had grown considerably over the course of the evening, and a swell of people pushed back in their direction, headed for the bar, forcing her closer to Spencer. Her breath caught as her body brushed against Spencer's.

"Sorry," she said.

Spencer stood about a couple of inches taller than her, and standing so close, Faith had to incline her head just slightly to meet Spencer's eyes. She could feel the rise and fall of her chest, and Faith's heart pounded so hard against her ribs she was certain that Spencer could feel the steady drum.

"Ready to set up our gear?"

Spencer pulled back an inch, and Faith turned to see Mari standing there with a stony, unreadable expression.

"Absolutely," Spencer said.

Spencer turned back to Faith.

"I guess that's my cue to go. I'll come find you after our set. You're okay here?"

"I'm fine," she said, but she felt Spencer's absence acutely, already.

She quietly sipped her beer, wondering at the change in their relationship. A week earlier, everything had been cold and awkward. Her past actions had been an insurmountable barrier. Now, suddenly, here they were. As what exactly? Not friends. Something more? She almost felt as though she'd been skyrocketed back in time, back to their teenage romance. Whatever had grown between them had the same warm and intimate glow to it.

The lights dimmed. A heavy electric note began to swell from the speakers and a jolt of excitement swelled within her along with it. Suddenly, her vantage point at the back of the venue felt too distant, and while she wanted to avoid getting trapped in any kind of mosh pit, she set her empty beer on the bar and worked her way forward, getting as close to the stage as she could before the dense crowd became impenetrable.

A single guitar chord cut through the ambient pulse of noise, sharp and electric, and then its edges blurred as it melted into the background pulse of electricity. The lights were still down, and all she could make out was a shadow of Spencer, standing to the left of the stage holding her guitar in a still and stoic position, legs slightly parted, head bowed.

And then, all at once, the stage lights blasted on and the band began to play with a heavy-charged energy. Spencer came alive. She leapt in the air with the initial surge of music and threw her head and torso forward into the chords as she strummed. She didn't play guitar with her hands; she played guitar with her entire self.

Faith was familiar with the song. It was one of the heaviest ones on their album: not one she tended to gravitate toward because of how loud and aggressive the music was. Seeing the song played live, however, gave it a different life. She knew she would go home and listen to it again and again, and each time she would remember the way Spencer jumped along with the sharp staccato strumming pattern that led into the chorus. She'd remember the way Spencer leaned back, eyes closed, as her fingers flew across the strings, moving quickly up the neck of the guitar and back down in a quick choreographed tap dance. She'd remember the way Spencer tossed her head forward into the music, the lavender tips of her hair blowing back and forth as she did so, illuminated almost silver in the harsh stage lights. Every cell in Spencer seemed attuned to the song.

Without even realizing it at first, Faith wondered what it might feel like to be the cause of such complete abandon in Spencer. She watched Spencer's fingers dance across the fret board and felt a shiver at the ghost of those fingers dancing over her skin instead, and as she watched Spencer's body thrust forward and backward with each strum of her guitar, she felt that rocking rhythm somewhere deep and primal inside of herself.

I'm gay, Faith thought with sudden, stunning clarity. Her teenage romance with Spencer had been childlike and innocent, but there was nothing innocent about her thoughts now. Maybe the realization should have scared her, but it didn't. It felt as though she had finally figured out the pieces to the puzzle of herself. They hadn't fit right, and now suddenly they clicked into place.

She had been so excited to see Shattered Ceiling play live, but all of a sudden, their set felt agonizingly long. She wanted to go to Spencer with her newfound clarity. She wanted to feel the ripple of muscle beneath her fingers, as she traced all of Spencer's hard edges and soft curves. She wanted to taste the salt of sweat as her lips moved over Spencer's body.

The want grew with each song. She tried to ground herself by focusing on the music, but Spencer was all she could pay attention to. Fire and fury burst out from inside of her as the band played their heavy, political punk songs, and a free-spirited and playful side came out during their more light-hearted songs. Faith wanted to know every side of her.

When the set finished and the stage lights turned off, she was disappointed to see the show end, but more than that, she was overwhelmingly relieved. She moved through the crowd, eager to get to Spencer.

And then, over the heavy cheering and raucous applause, she heard the guitar once more, and nearly groaned at the realization she needed to wait until after the encore.

She stood itching with impatience for the first two songs, until Spencer played the opening notes to 'Bottle Rockets', and she let herself get lifted away into the music.

We're building bottle rockets in our basement
Just kids setting them off on the pavement
Light it, ignite it, this spark you shouldn't fight it…

Faith listened, *really* listened, like she had during their music group, but this time she didn't feel the weight of regret. She felt light and free. She couldn't live her teenage years over again, but her life wasn't over.

We only live once.

It might have been too late to correct course with Spencer, but then again, maybe it wasn't. Spencer had invited her to the show, after all.

It's only ever been you.

Spencer's words echoed in her mind, and she realized how true they had been for her, as well. It had only ever been Spencer.

The final note rang out while Wren pounded a short drum solo over top, and then thunderous applause replaced the music, shaking the small room. Faith cheered and clapped along with the others, but she had already begun working her way through the thick crowd toward the side of the stage.

She found Spencer and the rest of the group already dismantling the gear on stage. Wren was removing cymbals from their stands, and Spencer and Mari wrapped cables while Sienna drank down her glass of water and then began greeting the lineup of fans that had formed.

Of *course*, there was a lineup of fans wanting autographs. For a moment, she felt foolish in her desire. She felt small compared to Spencer's shining star. But then Spencer caught her gaze and smiled, a smile so direct and genuine that Faith felt anything *but* small, and the rest of the room faded away as she made her way over.

"So, what did you think?" Spencer asked, still breathing heavily from the exertion of the show.

Faith *felt* the adjectives to describe the set—*incredible, electric, powerful, bold, sexy*—but her brain couldn't function well enough to pull the words from her chest to her mouth.

Spencer pushed her sweat-slicked hair off of her forehead and arched an eyebrow when her question went unanswered.

Light it, ignite it, this spark you shouldn't fight it.

The song echoed in her mind.

We only live once.

She shifted forward. Spencer's eyes widened in surprise, and Faith studied them for any sign that she should stop. She registered the vulnerability and fear etched in the curve of Spencer's eyebrows, but she also caught the sharp inhale of hope and desire.

She took Spencer's face in her hands, holding eye contact for one last long moment before pulling them together.

Any remaining hesitancy or uncertainty on either end dissipated the minute their lips met. All the passion she'd kept buried over the years clawed through her, finally free, and she met Spencer's mouth with an almost bruising intensity.

Spencer's hands found her hips and tugged her closer, and she whimpered at the first touch of her tongue.

Then, as quickly as the kiss had ignited, they broke apart, flushed and breathing heavily.

Gradually the world came back into focus, and her cheeks warmed with the realization they were in a crowded room and a number of eyes were on them.

"So, yeah, I really enjoyed your set," she managed.

Spencer said nothing, her blue eyes dark and stormy with questions.

Faith indicated the lineup of people and added, "I should let you get back to your adoring fans."

Spencer looked over at the crowd, and the storm was gone from her eyes when she looked back to Faith. "Okay." Then she leaned in and lowered her voice as she added, "But I want to hear more of your thoughts later."

The implied meaning wasn't lost on Faith and she warmed with the anticipation of getting to spend some time alone with Spencer. It wasn't the night to make up for their past or for the lost years, and there was a lot she still needed to say, but as Spencer went back to her band, Faith touched a finger to her lips and knew she was on the right path.

Spencer avoided eye contact with the rest of her band and made quick work of unplugging and wrapping the remaining cables to her pedal board. She was well aware all three of her fellow band members had witnessed her kissing Faith, and while she didn't have a single regret, she also didn't have a single explanation.

Still, Mari leaned in and whispered, "*We'll talk later?*"

She nodded; sooner rather than later she'd be alone with her friends and all of their curiosity and concerns. She would probably share those concerns later, once the memory of Faith's lips, warm and yielding, faded from the forefront of her mind. In the meantime, the kiss was all she could think of, and she wanted more. She could still feel the warmth of Faith's hands on her cheeks, and the way Faith's thumb errantly traced her jaw, sending a hot shiver through her.

She forced herself to focus on her work—on taking down her gear and greeting fans—but all she really wanted to do was pull Faith somewhere private to finish what they'd started.

Still, she was hyper-aware of Faith's every move as she greeted fans and signed autographs, and she was sure there was more than one photo of her band with a fan where she was looking over to the side, seeking Faith's warm gaze.

Usually, she enjoyed this part of a show nearly as much as playing the music, and they didn't get the same opportunity to interact with fans in the large venues, but this time, she suffered through the whole event, which couldn't end soon enough.

It did end, though. Eventually the room emptied, and they found themselves settling up with Luci, collecting their share of the door proceeds, and packing the gear back into their van.

"Can I help?" Faith offered, as Spencer picked up the floor tom in both hands.

"I think we've got nearly all of it," Spencer said. She held the large drum to her chest and looked at Faith, so pretty in the dim light of the bar.

"Thanks for inviting me out tonight," Faith said. Her smile was shy but genuine, and the gentle sincerity knotted Spencer's stomach.

"Thank you for coming."

Spencer carried the drum out to the van, with Faith walking alongside her, and she set the instrument in the back.

"I have to teach an early dance class," Faith said, the disappointment palpable in her voice. "I promised I'd cover for one of our other teachers who is busy moving tomorrow."

"I get it." Spencer shoved her hands into her jean pockets, suddenly not sure what to do with them.

"I really wish I could stay and spend a little more time with you, but I probably *should* get some sleep."

"Let me walk you to your car," Spencer suggested, and Faith nodded, quietly leading the way while Spencer fell into step beside her.

"This is me," Faith said, all too soon, fishing out her keys and unlocking her Jetta.

Spencer fought the urge to ask her to stay a little longer. It wasn't as if she could realistically spend any more time with Faith, either. Now that they'd loaded up their gear, her band would probably be ready to leave as well.

"Thanks again for coming," she said, and when Faith turned to her, she stepped forward without hesitation, leaning in for one more kiss.

This time, there was none of the urgency or intensity, just a slow, sweet kiss goodnight that promised more to come.

Faith got in her car and Spencer stood back to watch her drive away, surprised at the depth of the loss she felt.

Then she went back to where the rest of the group was already getting into the van. Without a word she slid into the passenger seat.

When Mari turned and opened her mouth to comment, she held out a hand to cut her off.

"Not tonight."

Mari's eyes were a dark storm of questions, but she sat back behind the steering wheel, nodded, and turned over the ignition.

Spencer leaned back against the seat and looked out the window while they drove. Later, there would be questions, but tonight she would enjoy the happy glow.

Chapter Thirteen

Faith watched the group of preschoolers twirl and dance to "Show Yourself" from *Frozen 2*, ending the dance class with a few minutes of free dancing before dismissing the students to enjoy the rest of their weekend. From the moment the song started, each of the children began to make up their own routine, bending and moving to the music as though nobody was watching them. Some mornings, she enjoyed sitting back and taking in the scene, watching them as they danced freely and enthusiastically. This morning, however, she felt inspired to join in, and she began to twirl and bend alongside the carefree group, letting the music take over and move through her.

She had selected the song because the group, primarily made up of little girls, *always* requested songs from *Frozen*, and she had played the first soundtrack to the point that it made her ears bleed. But once she hit play, she couldn't help but hear the parallels to her own life. She remembered how she'd felt at the concert the night before, the realization she was gay hitting her with stunning, certain clarity. On some level, she'd probably always known, and she'd certainly wondered over the years, but now the truth burned so bright and so bold inside of her there was no way she could ever lie to herself, or even simply question herself, again. She was gay and she wanted Spencer. She felt both of those truths in her bones, and neither scared her anymore. They felt too right and honest to be scary.

One of the little girls twirled, arms wide open, and a huge grin on her face.

Faith had felt like that once. She'd been carefree and bold. She thought about all the layers of expectation she wore now and wondered when she'd allowed herself to be cloaked in them. It had started slowly, she was sure, one layer at a time, until they were all so heavy, she couldn't move or breathe. All of the pressures and expectations still existed for her, she knew, but in the aftermath of her realization at the concert, and the soul-searing kiss with Spencer afterward, she felt a little stronger beneath them all. She'd been the one to initiate the kiss, and it had surpassed any hopes or expectations she'd had of what kissing Spencer might be like. She hadn't stopped thinking about the feel of Spencer's lips on hers, and she wanted to hold onto the confidence she'd felt in that moment when she'd gone after what she wanted.

Her students' youthful freedom expressed through dance was an almost perfect reflection of the limitless feeling that Faith hoped to retain, and so along with her students she began to twirl, spinning, and spinning, and spinning, until she grew dizzy with delight, and at least some of the weight had spun off.

As she spun, she began to smile.

At first, she didn't recognize the joy as it radiated from her chest, out toward her limbs. The purity of such joy was foreign to her. But once she recognized the feeling, her smile widened, and she allowed the feeling to lift her and carry her through the rest of her dance.

And then, the song ended.

But as she said goodbye to each of the children, sending them off with a sticker and a high-five, she promised herself that even though the dance had ended, the joy wouldn't.

She went to the change room and began to pack up her belongings, saying a quick "hello" to Callie who was untying her shoes after teaching her pointe class.

"You look happy today," Callie commented, and it was only then Faith realized she had a smile on her face.

She nodded. "I am. It's a good day."

"That's what I like to hear!" Callie said, as bright and bubbly as ever.

"How are you?" Faith asked. The conversation felt unfamiliar and she realized she hadn't taken much time to really connect with anyone at the studio in... well, she wasn't sure how long. Months, at least.

"Oh, I'm good," Callie said. "My girls were all a little disappointed about their competition results, but I'm so proud of how far they've come."

There was no hint of disappointment in Callie's voice, which was a refreshing change. She thought of Mandy and how invested in her students' competitions she became, as well as all of her own instructors growing up.

"Anyway, dance is about having fun, right?" Callie continued, as she slung her bag over her shoulder and headed to leave.

Is it? Faith hadn't found that to be the case, but maybe she could get that spark of joy back.

Spencer knew she was going to be hit with a barrage of questions the minute she walked into band practice. Mari had sent her a couple of text messages over the weekend, and she replied to each with short, one- to two-word responses. The early messages had been light-hearted and curious, but she hadn't known what to tell her friend. Then, in response to her withholding information, Mari's messages shifted toward concern. Spencer had told her not to worry, she knew what she was doing, but her friend wasn't going to accept that answer easily. She hoped she could avoid some of the questioning by showing up late for practice, but her friends all stopped what they were doing the minute she opened the door. Three pairs of eyes landed on her intently.

"Sorry I'm late," she said, ensuring her voice had an air of exasperation to it, as though she'd rushed to get there and hadn't simply sat in her car for a good fifteen minutes, watching the clock and weighing when enough time had passed for her to go into the studio. "Don't let me interrupt. Keep playing and I'll jump in right away."

"Wow. You *really* don't want to tell us about Faith," Sienna teased.

Spencer felt her cheeks redden and she avoided eye contact, checking all the connections on her pedal board and pulling out her guitar tuner.

"I'm not really sure what to say," she admitted.

"What the hell are you doing?" Mari asked. Her voice didn't hold any playfulness like Sienna's had, and after a weekend of dodging her friend's messages, Spencer knew she deserved the bite behind the words.

She couldn't meet Mari's gaze. "I don't know, Mar. We've been working together, and… Things have changed."

This time, when Mari spoke, there was no judgment in her voice, only concern. "Spence, that's how it was before, remember? And she broke your heart."

Spencer *did* remember, and the memory of it knocked the air out of her chest. As a teenager, she hadn't had much good in her life, or even much to hope for. With Faith, suddenly she'd imagined a *million* futures, all of them together, and the thought of Faith ending things hit her like a truck—one she hadn't even seen coming. Now, she wanted to pretend she was stepping toward Faith with her eyes open, but the truth was, even with her eyes open, there was a good chance she'd get run over again. She could practically see the truck barrelling toward her.

"I'm worried about you," Mari said. "I don't want to see you get hurt."

Spencer wanted to tell Mari she had everything under control, but she'd be lying and they'd both know it.

"You looked really happy when she showed up yesterday," Wren said, and Spencer was grateful for the voice of support.

"I had a great time with her last night. The kissing was unexpected, but that wasn't why I invited her."

"You totally want there to be more kissing," Sienna said.

Spencer held her thumb and forefinger close together and let the happiness she felt at the thought bubble into a small laugh. "Yeah, a little bit, I do."

Mari visibly held her tongue, and some of the happiness dissipated again.

"What if things are different this time around?" she asked, and the words popped the remaining happiness. She heard them echo back, and she heard her mom say the exact same sentence. She'd used that same justification each time she'd gotten back together with Spencer's dad. *This time will be different.* Things were never different. People didn't change. *When somebody shows you who they are, believe them the first time.*

Spencer tried to push those thoughts from her mind, clinging instead to the happiness she'd felt the night before. Her relationship with Faith had always been special. She'd never connected with anyone else the way she'd connected with her. She didn't want to give up the tenuous new connection forming between the two of them. They weren't kids anymore, and Faith had shown that she *had* started to take ownership of her life. Maybe she would fight for their relationship this time. Spencer could see the potential for heartbreak, the truck barrelling toward her, but she planned to put one foot in front of the other and hope that instead of getting run over, she could reach that imagined future she'd always dreamed of.

She couldn't get there without the risk and standing still no longer felt like an option.

Faith took a sip of the sangria that she'd chosen for her weekly cocktail selection, turning each of the fruity notes over on her tongue as she looked out at the ocean. The setting sun cast a golden glow across the water, reminding her of the natural golden tones in Spencer's auburn hair. Even though they hadn't seen each other since the concert, Spencer had been a constant presence in her life all week, occupying most of her thoughts. The feel of the kiss still lingered on her lips, desire tugging at her core. She relished the memory, replaying in her mind each delicious moment. But as the days stretched between them, she found herself increasingly left wanting.

While her desire grew by the day, so did her concerns. Communication between her and Spencer had been limited since the concert, friendly but sparse. The distance was equally on her as she'd been busy with her work week, but it made it hard to gauge where they stood. Her kiss had been met with enthusiasm, but that didn't mean Spencer hadn't had a surge of doubt in the days since. Faith knew the fear was warranted, and she hated herself for it, but she hoped Spencer could see she was not a kid anymore, she was a grown woman, still figuring herself out, only now she had a hell of a lot more agency and backbone.

"And anyway, I would have rather gone to Mexico for vacation, seen something new, but Chad is adamant Hawaii's the better option. He's got this fear of the cartel that I think is overblown, but the beaches in Hawaii *are* nice, and really, who are we kidding? I really just want a nice beach and a fruity drink, and I'll be happy."

She sensed Mandy was nearly done talking and turned her attention back to the conversation. She loved her friend, but she didn't feel like weighing in on which beach she and Chad should visit for their annual winter getaway. She didn't even know why it was a debate. The two never went anywhere other than Florida or Hawaii. Mandy had recently decided she wanted to add Mexico to her bucket list after seeing some photos of a trip one of the other dance instructors had taken, and she seemed to think it meant she was being adventurous and branching out, but in actuality, it didn't matter where they went. If she and Chad went to Mexico, the two of them would never leave the resort.

Faith couldn't think of a worse way to spend a vacation. If she ever went to Mexico, she'd visit the Mayan ruins, try authentic mezcal, and eat tacos from street carts. She wanted to see the whole world, not just one or two beaches.

"I'm sure you'll have a good time either way," she managed.

Mandy looked thoughtful and nodded. "Yeah. Maybe I could even convince Chad we could take two trips this winter."

Faith smiled at her friend, but she knew it didn't reach her eyes. "There you go."

Mandy didn't appear to notice Faith's lack of enthusiasm for her vacation planning. She was looking off into the distance, clearly thinking over her new plan.

"Anyway," Mandy said at last, returning her focus to the table. "Tell me about your week. I hate that we haven't talked much, but with regionals coming up, well… you know how things get."

Mandy had days where she was a great listener, but on weeks when she had a lot on her mind, she possessed a remarkable ability to simultaneously express interest in others while continuing to steamroll the conversation. It didn't typically bother her, but she had too much she wanted to talk over with her friend to let the conversation be redirected to dance competitions and rehearsals.

"I went to see Spencer's band play at The Lighthouse the other night," she began.

Mandy interrupted her with a chuckle. "I'm trying to picture you at a punk concert."

She bristled, even though Mandy had said the comment in a good-natured tone. She was happy. Why couldn't her *best friend* hear, and help protect, that happiness? She swallowed the acrid taste of Mandy's response and kept talking, wanting to share her joy. "They were incredible, Mandy. I wish you'd been there. One of the opening acts was a little aggressive for my tastes, but overall, it was a really fun night. Spencer and I watched the first two acts together, until it was her turn to play, so it wasn't like I was standing there sticking out like a sore thumb all night."

Mandy studied her for a minute longer than was comfortable before she said, "So you and Spencer are spending time together again."

She flushed at Mandy's words. There it was. The *real* reason Mandy laughed off the idea of her at the concert.

"She let me know she had a show coming up, and I thought it would be a lot of fun to see her play live." She was downplaying the relationship forming between Spencer and herself, but with everything so new and fragile she didn't want Mandy's scrutiny. It would be different if they were officially together, she reasoned. They'd barely kissed twice, and she still didn't know how Spencer felt about that fact. It was premature to tell Mandy anything.

Still, shame crept up her neck. She shouldn't *have* to defend herself, but she hated herself for not trying.

"Well, I'm glad you enjoyed the concert," Mandy said without any enthusiasm in her voice. When Mandy changed the subject back to herself, Faith let her.

When she got home at the end of the night, however, she was eager to escape her life, and she sank down under the comfort of her covers and pulled her book into her lap. Soon, she was on a sailing adventure, hurrying to dock in the Bahamas before the looming hurricane hit the area. Or, at least, that's what the family in the book was doing. Usually, when she opened the pages of her travel adventure books, she was able to be transported on all of the adventures alongside the author. This time, she felt the separation. They were doing the big, fantastic things, while she read about them.

She felt the sharp pang of jealousy as she read the nonfiction account of a family sailing around the world. The author, along with her husband and two school-aged children, had left everything behind for a year on the seas. The kids traded homework for a real-world geography lesson, and the four made invaluable, lasting memories. For all intents and purposes, the author had every reason to *not* go on the sailing trip. She'd been establishing her career, her parents were aging, and she had two young children. She had *more* excuses than Faith, certainly, but she hadn't let any of them stop her. She'd had a dream and she'd made it a reality.

Meanwhile, Faith read about others' adventures, while her own life remained stagnant and filled with "one-day" dreams.

One day she would try sailing. *One day* she would stand on the equator. *One day* she would visit the Great Wall and the Terracotta Warriors.

She was happy, really. She liked her life. It wasn't everything she would have hoped for, but it was comfortable and warm and safe— things she hadn't been able to say in the years she'd been with Brett. She had a fulfilling career, and she enjoyed the time spent with her parents and friends and teaching dance classes. If she ever got the opportunity to live in Ecuador for a year, it would no doubt be amazing, but if she didn't, it wasn't like her life was lacking in any way.

So why, then, was she suddenly so unfulfilled?

She knew the answer. Her conversation with Mandy had left a bitter taste in her mouth. They were best friends, but sometimes, it felt like they had nothing in common. She knew what Mandy would say if she were to tell her about any of her travel aspirations. She'd heard it all before—from Mandy, from Brett, from her parents. *You want to go on an Amazon river cruise? Why? You'd be in the middle of the jungle. Can you even imagine the bugs? You'll come back with dengue fever. It's not safe.*

Mandy didn't understand or respect her goals, and, truth be told, Faith didn't understand or respect Mandy's. She had no interest in debating the merits of various snowbird destinations or whether they should drink mai tais or margaritas. It all felt so frivolous and empty.

She thought back on the derision in her friend's voice when she mentioned going to see Spencer's band play live. Spencer was threatening, and not just because of her gender or sexual orientation. She'd always encouraged Faith to imagine a life outside of the neat little existence that had been prescribed, while Mandy wanted a friend who conformed to all of the same societal pressures she did. Maybe having Faith caged alongside her gave Mandy the illusion of freedom, or maybe she actually found comfort in the constraints imposed on her life. Either way, Faith felt herself shrinking within the confines of their friendship.

Shame simmered inside as she thought about how abruptly she'd ended things with Spencer back in high school. She had many regrets in life, but that moment was the biggest. She'd known it to be a mistake as soon as the words fell from her mouth, and after spending the night crying, she'd gone to school the next day hoping to get a chance to repair some of the damage with Spencer. Instead, Spencer had disappeared, and when Brett asked her out for the fifth time, she'd numbly accepted. She had been selfish and cowardly— she knew now, and she'd known then. She'd hated every second of her first date with Brett. She'd hated the possessive way he always took her hand when others were around, or the way he'd make sure to kiss her when others were watching. Their entire relationship was founded on hate—specifically, the hate she'd had for herself. Then, by the time she was done punishing herself, she was in so deep that she hadn't known how to get out.

If she got a second chance with Spencer, she wouldn't make the same mistake again.

As if on cue, Faith's phone buzzed and she set down her book, turning to see Spencer's name light up across her screen. Instantly all of the shame and tension dissipated, replaced with the light, airy feel of joy.

I hope you're having a good week, the message read. *I'm really looking forward to seeing you in group tomorrow.*

She smiled to herself and read the message three times before responding. *This week has felt too long. Tomorrow can't come soon enough.*

I'm still thinking about that kiss. She hit send before she could second-guess herself.

The response came quickly. *So am I.*

She wished she had some insight into those thoughts, at least to know if Spencer had enjoyed the kiss or whether she regretted it, but she didn't know how to ask, so instead she chewed on her bottom lip as she typed and retyped her next message. *You took me skydiving. Tell me something that's on your bucket list.*

There was a long pause before a response came through, and she imagined that it was hard for Spencer to come up with anything. Spencer wasn't caged like she was, and her life had afforded her the opportunity for all sorts of travel and adventure. Faith expected her to reply and say she couldn't think of anything but was unprepared for the vulnerable answer she received.

In all honesty, I have a really boring bucket list. I want the quiet experiences that I never had growing up because my childhood was so tumultuous. I want one really happy Christmas morning. I want to toss a frisbee around with my kids one day. I want a day to just feel like a kid again, myself.

She read the message a few times, wishing they had more than a cell phone connecting them. She wanted to run her fingers through Spencer's hair while listening to stories of her life, physically anchoring them together as they dared to travel back in time. She didn't want Spencer sitting alone, all the way on the other side of Vancouver. She wanted to ask her to come over, but she knew Spencer was likely not ready to *really* open up, so instead, she typed back, *A day to feel like a kid again. Let's do it.* She didn't know what exactly she would plan for them to do, but she would come up with something.

A long moment passed, and Spencer didn't answer. At first, Faith was simply eager for a response, but then with each second that went by worry began to mount, and she found herself wondering if even that simple response had somehow pushed their tenuous connecting too far.

Let's do it, Spencer finally typed back.

She leaned back with a smile, her stomach knotting in anticipation. *How's Saturday?*

Sounds perfect.

That gave her two days to come up with the perfect bucket list day of childhood for Spencer. It *had* to be perfect.

I'll see you tomorrow, Faith, Spencer typed. *Sleep well.* She followed her text message with a little kissing emoji and Faith stared at it with a stupid grin on her face.

She wasn't sure she would sleep at all.

Chapter Fourteen

Spencer arrived at Sunrise House a few minutes earlier than usual and pressed the buzzer with an eagerness she'd have never thought she could muster for the shelter. She'd been excited for her music program when she'd first returned, but the echoes of her own long-silenced traumas had been stirred up in the hallways of the old, familiar home. Now, as she entered, she only heard the echo of Faith. The rest was all a distant memory of another life.

That was how things had always been with Faith: like opening the windows and letting light chase out all the ghosts.

She found Faith already in the recreation room, clearing it for their workshop. She stepped inside and began helping.

Faith smiled over at her, warm and wordless, as they fell into a natural, easy rhythm.

"So, are you going to tell me what we're doing on Saturday?" Spencer asked at last, as she finished setting the chairs in a circle. Faith had promised her a day where she could feel like a kid again and sent a couple of teasing messages since that conversation, leaving her wracking her brain trying to guess what they might be doing.

Faith shook her head. "You'll see this weekend."

"Come on. A little hint?"

Again, Faith shook her head, a teasing smile tugging at the corners of her mouth. "I like keeping you on your toes too much to give anything away."

Spencer had come to learn Faith's voice dropped a note when she was flirting, and the recognition of that ever so slightly altered tone tugged at her. Faith's hair was loose, falling in soft blond waves over her shoulders, and Spencer ached to close the distance between them and knot her fingers in Faith's hair while she pulled her mouth to her own.

Instead, she sat down and took out her guitar, needing something else to do with her hands. She was fully aware she was at Faith's place of employment and any minute a group of teenagers could walk in the door.

"Well, I look forward to seeing what you have planned," she said. She finished tuning her guitar, and without thought she began to play the song she'd written for Faith once upon a time. The notes spilled from her, quiet and effortless, unable to be contained, just like her feelings for Faith.

She'd just started playing the chorus when she noticed Faith studying her and realized what she was playing.

She stilled her fingers and set her guitar in her lap.

"I remember you playing that for me," Faith said, her voice barely above a whisper.

Embarrassment coloured Spencer's cheeks. She hadn't intended to play the song. "I figured you'd have forgotten it by now."

"I've listened to it in my mind a thousand times," Faith said, speaking slow and careful. "It's so strange to hear you play it again."

Faith's words rooted in her heart and blossomed warmth in her chest. And at the same time, hurt and embarrassment simmered in her stomach. She remembered that warm spring day when she'd first played the song for Faith. She remembered the way the sun highlighted the golden tones in Faith's hair, and how she'd leaned back and closed her eyes to listen. She remembered how hopeful and in love she'd felt, with no reservation or fear. How she'd trusted Faith completely.

And then—

"I'm here to play the guitar?"

She looked up and saw a gangly teenaged boy standing in the doorway wearing ripped skinny jeans and an oversized hooded sweatshirt.

"Come on in," she said.

Soon another couple of teenagers joined the group and the music program was underway. Spencer tucked all of her feelings for Faith— all the hope and all the hurt—back into the boxes where they belonged and focused on teaching the basics of guitar.

She could deal with the feelings later. Or never. The hurt could stay boxed away, as far as she was concerned.

Spencer sat in her nest chair, looking out at the gray and rainy skyline, while she plucked at the strings of the guitar in her lap. She was almost thankful for the gloomy weather that helped temper some of the nervous excitement that vibrated inside her every time she thought about the date Faith was taking her on as soon as she was done teaching her morning dance lessons. Watching the water run in rivulets down the windowsill had an almost meditative effect, and she studied the little trails of water while she let her fingers move over the strings, creating a new melody, one that was soft and hopeful. She wanted to believe that the stain of their past could be washed away, and that she and Faith could truly have a fresh start. She wanted it so bad she could feel the ache of it in her chest.

The musical ringtone on her cell phone interrupted her thoughts, and she glanced down, smiling when Faith's name lit up her screen.

"Hey, you," she said, as she quickly hit the answer button.

"How is your Saturday morning going so far?" Faith asked. Spencer sunk down into her chair as though sinking down into the warmth of Faith's voice.

"It's going better now that I get to talk to you," she admitted. "You?"

"It would be better if it weren't for the rain which is putting a damper on all of my carefully laid plans."

Spencer sat up a little bit straighter, looking with disappointment at the rain she had found so contemplative and relaxing just minutes earlier.

"I had organized some outdoor activities for us, but it looks like those won't be happening, so I started thinking about rainy day activities. I was wondering if you'd prefer I come by your place, or would you rather come to mine?"

"Are you going to tell me what the rainy-day activities are?" Spencer asked.

Faith's musical laughter came through the phone. "Still a surprise, but I promise you are going to get the day of childlike fun that you've been wanting."

Already she felt some of that youthful joy radiate through her, the eager curiosity reminiscent of her few good Christmases, where she couldn't wait to wake up in the morning.

"Why don't you come over here?" Spencer suggested. "You plan our rainy-day activities, and I can plan our rainy-day dinner."

"Deal," Faith agreed, "*but* it has to be a dinner that you loved as a child. No fancy gourmet adult dinner. I'm talking Kraft dinner, piggy-in-a-blankets, grilled cheese sandwiches... Something along those lines."

"Yes, boss." She gave Faith her address and then she hung up the phone.

She quickly scanned her apartment, relieved to find it relatively orderly. There were a few piles of clutter—music magazines and guitar picks mostly—that she quickly tucked away, but she generally kept things neat and tidy, so she didn't have to rush to clean anything for Faith.

"She's coming *here*," Spencer said out loud, the weight of that realization settling on her. Faith would be there, *in her home*, and she was overwhelmed with how that felt both incredibly special and deeply vulnerable.

She had a little over an hour to prepare before Faith arrived. She made a quick run to the grocery store to pick up what she needed for their dinner, and then she got back to the apartment with time to spare... and stare at the walls, and pace, and have her nervous excitement build upon itself.

She jumped when the sound of her buzzer finally cut through that rising tension.

"Come on up," she said into the intercom. Then, she buzzed Faith in and waited eagerly by the door for her. She had to stop herself from opening the door and standing in the hallway to greet Faith, not wanting to run the risk of appearing too eager.

She took a breath and tried to calm her racing heart, suddenly reminded of the visceral fear she'd felt as she'd been about to fall through the sky after Faith. The intimacy of having Faith in her place felt almost equivalent.

When Faith knocked on the door, she quickly ran a hand through her hair and straightened her shirt, and then swallowed her fear and greeted Faith, a laugh bubbling up out of her chest the minute she saw her.

Faith was dressed in patterned pajama bottoms depicting various cartoon Star Wars scenes, and a soft gray t-shirt with Yoda on the front.

"Don't worry," Faith said over Spencer's laughter. "I have a pair for you, as well." She held up a bag and Spencer's laughter died down.

She shook her head. "I'm good. My jeans are comfy enough."

Faith, though, pressed the bag into her arms. "Oh no. We're doing this. You wanted a day to feel like a kid, and the first thing we're going to do is get dressed up in ridiculously comfy and ridiculously silly pajamas, because it is impossible to take yourself too seriously when you're dressed like this."

Spencer couldn't think of anything to say other than, "But Yoda? I wouldn't have pegged you for a Star Wars fan."

"I was hoping for something with Queen Elsa," Faith admitted, "but the cartoon character pajamas were limited in adult sizes. I took what I could find at the last minute."

"You know, you really didn't have to take this whole 'day to be a kid' thing quite so literally."

"Just go change," Faith said.

Spencer rolled her eyes, but she could already feel the happiness spread from her chest out toward her limbs. The day was guaranteed to be silly and fun and exactly what she'd wanted. She took the bag with the pajamas Faith had bought for her, and went to her bedroom to change.

She also had a pair of cartoon Star Wars pajamas, but hers were darker fabric, and her gray tank top had Darth Vader on the front.

She shook her head at the outfit, but she was aware of the smile that wouldn't leave her face. She changed from the jeans and t-shirt she'd agonized over before Faith arrived into the ridiculous pajama set, and looked at herself in the mirror. She had to admit she *did* feel more comfortable and lighthearted. Her nerves for the date dissipated, and she ran a hand through her hair, ruffling it just slightly to add to the casual look, before she stepped back into the living room.

"Well." She held out her arms. "How do I look?"

Faith's gaze was appreciative as it traveled over her body, sending a shiver down her spine and arms.

"You look amazing." Her voice was low and lacked any of the jovial spirit Spencer was sure had been intended by the pajamas.

At the shift in mood, she couldn't help but notice the way the cartoon top hung from Faith's chest, the soft fabric clinging to her in all the right ways.

"So." She cleared her throat a little as she spoke. "What did you have planned for us today?"

Instead of answering, Faith pushed past her and went to the living room, setting down the second bag she had brought with her. She moved the coffee table out of the center of the room, and then took a seat on the floor.

"Come join me," Faith said, and as Spencer made her way to the middle of her living room, Faith pulled an unopened board game out of her bag.

"Candyland?" Spencer asked with a laugh at the unveiling of the colorful game.

Faith nodded and somehow managed to maintain a serious expression. "This was only my favourite board game ever when I was a kid, and so I had to pick it up for the two of us to play. But I will warn you, I am a boss at Candyland."

"Is there even any skill involved in the game?"

Faith *tsk*ed at her while opening the box and setting out all the pieces.

Spencer was fairly sure she'd never played Candyland before. She knew of it, of course, but she hadn't exactly played a lot of board games growing up. She'd spent the majority of her childhood in self-preservation mode.

She watched Faith unbox the game, focusing on the way Faith's hands smoothed the game board open, and the delicate movement of her fingers as she shuffled the cards. Faith had understood *all* of what she'd meant when she had said she wanted one day to feel like a kid again—a day spent making memories that could replace the shadow-stained version from her past.

Faith was going to give her the one really fun, really silly, and really carefree day she'd never had.

She selected the blue playing piece and set it near the start space on the board, as Faith once more reached into her bag and pulled out a big bulk bag of assorted gummy candies.

"We can't play Candyland without candy." Faith reached into the bag and set candies around the game board.

Spencer reached for a gummy bear near her side of the board, but Faith was quick and smacked her hand away. "These have to be won."

She scowled, but then felt herself melt beneath Faith's playful grin. "You're on, Siebert," she said.

Faith quickly explained how to play, complete with her modified directions for how to win, lose, and steal candy; selected the yellow game piece and set hers next to Spencer's, and then motioned to the cards. "I'll give you the advantage of going first. Pick your card."

Spencer picked a card with an orange square and moved her game piece to the first orange square on the board, feeling her competitive spirit rise inside of her.

She was the first to reach the candy castle, and she nearly leapt up from the floor, taking the little pile of candies that she'd won and popping a couple in her mouth while she pumped a fist in the air.

"Beginner's luck," Faith said, shaking her head with a laugh.

Spencer tossed a couple candies at her, which she tried unsuccessfully to dodge.

Then they reset their pieces and began their second game.

By the time they finished playing, both of them were laughing and fighting over candies. Spencer felt a buzz from the rush of sugar that made her feel slightly elated and giggly. Words that she would *never* have used to describe herself.

She stole the last gummy worm from the bowl and popped it in her mouth before flopping back against the sofa and closing her eyes. Faith sat across the game board from her, but they'd both stretched out, and their legs intertwined over the game. She was sure their legs hadn't come together intentionally, but she became hyper-aware of every point of contact.

"This was perfect," she said. "Thank you."

"We've played one board game," Faith said. "That hardly constitutes an entire day to feel like a kid again."

Spencer opened her eyes lazily, feeling the high from the sugar begin to dissipate. "Oh yeah? What else did you have planned for us?"

"How do you feel about blanket forts?"

"I can't say I have feelings one way or the other."

"Well, prepare yourself," Faith said. "We are going to build the greatest blanket fort of your life."

Spencer felt the loss when Faith stood, and she wanted to beg Faith to sit for a while longer so she could continue to soak in the moment, but Faith had already started rearranging her furniture, pushing on the sofa she was leaning against, and forcing her to sit up while Faith moved the sofa closer to the nest chair.

"What are you doing?"

"Come help me," Faith answered.

Spencer did as she was told. She followed Faith's lead, rearranging her living room to create a frame of furniture for them to drape blankets over. Once she had a good sense of Faith's vision for the fort, she began to take some initiative with the build. She pulled the cushion off her nest chair and rested it vertically next to the sofa to form another wall. Then she went to the kitchen to grab a couple chairs to complete the frame.

Without needing direction from Faith, she emptied her linen closet and began to round up every spare pillow and blanket she owned.

"You're a good apprentice fort builder," Faith said, happily taking an armful of blankets and beginning to drape them over the haphazard structure.

"I hope to graduate from my apprenticeship in no time."

"Whoa." Faith stopped her work and held up one hand. "Graduating to solo fort building is no small feat. You're still going to need a *lot* more supervised practice."

Spencer tried to maintain a serious expression as she nodded, but it was hard not to smile at this rare, playful side of Faith. She was enjoying Faith's carefree mood perhaps more than her own.

Spencer weighed the corners of the blanket roof down with books to hold everything in place, and then she stepped back to admire their creation. In the end, it had turned out to be a somewhat decent structure.

"Do you have any flashlights we can use inside?" Faith asked.

"Hold on. I'll go look."

She searched her storage closet and found an unopened package of plastic battery-operated tea light candles she had purchased a few years ago with the band while they had been experimenting with lighting options for the small venue shows. "How about these?"

The smile that formed on Faith's face at the sight of the candles was bright and unrestrained. It was clear Faith wasn't merely building a blanket fort for Spencer's sake. She was genuinely having fun, as well.

"These are perfect," Faith said.

Spencer opened the package and turned on each little candle before passing them to Faith who crawled into the fort and placed them along the perimeter.

Then Spencer turned off the living room lamps, before kneeling down and crawling into the fort herself.

The daylight was starting to wane, and the gray of the clouds made it seem even darker. Beneath the blankets, the light had gone quite dim, and the little plastic candles emitted a soft, flickering glow. Suddenly, the pillow fort, which had seemed childlike at first, appeared small and intimate

Faith lay down on her back, resting on one of the couch pillows, arms behind her head. She studied the blanket above her as though the plaid pattern was really a constellation of stars.

Spencer lay next to her, and the closeness made her breath catch in her chest. Faith was so near Spencer could feel the warmth coming from her. She wanted to sink in and lose herself in Faith.

"So, what do we do now?" She propped herself up so she could look over at Faith. "What's next in our day of fun?"

Faith rolled her head to the side to meet Spencer's gaze; the playful spark was gone from her eyes.

"Now," she said, her voice barely above a whisper, "you tell me a story."

"What kind of story?"

"A real one. Tell me something about you. Something you've never told anyone before. Something you can only say in the sanctity of this blanket fort."

Emotion tightened around Spencer's chest. Stories she had long since buried clawed up her throat, fighting to be heard. There were so *many* stories she found herself wanting to tell in the safety of Faith's presence. Stories that the frightened little girl she'd once been almost ached to speak into the world, in a safe space, so the power could be taken from them. But still, a part of her wasn't ready. Faith had left her. Spencer wanted to trust her, but she wasn't ready yet. Not fully. Not with those stories.

"At the start of grade twelve, I don't know if you remember, but somebody egged Principal Webb's car."

Faith nodded. "Of course, I remember. He never figured out who'd done it so he canceled the fall dance for everyone."

Spencer waited while the realization dawned on Faith.

"Oh my God, it was you?"

She shrugged. "Webb was an asshole."

She hadn't had a good reason for why she'd egged the principal's car. He hadn't done anything to her. She'd simply been tired of seeing the way he talked to others, students and staff alike. He'd had a smugness to him that had reminded her of her dad. That same way of acting untouchable, like everyone should defer to him. He hadn't done anything specific, but there was that quality about him... And she hadn't exactly been able to go out and egg her dad's car, so Principal Webb had served as the next best outlet for all of her anger.

She didn't say any of that to Faith, though.

"Your turn," she said instead.

Faith leaned back against the pillow and closed her eyes, thinking for so long she almost appeared asleep. Spencer was just about to nudge her when Faith spoke.

"I cheated on Brett," Faith said.

Of all the words Faith could have spoken, those were the last ones Spencer ever expected, and she felt the air rush out of her lungs at the softly spoken admission.

"Just one time, and he was already cheating on me by that point, not that any of that makes it better."

Spencer reached over and rested her hand on Faith's leg, not sure what she could or should say, instead giving Faith the space to tell her story.

"Every year Brett's work had a week-long convention that he'd have to go to, and I had decided that this time, while he was out of town, I would take a weekend trip to Victoria and check out a gay bar. I wasn't looking for a hookup. I really wasn't. I was looking for a sense of belonging somewhere. I'd had a few drinks to try to relax my nerves when she started talking to me. I think her name was Trina or Trisha or something like that. I can't even really remember. How bad is that? What I remember is the thrill at feeling wanted by this woman and wondering if I had sex with her if all of the questions about myself would finally be answered. When she suggested we find somewhere more private, I offered my hotel room."

"And?" Spencer hated the jealousy she tasted in the back of her throat.

"And she wasn't who I wanted to be with."

She turned to Spencer with naked honesty darkening her hazel eyes.

Spencer swallowed hard at the implication, but she needed more. She needed to know that Faith was going into this, whatever this was, with her eyes open. She couldn't be another experiment.

"But did it tell you anything about yourself?"

Faith shook her head from side to side. "She was assertive almost to the point of aggressiveness, and the whole event felt rushed and uncomfortable, especially with my guilt layered on top."

Spencer tried to think of how to respond, but Faith spoke again.

"I imagined she was you, and I came harder than ever before. I told Brett I wanted a divorce the next morning."

The words stunned Spencer, both in their boldness and meaning, and she propped herself up on one elbow, leaning to look down at Faith. She could see Faith's flush of embarrassment in the plastic candlelight, but Faith didn't avert her eyes or offer any words to detract from her blunt statement.

"Faith—" Spencer began.

Faith propped herself up as well, holding her gaze when she said, "It's always been you, for me too, Spencer."

Those words were Spencer's undoing. She wanted desperately to believe them. They were the words she'd ached to hear for the past decade, despite trying to bury that longing so deep within her she no longer felt it.

She gazed at Faith for a long, unbroken moment, wanting to close the distance between them, but feeling paralyzed by the level of intimacy right then. In that moment, she realized she'd been wrong. She thought Faith didn't really *live* because she let fear win. But while Faith perhaps didn't live large, she did live fully. Her life might have been quiet, but it was far from empty. She thought of the beautiful day Faith had given her because she took in all of the simple details and nuances of life. She'd accused Faith of missing out because she didn't travel the world, skydive, or go on grand adventures, but in that moment, she realized *she* had been the one missing out. She went on adventures, but she used them to cover up all of the small moments and vulnerability she was so good at running from.

Now, Faith was lying there, and the moment was simple, and perfect, and utterly terrifying.

And it was her turn to be brave.

Heart pounding so hard she thought it would leap out of her throat, she leaned in and kissed Faith.

Faith inhaled as Spencer's lips caught hers, as though she was about to go underwater and knew she'd need air. She didn't want to surface. She wanted to drown in their kiss.

Spencer knew exactly how to kiss her, the perfect tempo and pressure—slow and deep. Agonizingly slow. She tasted like the gummy candies they'd eaten earlier. Faith tried to deepen the kiss, wanting more, but Spencer took her time, brushing her tongue over the inside of Faith's upper lip in a tender, thorough exploration that communicated the years of longing.

Faith reached for her, pulling Spencer over top of her, wanting to be closer, to feel their bodies against one another. Spencer settled her weight over Faith, but continued to take her time, and she wanted to groan at the need that welled within her.

"I've wanted this for so long. I'm not going to rush it."

Faith's eyes slammed shut at the words. She fought the urge to beg. She didn't want to rush things either, she wanted to spend the entire time learning Spencer's body. But the need was so sharp and acute she couldn't see beyond it.

Finally, Spencer deepened the kiss and all the pent-up passion presented itself in bruising intensity for one long, perfect moment. Then, she pulled back, and Faith almost cried out at the loss.

Spencer's lips brushed over her chin, jaw, and neck. Too tentatively, as though uncertainty still lingered in her mind.

"I want you," Faith said, her words breathy and raw. She rocked her hips upward, desperate for contact. With anyone else, she'd have felt embarrassed at her blatant desire, so it seemed impossible Spencer *wouldn't* know, but she said the words anyway.

Spencer pulled back and straddled her, settling her weight right where Faith needed her most. She could feel the heat coming from Spencer, and she wanted to reach inside her pants, finding her wetness.

Instead, her hands went to Spencer's sides, and she allowed her fingers to dance up the inside of her shirt. Even the lightest of her touches caused muscles to tighten. She brushed a thumb over Spencer's belly, marvelling at the ripple of abs, and then Spencer lifted her arms. Faith took the hint, helping push the shirt over her head, leaving her chest clad in only a sports bra.

The dim light from the plastic candles flickered over Spencer's skin, and Faith traced her eyes over the contours of muscles visible beneath the tattooed skin of her arms.

She wondered if Spencer could feel how wet she was, even with the clothing still between them.

Spencer took off the sports bra, and Faith was distantly aware of the appreciative hum that escaped her lips, as she brushed her thumb over one of Spencer's hard nipples.

She managed to tear her gaze from Spencer's chest, and the

want she saw was intoxicating. Spencer's head was tilted back slightly, her eyes were closed, and her lower lip was between her teeth. Faith marvelled at how her brow pulled together as Faith rolled her nipple between her thumb and forefinger.

She'd never had that effect on anyone before, that ability to bring intense pleasure with the slightest touch. Emboldened by the way she so visibly impacted Spencer, she propped herself up to replace her fingers with her lips, gently kissing one nipple before sucking it hard into her mouth and flicking her tongue across Spencer's skin, causing a loud, guttural groan.

Before she could explore further, Spencer pulled her in, bringing their mouths together hard, while her hands tugged at Faith's shirt.

She broke the kiss only for a moment to help shrug off the shirt, and then their mouths came together again, each of them fighting for control.

She was only distantly aware of Spencer unclasping her bra, but then their bare chests pressed together and every inch of her felt like fire.

Spencer pushed her down, this time without hesitancy. She removed Faith's remaining clothes, urgent and certain.

Spencer's hands began exploring her thighs, teasing their way up and then back down, and Faith's desire became nearly too much to take. She writhed, begging for more with her body, unashamed of how desperate she looked. She *was* desperate. Finally, Spencer ran one finger along her opening, and Faith cried out at the touch.

"You're so wet," Spencer said, her voice thick with awe.

She couldn't reply. She needed Spencer inside of her.

But Spencer didn't comply, even as her name escaped Faith's lips again and again.

And then, her mouth closed over Faith, and she arched in surprise at the hot wet press of Spencer's lips against her clit.

She heard herself as though from a distance, unable to help the sounds that were pulled from her.

Finally, Spencer pushed two fingers inside of her, and the sensation mixed with the feel of Spencer's mouth pushed Faith over the edge. The orgasm ripped through her and she cried out loudly as her whole body came around Spencer.

And then Spencer held her as the waves of pleasure subsided, and she was left spent, heart pounding against her rib cage. Spencer slowly slipped her fingers out from inside her and curled up beside her while she sucked in air.

"That was…" she began, but she couldn't find the right word to complete the sentence.

Spencer didn't answer, she just held Faith, until she finally had the energy to move and continue their exploration.

Chapter Fifteen

Spencer woke in a tangle of limbs, with Faith's head tucked against her shoulder and a hand cupping her breast. She was stiff from sleeping on the floor, but her body was otherwise heavy and satisfied. The plastic tea lights still flickered around them, but sunlight penetrated the blanket fort, rendering the little candles nearly useless.

Faith stirred slightly against her and she held her breath, scared of waking her. The perfection of the moment felt fragile, like a bubble that could pop at any moment. She felt somehow certain Faith would wake, unprepared for the enormity of what had transpired between the two of them, and then she would leave again. This was the type of moment that Spencer's experience had taught her could never exist.

But then, Faith blinked open her sleep-lidded hazel eyes, stretched a long, contented stretch, and said "Good morning," with no indication of panic in her voice. The relief hit Spencer so acutely that emotion lodged in the back of her throat.

"Did you sleep well?" She hoped her voice didn't betray her nerves.

Faith sat up and brushed her blond hair with her fingers while she gazed down at Spencer with adoration.

"That was the best sleep I've had in a long time."

Spencer had to laugh. She'd also woke feeling rested, which seemed ridiculous given how little sleeping had actually occurred.

"I have a bed, next time," she said, before she could think through the implications of that sentence. She froze momentarily with panic, but then Faith smiled, and she let the tension fall away.

"I look forward to getting to see it," Faith said.

Spencer hadn't even realized how deep her fear ran until that moment when she could let it go. The relief was immediate, sharp, and overwhelming.

Faith pulled on her shirt and underwear then pushed her way out of the blanket fort, and Spencer did the same, blinking against the bright sunlight that filled the room.

"Oh my God," Faith said. "Your view is incredible."

She stood at Spencer's large windows which overlooked Vancouver's harbour, with both the oceans and mountains in the distance. The previous day, the clouds and rain had turned everything into a boring gray slate but on a clear day, Spencer would admit, the view from her apartment was spectacular.

"It was the selling point for me," Spencer admitted.

"No kidding." Faith continued to stand and gaze out at the horizon in awe.

"Are you hungry? I could make us breakfast and coffee."

"That would honestly be amazing. I don't think I ate much else besides candy yesterday."

Spencer thought back on their feast of gummy candies and chocolates. "We never did get to the Alphagettis I had planned for our dinner."

As if suddenly reminded of its need for food, her stomach rumbled loudly.

Faith stepped closer and added, "We also worked up quite the appetite last night." The words were husky and low, hitting Spencer's core.

Suddenly she wasn't hungry for food, but Faith headed for the kitchen before she could close the distance between them.

Spencer filled her kettle and set it on the stove to boil water for her pour-over coffee pot. Then, she pulled her coffee grinder from the cupboard and hand ground some of the Bottle Rocket Blond roast from Black Soul Coffee. In recent years, she'd become a bit of a coffee snob, in part because she much preferred the taste of a quality cup of coffee over the motor oil that seemed to come out of every drive-through, and in part because she enjoyed the morning ritual. It was an almost sensual experience to pour boiling water over the hand-ground beans, listening to the coffee drip into the carafe below while breathing in the rich aroma. She found the process soothing and almost meditative, and it had become an important, grounding part of her morning routine. This morning, the simplicity of the coffee preparation helped calm her storm of emotions: fear, desire, hope… something stronger she wasn't ready to name . . .

Meanwhile, Faith set to work on breakfast, opening Spencer's fridge and pulling out various items.

"May I?" she asked, indicating the food she'd laid out on the counter.

Spencer had to chuckle. "Go for it. You're welcome to use whatever you can find."

They moved around the kitchen together, comfortable and familiar, as though it was how they'd already spent countless mornings. Faith chopped some bacon and tossed it in a frying pan, dicing onion and potatoes afterward while the bacon sizzled in the pan. She made herself at home, searching Spencer's cupboards until she found the frying pan, knives, cutting board, and spatula, and Spencer was able to anticipate what Faith needed, helping find those items without her needing to ask.

Faith tossed the onion and small cubes of potato in with the bacon while Spencer poured them each a cup of the coffee.

"How do you take yours?" she asked.

"A splash of cream and about a teaspoon of sugar."

Spencer added both and then extended the mug toward Faith, who set the spatula down and took the coffee in both hands, breathing it in.

"Thank you." Her eyes closed as she tried her first sip. "Oh my God, this is amazing."

Spencer grinned. "I like to give coffee the respect it deserves."

"It deserves all the respect," Faith agreed, taking another sip and letting out a soft moan.

Spencer laughed, but her body reacted to the sound, which recalled memories from the night before.

"What do you have on the go for today?" Spencer asked, trying to gauge how much time she and Faith had and whether or not she could take her into the bedroom for an encore.

Faith's shoulders slumped forward, and she said, "I have to be at the studio by noon. One of the soloists booked extra private lessons over the next few weeks leading up to her competition."

A quick glance at the clock told Spencer the encore would have to wait. They had enough time for breakfast, but that was about it. She hid her disappointment with a joke. "There's no rest in the world of elite ballet, is there?"

"Not this weekend, anyway," Faith replied. She didn't bother to hide her disappointment.

"What can I do to help with breakfast?" Spencer asked, realizing Faith was doing all of the cooking.

"Do you have another frying pan? The potatoes are just about done. We can fry up some eggs."

Spencer set to work helping Faith cook. When she took her first bite a few minutes later, she realized how truly ravenous she was, and she devoured her breakfast quickly, hardly stopping to talk with Faith. "I almost never eat breakfast," Spencer said, as she finished the final potato on her plate. "At least not before noon."

"Not a morning person?"

She tipped her head from side to side. "I think I would be if left to my own devices, but it's hard to be a morning person when touring. When we're on the road, half the time I don't go to bed until the sun is coming up. I've become nocturnal."

"Do you like touring?" Faith asked, leaning forward with interest.

"I love it," Spencer said. "I never had the opportunity to travel anywhere growing up. I'd never even been out of province. I've seen so much more of North America than I'd ever thought I'd get the chance to, and with our next album's release, we're starting to book international gigs. I can't wait."

Faith's eyes sparkled with interest. "That sounds amazing."

Spencer remembered Faith telling her how she wanted to see the world, and for flash of a moment she envisioned what it might be like if Faith joined her on tour: sleeping against one another on the tour bus as they drove between cities, trying all of the local foods and coffees, and exploring new places together. She could see that future so clearly, and it terrified her, how badly she wanted it.

"I should get going." Faith frowned as she looked at the clock. She stood and took her plate to the sink, and Spencer begrudgingly walked her to the door.

"Thank you for yesterday," Spencer said, as Faith lingered for an extra moment in the doorway.

Faith didn't answer with words. Instead, she stood on her tiptoes and kissed her, slow and sweet, promising more.

Then, Faith left, and Spencer watched her walk down the hallway toward the elevator, realizing just how deep in this she was.

Chapter Sixteen

Faith watched as her student, Heather, pirouetted across the room, then stopped and shook her head before Faith could point out the improvement in the girl's spins.

"They're still not perfect," Heather said, speaking more to herself than Faith.

"They've become a lot tighter. Do you remember how wobbly your turns were at first? Pirouettes on pointe are miles more difficult than pirouettes on flat toes, and you've only been on pointe for a year."

Heather's perfect posture collapsed in. "Exactly. I've only been on pointe for a year. I'm *fourteen*. The other girls my age have all been dancing pointe for at *least* two years. Some for three."

"I know you were disappointed to get the approval for pointe shoes so late," Faith began.

"Disappointed?" Heather's voice rose. "I was humiliated. If I want to prove I'm on the same level, I have to nail this competition."

Heather took a couple sharp breaths and then began trying the turns again, but her anger threw her off balance and each attempt grew worse than the last.

"Stop," Faith said, and Heather did as instructed, looking to her as though awaiting the magic instruction that would make the move come together perfectly. But she didn't have it in her to adjust the girl's posture, or tell her to turn her knee out more, or suggest she propel herself a little less aggressively. "We're done with pirouettes for today. You're tired and upset. We can circle back to them next week."

Tears welled up in Heather's eyes, and she swiped angrily at them with the back of her hand, but that only seemed to make the tears come faster.

Faith guided Heather toward the front wall, then sat down and indicated for the girl to take a seat beside her. Heather slumped to the floor resting her elbows on her knees and her chin in her hands, while she fought off more tears.

The emotion radiating off of Heather woke visceral memories of her own big teenaged emotions. She remembered what it felt like to have everyone's eyes on her, offstage just as much as on. She remembered all the expectations and pressures, and how she'd bent to what others wanted her to be.

"This all feels so much more important than it is," she said.

"Tell that to my mom," Heather said with a sniffle.

"I will," Faith promised.

She was prepared for her response to horrify Heather, but Heather turned her gaze to her and she saw the flash of hope and relief before the anger and humiliation replaced those feelings.

"Why do you dance?" Faith asked.

"What do you mean?" Heather asked, and it became clear to her that the girl had no idea anymore. Once, she might have had a reason, but ballet had likely long ceased being something she *chose* for herself. She'd fallen into it, and all of the pressures and expectations had fallen right on top of her.

"Why did you start dancing?" Faith amended.

"Because I love it," Heather said, her voice small. "When I was little, I used to always dress up like a ballerina, and I'd dance to any music that came on."

"Do you still love it?" Faith asked.

Silence answered her.

"Nobody in this studio is going to make a career out of ballet," Faith said.

"I'm not trying to make dance my career," Heather argued. "I want to be an interior designer like my mom."

"Then who cares about this competition? Who cares how old you were when you started pointe? Who cares if your pirouettes are exactly perfect?"

"My mom cares. The other girls all care."

Faith held Heather's gaze as she said, "Fuck 'em."

Heather's eyes widened in shock at her use of the expletive.

"Dance isn't supposed to be about any of that. It's supposed to be about having fun, moving your body to music, and creative expression. If you don't love it, then it isn't worth it. That goes for anything in life."

She heard the hypocrisy as she said the words, and hated that the advice, which seemed so clear as she offered it to Heather, was so hard to implement in her own life.

"I don't want to quit," Heather said, her voice small and sad.

"I'm not suggesting you quit. I'm suggesting you find a way to connect with what you originally loved about dance. You don't *have* to compete, you know?"

Heather gave a single bitter laugh. "Yeah, right. My mom would kill me if I didn't. How else can she measure my success?"

She heard herself echoed in the girl's words. All the fears, the pressures--they wouldn't just disappear because of a conversation. Not for Heather, and not for her.

"I'll talk to your mom," she promised again.

This time, Heather nodded, and then she said, "Good luck."

She bumped the girl with her shoulder. "Forget the practice. What's your favourite song? Let's dance."

She watched a small ghost of a smile cross Heather's face.

She'd talk to Heather's mom. And then, sooner or later, she needed to talk to her own.

Spencer arrived at the jam space early, but Wren had beat her there and was already warming up, her jaw set with steely focus as she moved around the kit in a percussive loop. She stopped playing when Spencer moved to her stool and slung her guitar case off her shoulder.

"Don't stop on my account," she said, but Wren was already pulling her earplugs out. "I can get set up while you play."

"I'm all warmed up," Wren said and set her sticks down on her snare drum. "How was your weekend?"

After their last conversation about Faith, Spencer had decided she wasn't ready to tell the band about their date, but the smile that tugged at her lips at the memory betrayed her.

"It was good," she said, hoping Wren wouldn't press for more details. "You?"

"Uneventful," Wren said, studying her for a long moment before asking, "What's got you so smiley?"

Spencer pulled her guitar out of its case as she debated how much to share. She and Wren hadn't had many heart-to-hearts in the time that they'd been in the band, but from the few conversations they'd had, she had found her to be a good listener and a stable sounding board. Sienna led with her heart and sometimes needed someone to be her head, bringing her out of the clouds. Mari led with her head, thinking through everything logically, and sometimes needing someone to remind her that emotions weren't things to be feared. Wren always remained balanced, able to get to the core of an issue and help untangle the different demands of the head and the heart. And Spencer so desperately wanted to tell *someone*. She had so many thoughts and feelings that she wanted help sorting through.

"Faith came over Saturday. She ended up staying the night."

Wren leaned back against the backrest of her drum stool and set her feet on top of her bass drum. "Wow. That's pretty huge, isn't it?"

Spencer nodded, and her happiness was overwhelmed by fear. It *was* pretty huge. Over the years she'd been with a number of women, but few had ever been invited over to her place, and even the few she'd let in had not lasted long. Relationships scared her. She'd watched her mom give herself away to relationships, only to get hurt. Then, she'd given herself to Faith, and she'd been hurt. Love was dangerous.

"It's a good huge, though, right?" Wren ventured, as though trying to decipher Spencer's thoughts.

Spencer thought about how connected she'd felt to Faith, how comfortable and right the night had felt.

"Yes," she confirmed. Then she thought of all her fears and added, "I think it's a good huge."

"I can tell you really care about her."

"Mari will tell me to run the other way, but I don't think I could if

I even wanted to. This girl . . ." she exhaled. "She's everything."

"Then you owe it to yourself to pursue this." Wren said it so matter-of-factly, as if it was simple as could be, and Spencer fought the urge to spill all of her fears. But she didn't want to voice them and give them any weight.

"Do me a favor?" Spencer asked.

Wren nodded.

"Keep this conversation between you and me? I want some time to figure out where this is headed, if anywhere, before I share it with the rest of the band. After how Mari reacted to me kissing Faith at the show... I need to *know* this is going somewhere before I try to convince Mari of that fact."

Wren mimed zipping her lips shut and tossing the key.

"Thanks." She began tuning her guitar.

The rest of the band would come in any minute, and they'd already decided they were going to spend the day finalizing the details on the song she'd written for Faith. The new album was almost complete, and the band all agreed the song was the perfect ballad to round it out. It brought a depth to their second album that their first had lacked.

Faith was everywhere lately. Spencer couldn't have stopped the course they were on if she tried.

Chapter Seventeen

Spencer sat naked on her bed with her unplugged electric guitar in her lap and plucked a sweet melody while Faith leaned back against the headboard and watched her play.

"This is the best way to wake up." Faith's voice held a dreamy quality.

Spencer didn't disagree. She had never considered herself a morning person, but with Faith, she'd been eager to start another day. Faith had assured her that this time, she didn't have a student coming in for an afternoon lesson, and they got to sleep in and spend the day together. Spencer's heart was full and happy.

"Play 'Bottle Rockets' for me."

She began to strum the opening power chords. The notes were muted and lifeless without the amp, but the song was still recognizable, and she watched as it brought a smile to Faith's face.

"You really like this song," Spencer said as she played through the intro, pride expanding in her chest.

"It's catchy."

Faith bobbed her head along with the beat and she felt all the youthful joy that they'd attempted to bottle with the song. She got into it, as well, moving her body to the music as she played.

"We're building bottle rockets in our basement," Faith sang when it was time for the lyrics to come in.

She watched as Faith closed her eyes and sang out the lyrics. She sat straight, head tilted back slightly as she sang, blond hair cascading in waves over her shoulders and the tops of her breasts. She had never been sexier.

"Just kids setting them off on the pavement."

She thought of all of the fun she'd had in her youth in the years following high school, like the going-away party she and Mari had attended for their friend Arly before she'd moved to Toronto for work—the party where they'd built a homemade firework and set it off in the street, the story that eventually inspired 'Bottle Rockets'. They'd all been so giggly watching Arly light the thing and then run, while they covered their ears against the bang. It had been such a stupid thing to do, and they'd been lucky nobody had been hurt or arrested, but it had always stuck in her mind as one of her happiest nights.

It paled in comparison to her time with Faith.

Spencer reached the chorus and Faith's confidence grew with the song, her singing becoming more animated.

"We only live once."

She couldn't wait any more. She stopped strumming and leaned forward, capturing Faith's lips with her own, cutting Faith off mid-lyric.

Faith inhaled in surprise and then immediately melted into the kiss, her hands finding Spencer's face as she anchored herself to her.

The thrill she felt kissing Faith was sharper and more acute than the thrill she'd felt setting off bottle rockets with her friends. The moment she had distilled into a youth anthem paled in comparison to the sparks between them. She thought she'd been living, but if that were true, how was she now coming to life?

She unhooked her guitar strap so she could slide the instrument off her lap and onto the floor without breaking the kiss, then she pulled Faith into her lap, tangling her fingers into her hair while she poured all of the years of longing into the kiss.

Faith reacted audibly to each touch of her tongue, and each sharp gasp and light moan emboldened Spencer, until she needed more than Faith's mouth. She knotted Faith's hair around one hand and tugged her head back, leaning in to kiss the long elegant expanse of her neck. She wanted to kiss every inch of Faith's body and trace its contours with her tongue until she understood her like a language.

But when Faith's hand reached between them, and her fingers slid through Spencer's wetness, teasing at her opening, she lost track of her own exploration. She leaned back, using her arms to prop herself up in a sitting position, while rocking her hips forward to urge Faith inside of her. Her eyes closed against the sensations that flooded her.

The intensity of her need caught her off guard. A moment earlier, she'd been playing guitar, and a couple light strokes of Faith's fingers already had her near the edge, desperate for those fingers to fill her while she came around Faith's hand.

Faith, however, didn't oblige. Her fingers danced over Spencer's thighs, through her wetness, and over her clit, but didn't penetrate her.

"Please," Spencer begged, releasing any semblance of control with a sharp exhale of desperation.

She met Faith's hazel eyes which were focused intensely on her, confidence and desire darkening their depths, and it was only then that Faith pressed inside, slow and deep.

She closed her eyes again, but Faith stilled her hand. "Look at me."

She swallowed hard and did as she was told; Faith's fingers pulled her desire higher and higher. The orgasm hit like a tidal wave, hard and without warning, and she collapsed backward onto the bed. Skilled fingers stilled inside of her, holding her in that wave of pleasure.

And then Faith was there, her body pressed against the length of Spencer, kissing her face and nibbling her earlobes, while her breathing came back down to normal.

"I don't know if I can move," she said at last. Her limbs felt like weights, tired and sated.

Faith's smile was sparkly and playful when she replied, "I guess I should go get dressed then."

Spencer responded by tackling her back onto the bed, the sound of Faith's laughter wrapping around her like a blanket.

It wasn't until way later, once they both lay satisfied on their backs, that Spencer rolled over and said, "Let's go get waffles."

"Waffles?" Faith asked, as though she had spoken a foreign language.

She nodded. "There's a great waffle truck that parks a few blocks over, out by the ocean. We could get waffles and watch the waves."

"That actually sounds perfect," Faith said.

She didn't realize she'd been holding her breath until Faith replied, and the palpable relief highlighted the tension she'd been carrying as she'd expected Faith to decline. Their relationship had always existed in private, and Spencer's reaction to Faith agreeing showed just how badly she needed to know their relationship could exist in the open this time.

They both dressed, and Faith tied her hair back in a neat French braid, and then they walked toward the ocean. Faith took her hand while the sun shone down on them, people walking past, and Spencer wondered if perhaps she hadn't yet woken up and the moment was all a dream. This was everything she'd ever wanted in life, and then some. She had thought she was happy. She thought she'd achieved everything she'd wanted. Now, spending her morning with Faith, she realized just how much she'd still ached for.

The waffle truck parked on top of a little hill that overlooked the sea. It was one of Spencer's favourite places to go on a lazy weekend, and she was excited to share a little piece of her life with Faith.

She could smell the sugary, sweet toasting liege waffles as they approached the truck, and her mouth watered in anticipation.

"Oh my God, they smell amazing," Faith said.

"These are the best waffles you'll ever taste," Spencer promised. "They'll ruin you for all other waffles."

"I'm not sure I'm ready for that!"

"You'll thank me later."

They stepped close enough to the waffle truck for Faith to read the menu.

"There are so many choices," she said with a frown.

Spencer often forgot how many options the waffle truck had, as she always ordered the same thing—the simple liege waffle with chocolate syrup, whipped cream, and strawberries. She found the combination simple, indulgent, and perfect, so she never bothered branching out, but the waffle truck offered a whole host of waffle creations, both sweet and savory.

"I think I'll try the waffle Benedict," Faith said, though she kept reading the menu.

"Ooh," Spencer murmured. "A bold choice."

She went to the window of the truck and placed their orders, and then walked with Faith over to a bench overlooking the water while they waited. Faith leaned her head against Spencer's shoulder, and Spencer drank in the perfection of the moment, neither of them saying anything for a long stretch.

"I'm really envious of your life," Faith admitted quietly.

"Why's that?" She turned to look down at Faith, who didn't meet her gaze. She knew why people were often envious of her. She had made it big as the guitarist in a well-known band, getting to travel the world while doing what she loved. But Faith wasn't a wannabe musician, so that was likely not the cause of her envy.

"I'm jealous of the freedom you have," Faith stated. "You're *you* all the time. I don't know how to get out from under all of the expectations piled up on me."

Spencer thought about what to say for a long time. "It hasn't always been easy for me to live authentically, either. If I have freedom now, it's because I fought for it."

Faith sat up and shook her head. "You don't understand. My parents..." she trailed off.

"I watched my mom shrink herself beneath my dad's imposing shadow and I swore that would never be me. People can love me, or they can leave me. I'm not going to change for anyone. Is it really loving me if they expect me to change anyway? Is it really loving *you* if they expect *you* to change?"

She watched as Faith mulled over her words. "They love me. In their own way."

The owner of the food truck called Spencer's name, and she was relieved for the reset button on the conversation before she told Faith what she really thought about her parents. It was hard to listen to Faith talk about how envious she was, or how disappointed she was in her own life, and not point out that nothing would change if she didn't step up and decide to change things. Harder still to know that those expectations Faith alluded to had cost her their relationship in the past and could have the same price again in the future.

Spencer picked up the two plates of waffles from the counter, and handed Faith the one topped with bacon, a poached egg, and hollandaise sauce.

"This looks amazing." Faith took a bite and moaned her confirmation. "You were right. This does ruin all other waffles for me."

"I told you so." Spencer took a bite of her own waffle, enjoying the sweetness of the dough and berries and chocolate.

"You're right," Faith said as she neared the end of her waffle. "About me. I *know* you're right."

Spencer looked over at her and saw a spark of something in Faith's eye—a glimmer of determination, a spark of motivation for things to be different.

"It's not easy going against the current when you've spent your whole life getting swept a certain way by the tide," Faith said. "But that doesn't mean I'm not going to try."

"Good," Spencer said. "You've got so much to offer the world. Don't make yourself small."

"I'm not going to make the mistakes I made before," Faith promised. "I'm here with you. I'm not going to let anyone change my mind about that."

Spencer took a bite of her waffle to hide the emotion that welled up inside of her. She'd needed Faith to say those words, and she wanted desperately to believe them.

"Take me to get a piercing after breakfast," Faith said.

"What?" Spencer asked, sure she had misheard.

"I've been wanting to get my nose pierced forever, but I haven't had the guts to do it. Come with me."

"You don't have to get your nose pierced to prove anything to me." Spencer wasn't sure where the sudden request had come from.

"I'm not going to," Faith said, with steely resolve. "I don't want to get a piercing for *you*. I want to get a piercing for *me*."

Spencer studied Faith and saw a fire in her eyes.

"Well, all right then," she said.

If that was what Faith wanted, then of course she'd go with her.

Faith's heart beat a little faster as she pulled open the door to the small piercing and tattoo parlour, stepping into the small building that smelled of antiseptic, but the blast of familiar punk music instantly eased her tension.

"They're playing your band," she said, turning to Spencer. It was one of the B-tracks, not 'Bottle Rockets'. The shop was playing the album; they hadn't merely stepped inside while coincidentally, the song happened to be on the radio. It still amazed her when she took the time to really recognize the level of success Spencer had achieved in her career and in her life.

Spencer, however, didn't look surprised when she smiled and nodded, and before Faith could say anything more to express her awe, one of the staff clapped Spencer on the back and said "'Sup Spence? What can I do for you today?"

"We're here for a piercing," Spencer hooked her thumb toward Faith.

He frowned and shook his head. "I'll go get Kelly."

"I'll be back in for some new ink soon," Spencer promised.

"You'd better." He headed to a room in the back of the building.

A moment later, a female staff person—Kelly, Faith presumed—greeted them. She had a petite build but a big presence, with full tattoo sleeves colouring her arms and extending up her neck. Her ear lobes were stretched around large wooden hoops, and her hair was dyed midnight black.

"All right, what can I do for the two of you today?" She didn't seem to know Spencer, and she appeared a little awestruck as she greeted them.

"I'd like to get my nose pierced." Faith hated how tentative her voice still sounded. She wanted some of the confidence Kelly and Spencer both possessed. She hoped the nose piercing would be a first step. It was relatively low commitment, she could take it out any time, but it was something she could do just for her.

Kelly led her over to a display case of jewelry to choose from. "Are you looking for a ring or a stud? We've got a selection of studs on this side you can look through. Rings are on the other side."

Faith studied the jewelry and then turned to Spencer. "What do you think?"

Spencer shook her head. "This is your decision."

Her gaze caught on a small emerald, the perfect blend of bright yet subtle.

"That's the one." She pointed it out to Kelly.

She and Spencer were directed to a little room where she was asked to take a seat on a raised black leather bench. Spencer stood beside her and held her hand.

"Breathe," Spencer reminded her, and it was only then that she realized how tense she'd become.

She let out a long, shaky breath, but she was smiling despite the nerves. She needed a change in her life, and this was the perfect step: small, but bold. A way for her to claim her identity and take back a bit of herself.

Kelly took Faith's face in her hands and studied her nose, then wiped it with antiseptic and drew a small dot on one side. She held up a mirror and asked, "How's that look?"

She imagined the dot replaced with the emerald stud. "Perfect."

Kelly set a tray of tools beside her and tore open the sterilized package that contained the piercing needle. Then the nervousness set in. She'd had her earlobes pierced, but she'd been seven and she could hardly remember what it felt like. She only had a vague recollection of the piercing gun at the shop in the mall. She did, however, imagine noses must be much more painful to pierce than ears.

She refused to let herself think about what her parents might say, or Mandy, or anyone else. She was doing this for herself, and she refused to entertain other's worries. She had enough worries of her own.

Spencer must have sensed her apprehension, because she gave her hand a reassuring squeeze, and Faith steadied herself by focusing on Spencer's hand in hers.

"Ready?" Kelly asked.

Faith nodded.

"All right. I'm going to get you to breathe steadily through your mouth and try to relax."

Faith focused on her breathing while her heart hammered against her ribs.

Kelly clamped her nose and quickly pierced the needle through

149

the cartilage with surprisingly little pain. She felt a slight bit of pressure as the jewelry was threaded through the hole, then Kelly tightened the bead and stepped back. The entire thing was over before she knew it.

"That's it," Kelly said. "Go take a look."

She hopped off the counter with a burst of adrenaline and took in her reflection in the mirror. The green stud shone bright and bold, a little mark of her confidence. She loved it. She almost couldn't tear her eyes away.

Except she did look away to find Spencer grinning at her with pride. Faith didn't hesitate to pull her into a hug, wrapping her arms around her neck.

"Thanks for coming with me," she said, then she turned to Kelly. "It's perfect."

"It suits you," Kelly said.

"It's totally you," Spencer agreed.

She looked at the piercing again in the mirror and nodded, a huge grin on her face. It *was* totally her.

Chapter Eighteen

Spencer played the opening riff of the song she'd written for Faith in high school. It was the exact same riff as the one she'd first come up with over a decade earlier, and the lyrics had been mostly untouched, and yet the song had grown into something completely different—better and stronger than the original. Mari's bass notes grounded it with a deep and steady resonance, Wren's drum pattern added texture, and the guitar effects Spencer now had access to gave the entire song an ethereal quality. As she played through the piece, listening to its complexity and fullness, she couldn't help but reflect on how the song, which had been written about her relationship with Faith, very much resembled her relationship with Faith. They were the same people, and yet the relationship had grown into something completely different than before—something better and stronger than the original.

Sienna waved her hand and the band stopped playing, looking to her in confusion.

"How do you imagine the lyrics sounding? I have them here in front of me, and I have a couple ideas for vocal lines, but you wrote it. I want to hear how you envisioned it before taking over."

The vocal line was the one part of the song the band had yet to settle on, and it was the final piece they needed to polish before they could count it as complete.

Spencer had a very clear idea of the vocal line in her head, but she shrugged. Singing in front of the band felt way too personal and vulnerable. She preferred to give Sienna the lead on creating a vocal melody. "I'm sure you'll come up with something great. You're the singer, not me."

"Nothing I'm coming up with feels true to the song," Sienna said. "I need to know how you originally wrote it."

Spencer wanted to argue with her, but she didn't actually disagree. Sienna had sung the lyrics over top of the song a few times, and while she'd sung pretty melodies the song hadn't ever sounded right. It hadn't sounded like *her* song. The rest of the band waited, and she begrudgingly pulled a microphone stand over to her.

"Just know I'm not married to this melody," Spencer said. "You're welcome to change it however you see fit."

Sienna leaned forward eagerly, and Spencer began to play again.

This time, Mari and Wren didn't join in, presumably giving Sienna a chance to really hear the melody behind the lyrics, but without the backup instruments, the song was raw and intimate. Spencer's heart was on display in the center of the room, and she trusted her friends to protect it.

She began to sing, her voice rattling with the first couple notes before finding stability.

She poured every ounce of vulnerability into the song, as though she was back on the bleachers behind her school, playing for Faith on her beat-up old acoustic. She felt every bit of the fear she used to feel, sitting in her room and listening to her parents fight, and the glow of her feelings for Faith had settled around her like a shield. Faith had been her safe place in the middle of a war zone.

She'd *loved* Faith.

And now, she loved Faith again. Or maybe she loved Faith *still*. Perhaps, in all of the years that had passed the feeling never fully left. She wasn't sure which, and she wasn't sure it mattered. Whether the feeling had ever left or not, it was there now. She was in love with Faith, and she wanted to convey the depth of those feelings with the music.

When she reached the end, she set her guitar down and the room once again came into focus. Suddenly, she was hyper-aware of her friends sitting by their instruments, wordless, all eyes on her.

"So, um, that's how I've always played it." She fiddled with the tone dial on her guitar to avoid meeting their gazes.

There was a long moment of silence and then Sienna said, "You should sing this."

Spencer's eyes snapped up as she shook her head hard. "What? No. No way. I'm not a singer. No."

"I could hear the emotion in your voice when you sang," Sienna said. "It's yours. I could never properly capture all the emotion behind the words. And besides, you have a lovely voice."

Spencer shook her head again, but when Mari and Wren began to speak up in support of Sienna's idea, she knew she was fighting a losing battle.

"It's clear both the song, and the girl you wrote it for, are important to you," Wren said.

Mari nodded, and Spencer expected her to jump in with words of caution, but she only said, "When you sang, I could *feel* the words."

"And what would you do while we play?" Spencer asked Sienna. "Stand around and look pretty?"

"She *is* good at looking pretty," Mari pointed out.

"Nobody would disagree," Spencer replied. "But my point remains; we can't cut Sienna out."

"Maybe I could add some keyboard over top," Sienna offered. "Or we could start the encore with this, and I could take an extra couple minutes to have a drink and rest while you three play."

Spencer shook her head, but she was already imagining singing the song in front of a live audience. She was surprised at how little terror she felt at the thought. The image felt right. The song *did* have a special resonance for her, and a large part of her wanted to be the one to perform the piece.

She imagined playing it at their next live show with Faith in the crowd and it was decided.

"Okay," she said, "I'll do it. But when we go over budget at the studio because I'm not a vocalist and can't hit the notes properly without a million takes, don't be too hard on me."

Sienna clapped her hands together in delight. "You're going to be amazing!"

Spencer wasn't certain of that, but she was excited to bring Faith's song to life.

They ran it a few more times, this time with Spencer singing the lyrics, until they all decided there was nothing more they could do to improve the piece that day.

Mari caught Spencer on the way out.

"Hold up," she said, as Spencer was about to get into her car.

The anxiety coiled around her chest, preparing for words of caution, but Mari simply pulled her into a hug, holding her tight for a long moment.

"I'm happy for you, Spence." Mari stepped back. "I can tell you love her. She'd damn well better not hurt you, but I wanted you to know I'm happy for you. And I'm sorry if I haven't been the most supportive. I just worry about you."

Spencer rolled her eyes but she felt that coil of anxiety release and she was grateful to have her friend on her side. "Wren talked to you, didn't she?"

"What?" Mari asked, appearing genuinely confused. "No. Sienna did."

"Sienna?" Spencer asked, just as confused.

"She made me read the lyrics. She said this was the type of love that didn't come around often, and I needed to be a more supportive friend. She's right."

"Thank you."

Mari hugged her one last time, then skipped off. "Go rest up those vocal cords. We've got work to do."

Spencer made a mental note to thank Sienna later and got in her car, heading home with a smile on her face.

Faith sat parked in her parents' driveway, studying her reflection in her rear-view mirror, trying to work up the courage to go inside the house for their Friday night dinner. The little green stud in her nose was not that noticeable. So far, most people either hadn't picked up on the piercing or hadn't commented. The only comment she'd received was from Callie who had noticed it a few nights earlier while they were both teaching at the studio, and she'd promised Faith the nose stud was *"totally her."* Not that people's reactions mattered, anyway.

She'd gotten the piercing for nobody but herself, and even five days later, she still loved it. But no number of reminders could bolster her confidence when she thought about her parents' reaction. She had no doubt they would notice the piercing the minute they saw her, and she had no doubt they would *not* love it. She was no stranger to her parents' opinions about things like piercings, tattoos, and dyed hair. She'd heard a number of comments over the years that had made it quite clear exactly what type of people they thought got piercings.

She'd thought about taking the piercing out for the dinner, but it was still healing and tender, so she didn't want to aggravate the healing process. Besides, the whole point of getting the piercing was that she was tired of living under others' expectations and wanted to live her own life.

If I can't stand up for myself over a piercing, how am I going to stand up for anything else that matters in my life? There was no taking the jewelry out.

With a long exhale, she stepped out of her car and walked into her parents' home.

The smell of roasting vegetables and chicken hit her as she stepped into the entryway. Dinners with her parents were never fancy or even, really, varied, but the familiarity was warm and comforting.

Her dad wasn't in the living room, which meant he was likely still working in his office down the hall, and she found her mom in the kitchen finishing the dinner.

Faith pulled herself up a little straighter, and then she stepped into the kitchen to help, just as she would any other Friday night.

"Hey, Mom. How can I help?"

She surveyed the food in various stages of completion and looked for a task she could take over, but her mom immediately let out a shrill cry. "What is in your nose?"

Faith blew out a breath. She'd known her mom wouldn't miss the piercing and wouldn't take fondly to it, but she'd somehow thought they'd at least make it through the greetings before the interrogation started.

"It's a piercing, Mom," she said, hoping to sound more confident than she felt. "I've thought about getting one for a while, and I really like it. Are the vegetables ready to take to the table?"

Her mom didn't move, and it was evident in the set of her jaw and her stony gaze that she did *not* intend to let the conversation go so easily.

"It's not a big deal. Can we go eat dinner? What can I help with?"

"What were you thinking?" Her mom almost choked on the words as they fell from her mouth.

Faith looked to the ceiling and shook her head. "I was thinking it would look cute and that I wanted to do something nice for myself. Can we please focus on dinner?" The request was futile and there was no way her mom would drop the subject, but still, she felt compelled to try.

"Cute," her mom echoed under her breath, the disdain thick in her voice.

She shrunk at her mom's reaction and she hated it. Anger simmered in her stomach, but it was overwhelmed by the hot burn of shame.

"Faith," her mom said, her tone soft and pleading this time. "Help me understand. Why would you want to put a piece of metal in your nose? You have such a beautiful face."

The implication followed, unspoken but understood: *And why would you want to ruin that?*

"I think it looks nice, Mom," she said, but she heard the embarrassment and uncertainty in her voice.

Her mom shook her head as though she were speaking to a child, and Faith felt like a child again.

"Do you know what people are going to think?"

Probably nothing, she wanted to say. She wanted to tell her mom that nose piercings were not uncommon anymore and nobody would make any snap assumptions about her. But she kept quiet. It was futile. Her parents were older than her friends' parents. They were from an era when nose rings were not common. They had always expected her to look and act and dress a certain way. Her mom's reaction was exactly in line with what she'd known it would be, and she almost felt as though she had no right to get mad when her mom's reaction was so consistent and true to self.

156

Her dad chose that moment to come into the room, and her mom instantly began recruiting him to back up her position.

"Do you see what Faith has done to her nose?"

She wanted to hide. If the world could have opened up and swallowed her, she would have gladly allowed it. She watched the surprise and then disapproval cross her dad's face, and she shrank even more. Her mom had always been the more emotional of the two, quicker to anger but also quicker to defuse. Her dad's anger was big and lasting, and his stony expression told her she'd lost. Her mom would have maybe come around, but her dad's disappointment was there to stay.

"You'll take it out," he said with a cold edge to his voice. "You're a professional and a grown woman, not some teenager with a rebellious streak. You are better than that."

"You're right. I'm not a teenager." She was a grown-ass adult who could make choices about her own body for herself.

"Then why are you acting like one?" her dad asked. "If you were eighteen, maybe I could understand. But Faith, you're a twenty-seven-year-old woman, looking and acting like a child."

Faith could never win. If she'd gotten a piercing at eighteen, she knew their reaction would have been equally, if not more, extreme. At eighteen, they'd still had power over her. They would have said if she wanted to make choices like that for herself, then she could learn to make other choices for herself and leveraged their financial support. They'd helped pay for her university, for which she was grateful, but it had always come with strings attached. And now her dad was trying to tell her she was too old to make those decisions for herself and she was acting like a child.

There was always a reason why she couldn't live her own life.

"I'm going to go," she said.

"Dinner is almost ready," her mom argued, as if they would all sit down and eat dinner together as one big, happy family.

"I'm not feeling very hungry."

"Faith." Her dad said her name in his stern parenting voice, the one that she'd always cowed to as a child. "Go sit down. Your mother worked hard to prepare dinner."

But she didn't want to go sit down. She had been sitting down her entire life. She wanted to finally stand up for herself.

"I'll see you at dinner next week," she said. "If you decide to treat me with the respect you would show to any other guest in your home, then I'll stay for that dinner. For tonight, I don't feel like joining you."

Both of her parents started in on the lecture, but she turned and headed for the door, her own swell of emotions deafening her to them.

Still, when she got home, she went to the mirror and took a long look at herself. Did the nose piercing make her look juvenile? She hadn't thought so, but suddenly she wondered. She'd heard their criticisms, and despite herself, she felt a little less confident in her decision, and the sight of her new jewelry no longer filled her with confidence, but rather, embarrassment and even a little bit of shame.

Maybe they were right.

Chapter Nineteen

"Can you believe it's week twelve already?" Taz asked. "It seems like just yesterday I was introducing myself to you and showing you around, and now here we are, wrapping up our time together. I know I speak for more than just myself when I say we'll all be sad to see you go."

Spencer sat across from her for their final debriefing, surprised at the strength of the emotion that hit her with the understanding this would be her final week facilitating the music group with Faith.

"The weeks have flown by," she agreed. She had complicated feelings about leaving Sunrise House this time, but far less to say about the matter than Taz. Though that was unsurprising, as Taz had more to say than anyone about anything.

She recalled the apprehension she'd felt when she'd arrived at Sunrise House. So much had changed that over the course of those three months, it seemed impossible to comprehend a time when she *wasn't* leading the music group with Faith.

"The group has been more successful than we could have even hoped for," Taz continued. "The youth and parents alike have all raved about it, and Faith has spoken highly of your ability to connect with and empower the teenagers."

Spencer straightened in her chair with pride as she thought of each of the kids she'd met over the twelve weeks. They each brought so much of themselves to the music lessons—all of their fears, hurts, hopes, angers, and vulnerabilities. She could remember every name, and she felt a rush of gratitude for each of them.

"If you wanted to continue on a more permanent basis, I know we would be really interested in having you." Taz let the sentence hang in the air.

"I wish I could," Spencer said, and she hoped Taz knew how sincerely she meant that. "The band is going to start doing some touring again soon, though, which means my schedule will get too chaotic to commit to anything on a weekly basis."

Taz nodded her understanding. "Well, we appreciate the time you *have* been able to commit. It's been a truly wonderful experience for the youth who have been able to participate. When your schedule settles down, we would love to have you back."

"I will absolutely keep that in mind," Spencer promised. The thought of returning at some point helped take the edge off the sadness of saying goodbye, though it baffled her that she could *ever* feel sad about leaving Sunrise House.

She thanked Taz for the opportunity and headed to the recreation room with a lump in her throat.

Faith was already moving chairs into a circle, and when their eyes met, Spencer saw her sadness reflected and was glad to know Faith was going to miss having her there as much as she was going to miss being there.

"I'll tell you what I won't miss," she said, picking up the thread of the unspoken conversation, "is the way this room almost always smells like teenage boy body odor by the time we're done."

Faith laughed, and the sound warmed Spencer.

"I know we'll see each other all the time anyway, but I've enjoyed having you here at work with me."

"It's been fun," she agreed, though fun was not exactly the right word. She couldn't bring herself to articulate any of her sadness about saying goodbye to Sunrise House and working alongside Faith. She wanted to acknowledge that the project had brought Faith back into her life, and she'd be forever grateful, but those words caught in her throat with a hard lump.

Faith took a seat in the circle, crossing her legs at the ankles, and Spencer sat across from her. She tuned each string on her guitar, and then looked up to find Faith practicing chord formations, concentrating hard on where to place her fingers.

For a long moment, she allowed herself to simply gaze at Faith, wondering at the luck that had reunited them. She didn't believe in fate, like Sienna did, but she had to admit she and Faith seemed to have been willed together by more than mere coincidence.

Perhaps it was silly, but Faith going for the nose piercing had erased her remaining doubts. It was the indicator she needed that this time things truly were different. The Faith she'd known before would have never done anything so impulsive and so totally for herself. Skydiving had taken bravery, but it had been a one-time bravery. Adult Faith being willing to get her nose pierced meant being willing to stand up and say, "this is me." If she could do that with the jewelry, Spencer hoped she could do the same in other areas of her life. It gave her hope for *them*. She dropped her gaze to Faith's nose and stilled. The little emerald stud was gone.

Maybe it's on the other side, she justified, trying to readjust her memory, but she knew she wasn't mistaken and when Faith looked up, any hopes she managed to cling to were dashed.

"You took out your nose piercing," she said quietly.

"Only for work," Faith answered, but her gaze didn't meet Spencer's. "I didn't want to look unprofessional. I'll put it back in when I get home."

Faith spoke the words so casually, like she was unaware of how they caused the air to rush out of Spencer's lungs.

It's just a piercing, she told herself, except in that moment, it *wasn't* just a piercing. It was one more rejection. The piercing represented so much more for Spencer, and seeing the little piece of jewelry missing took her right back to the bleachers, where Faith first said to her *I can't do this.* She hadn't fit into Faith's perfect image then, and she still didn't now.

"I'm back."

The sound of the small voice in the entryway pulled her from her thoughts and forced her back into the present. She immediately recognized the girl from their very first music group, twelve weeks earlier.

"Haley," Spencer said, and the girl's eyes widened in awe.

"You remembered my name."

"Of course, I did. It's good to see you again."

And then she realized what she'd said, and she immediately regretted the words. There was nothing *good* about Haley being back. Seeing Haley again didn't simply mean she'd returned to the music group, it meant she'd returned to Sunrise House. That alone told Spencer everything she needed to know about how Haley was doing. She couldn't even bring herself to wonder about the specifics of what might have brought her back to the shelter.

Haley took a seat next to Spencer and picked up one of the guitars. Spencer's eyes were immediately drawn to the trail of bright red cuts across Haley's left forearm and her heart broke. She wanted to wrap her up in a hug and protect her from all of the loneliness and desperation she could tell the girl felt. The guitar was the only weapon she had against those feelings, and in that moment, it felt entirely inadequate. Spencer wanted to do *more*.

A couple teenagers filtered in, and she fought to keep her attention focused on the present moment and the music lesson. Her thoughts kept ping-ponging between speculation about what Haley had suffered, and memories of her own past: the nights she had lain awake, wanting an escape from the pain at any cost. She could hear her own desperate pleas for her dad to just *stop*, when she looked at Haley's arm. Stop the violence. Stop the yelling. Stop the hurting. *Stop*.

Faith introduced the group and Spencer numbly transitioned into the lesson. In that moment, she was both inside of herself, able to recite the lesson, and outside of herself, trapped somewhere in time between the past and present, listening to herself speak as though she was an observer in the room.

"I've been practicing lots since I was last here," Haley said, when Spencer complimented her ability to move through the chord progressions.

She had so many questions she wanted to ask Haley. She wanted to first know the girl was safe, and then she wanted to hear every detail of her story, as though she could then take it from her. She felt a connection to her. But she forced herself to remain neutral and teach everyone in the group.

When their hour ended and the others cleared out, however, Haley hung back.

"I was wondering," Haley began, eyes on her feet as she spoke, "if I could show you the song I wrote?" Her eyes then turned to Spencer, her expression uncertain and hopeful and terrified all at once.

"Of course." Spencer noticed that Faith, who had stood to begin putting away the chairs, sat back down. She kept her distance, giving Haley the chance to speak to her, but Spencer was grateful for the silent support.

Haley turned her chair so she faced Spencer, took a few deep breaths, tapped a slow beat with her right foot, and then began to play.

She strummed a sequence of minor chords, moving through them haltingly still, with some difficulty in making her fingers bend the exact way she wanted, but when she began to sing, Spencer lost sight of the technical details of the music and got lost in the lyrics.

"We're here again. We've been here before. Why would you let him back in the door?"

The lyrics were rudimentary, like those lining Spencer's high school notebooks. Emotions laid bare over a simple rhyme scheme. No metaphor, just hurt. And the simplicity of that vulnerability carried her back in time.

She remembered coming home from school to find her dad sitting on their couch. He'd had both arms extended, resting upon the back of the couch as if to say *that's right, I'm still here*, and he'd grinned at her like he'd won. He had. She remembered looking to her mom, whose eyes had flashed downward in shame for the briefest of moments before she put a smile on her face and assured Spencer this time *things would be different.*

They were never different.

The song transitioned to the chorus, and Haley began to sing a little louder, anger injecting itself into her vocals.

"Him or me? Who's it going to be?"

How many times had Spencer wondered that same question? She hated herself for it each time, knowing that her mom didn't choose any of the violence that came her way. But still, the hurt child inside of her always felt somehow insufficient.

If she'd been enough, her mom wouldn't have taken him back.

She should have been worth protecting, but she wasn't.

Haley slowed the song as she transitioned to the last verse.

"You don't care that he comes at night. You let him use me to avoid a fight."

Spencer heard the words, even as her own memories deafened her, and her blood ran cold at their sickening meaning.

Suddenly, it wasn't her memories deafening her, it was the rage ringing in her head, and she was no longer in the past, but fully in the present, one hundred percent enraged over what Haley had been forced to endure.

She was vaguely aware Haley had stopped singing and was looking to her for feedback, but she had no idea how to form words in that moment.

Then, Faith was there, and she was talking in a soothing voice, getting all of the details of Haley's story. Spencer didn't know how Faith remained so calm, when white hot rage burned through her, but she admired the ability. She had never been more impressed by Faith than in that moment.

"Spencer?"

The sound of her name cut through her thunderous rage and she turned to Faith.

"I'm going to bring Haley with me to talk to the police officer on site so she can give a statement about everything she just told us. Are you okay to finish cleaning the room?"

She was grateful for the task and nodded. Then, she turned to Haley, wanting to offer the girl *something*. "That was really brave of you. You have a real musical talent, and I'm honoured you shared it with us. Keep playing."

A small, proud smile briefly lit up Haley's face, despite the heaviness in the room. "I will."

Faith and Haley left Spencer there with her storm of thoughts. She moved through the room robotically, putting away all the chairs and returning the room to its usual state. She had understood all of the teens coming to the music group came in steeped in trauma, but this was the first time she'd been confronted so intimately with the details. It felt wrong that it was the last of the music groups, and she headed out to her car, dissatisfied, feeling like she was leaving things unfinished.

This wasn't how I wanted my time here to end, Spencer thought, hating the self-pity. None of the evening had been about her, but she couldn't seem to step out of her feelings. She was worried about Haley. She wanted to know what would happen to her, and she wanted to be the one to take the girl under her arm and single-handedly fight off whoever would try to hurt her. Instead, fear and powerlessness overwhelmed her, to a degree she hadn't felt since she was a child herself.

She needed to do something, but all she could do was go home.

It didn't matter how many stories of abuse Faith heard; it never got any easier. Days like this one always had her simultaneously considering a career as a barista and feeling reaffirmed about her decision to go into social work. She would have a hard time shaking Haley's story. Like countless others, Haley's would come home with her, and she would think about it in the quiet hours of the night, wondering when and how the world had become so broken, with so many truly cruel people. On the worst days, she wished she'd selected a career she could leave at the office, but even when the job left her exhausted, both physically and emotionally, she never considered changing careers. She was in a position to help connect Haley with legal supports and advocates, as well as the counselling she would need to begin the slow and painful healing process. Faith could never take away what had happened, but she *could* help prevent it from happening to the girl again. That didn't always feel like a lot, but it had to be enough.

As soon as she left work, however, her concern shifted to Spencer, who had been visibly shaken by the disclosure, and pale when Faith'd had to leave. They'd locked eyes on her way out of the room, and Spencer's which were usually the blue of a summer day had darkened into cold depths. It had taken everything in her to remain neutral and professional and focused on Haley when all she'd wanted to do was comfort Spencer. Now, as she got into her car there was no question about going home. When she pulled out of the parking lot, she immediately headed in the direction of Spencer's apartment. She couldn't comfort her earlier, but now that she was done with work, she couldn't wait another second, knowing Spencer was on her own and hurting.

She parked in one of the visitor parking spaces and went to the buzzer, listening to the tinny sound as she pressed the button and waited for Spencer to answer.

"Hello?" she heard after a long moment.

"It's Faith. Can I come up?"

The door buzzed open and she got in the elevator. As it lurched upward, the anticipation tightened in her chest. Suddenly the awareness spread through her that it was not only Spencer she was hoping to comfort. She ached to hold Spencer for her own sake, sinking into the embrace until the day fell away from both of them. The thought echoed in the back of her mind that Spencer was who she wanted to come home to at the end of all her long days. She wasn't ready to fully acknowledge it, but she let the awareness register distantly, as she counted down the floors until the elevator slowed to a stop, a bell dinged to signify she'd reached the correct floor, and then the doors opened.

She walked briskly down the hall toward, and had to consciously slow her knock, trying to remain calm as she waited too eagerly for, Spencer.

When the door opened, however, she could *feel* the chill radiating off Spencer, and the distance between them, though they stood mere feet apart, was immediately apparent. Spencer stood in the entryway, shoulders squared with a stiff formality, and greeted her as though meeting a stranger. She didn't look happy or relieved to see Faith, nor did she look upset. Her expression remained trained in a perfect, stony neutral. She stood centered in the doorway and made no move to invite Faith inside.

"I, um, I just wanted to come by and make sure you're okay," Faith stammered, discomfort knotting inside of her. This was *Spencer*, she tried to remind herself. She didn't need to feel nervous. And yet, suddenly, she had no sense of how to proceed.

"I'm fine." The two words were spoken casually, as though the question had been asked on any regular day.

"Can I come in?" she asked.

Spencer moved aside to let her into the apartment, but it wasn't only the physical space she had been asking about. She had put up walls around herself, and they seemed thick and impenetrable. Faith shoved her hands in her pockets, unsure of where to put them. All the way over, she'd envisioned Spencer opening the door and the embrace being immediate, but it was clear she had no desire for touch.

"Haley is safe now," she offered.

"That's good."

Faith felt frozen, like a pause button had been hit between them and she wasn't sure how to press play and get them back in motion.

She reached out and put a hand on Spencer's arm, hoping the physical connection would break through the emotional disconnect, but when Spencer tensed, she pulled her hand back.

"Spencer," she begged. "Talk to me."

Emotion flashed across Spencer's face before her steely resolve returned. "There's not much to say. It was a long day. I'm tired."

"It *was* a long day," Faith agreed. "We haven't had a situation like that come up in group, and I want to make sure you're doing all right. I'm worried about you."

"There's nothing to be worried about."

She blew out a frustrated breath. She kept trying to open the doors of communication, but Spencer kept slamming them shut.

She reached out for Spencer's hand, despite the *don't touch me* barbs, but Spencer was quick to pull her hand away.

"You took out your piercing," she said.

Faith's thoughts shifted so abruptly it was dizzying. "What?"

Spencer nodded toward her and said again, "Your piercing. You took it out."

This time, hurt and rejection were thick in her voice. Faith sighed and shifted her weight backward, creating that extra inch of distance between the two of them. Truthfully, she'd known when she'd taken out the piercing that Spencer might have feelings about the little piece of jewelry being gone. She'd been nervous to go to the group that night without it, but after the disaster of a dinner at her parents' house, she'd been even more nervous to go anywhere with the piercing in.

167

"I took it out for work." It wasn't the whole truth, but it wasn't a lie either.

"Because you wanted to look professional." Spencer parroted her earlier words, then her walls began to crumble, and emotion stormed in her eyes.

Faith felt caught in the storm. She struggled to find the words to explain why she'd taken the piercing out, and she suspected there was no "right" answer.

When Spencer spoke again, her voice was much smaller. "What does that say about me?"

"It doesn't say *anything* about you."

Spencer scoffed. "Look at me. Would you say that *I* look professional?"

"You're the guitarist in a kick-ass band," Faith said. "You look the part. I'm a social worker. You're comparing apples to oranges."

Spencer shook her head, and this time, it was clear how deep the hurt went. They weren't talking about a piercing.

"You're always going to be a little bit ashamed of me." Emotion choking her words at the end. "In private, you make me feel like the most special person on the planet, but in public you're ashamed of me."

"Are you kidding?" Faith couldn't even wrap her head around the words. "I think you're incredible. I'm the farthest thing in the world from being ashamed of you. I admire everything about you."

It was clear, though, that the words didn't penetrate Spencer's defenses. She rolled her eyes. "Have you told your parents about me?"

"I plan to." Faith scrambled to keep up with each turn in the conversation. "When the time is right, and when we're not so new."

Spencer shook her head. "You say that now, but you broke up with me before when you got too scared. How am I supposed to believe you'll stand up for me—for *us*—this time? You took the piercing out."

"You don't understand," Faith said, the desperation swelling inside of her. "My entire life I've been told I'm my parents' dream come true. They thought they'd never have children, and I was their dream baby. Growing up, I was constantly reminded of all the great lengths they had to go to so that I could even exist. I never got the chance to be my own person. I belonged to them, and I've never quite lived up to their dream."

Spencer didn't soften at her words, and Faith could see she was deep inside of her own shame. She wanted desperately to connect but she struggled to tamp down her own anger at Spencer adding one more layer of expectations.

"I shouldn't have ended things in high school," she said. "I was young and scared. I should have stood up for us."

Spencer straightened, her walls pulling back into place, and she shrugged. "It's all good. You made the choice anyone would have made."

Except it clearly wasn't "all good."

"I think you should go now."

Faith felt the full intent of the words, and tears of both anger and hurt welled up in her throat.

"Spencer," she begged. "I know I hurt you, and I'll forever be sorry, but I thought we were moving forward with our second chance."

Spencer shook her head. "I can't be hurt again. I can't do it. I've seen time and time again where second chances get you. Ask Haley. Ask my mom."

Faith felt as though all the air had been vacuumed from the room. "Is that what you think of me?" In her head, she knew Spencer's trauma was doing the speaking, but the words pierced through to her heart regardless.

"I think you broke my heart once, and you'll break it again."

"I thought you were different," Faith said, no longer able to suppress her own hurt. "You were the *one* person who always made me feel like I could be myself. But you're just like everyone else, pressuring me and judging me. I feel so trapped."

"Then go be free," Spencer said. "I'm done."

"Spencer..." Faith let her name fall off her tongue with a final plea.

"Please leave now," Spencer answered, her voice breaking.

There was no use arguing or pleading her case, if she even *wanted* to. Spencer had made up her mind.

She quickly stepped into the hall before the tears could come, managing to contain them until she reached the elevator.

Chapter Twenty

Faith showed up for weekly cocktails nearly an hour early. She usually went home after work, but this time she didn't feel like returning to her empty apartment and her isolation, so instead she'd headed straight to their usual lounge. There were people there; she couldn't let herself dissolve into a puddle of tears.

She managed to snag a table overlooking the water, and sat with the drinks list, pretending to read the offerings but not actually seeing any of the words on the page, lost in the replay of her conversation with Spencer. She had sent a handful of text messages in the days since, trying to get Spencer to *talk* to her, but it was time to stop. Spencer's mind was made up, and she needed to respect that.

Spencer's decision wasn't undeserved, as much as she wished it was. When she'd left Spencer's apartment, she'd burned with self-righteous anger, but it had burned itself out quickly, leaving only heartbreak and regret. The truth was, she had broken Spencer's heart, and as much as she yearned for a second chance, she couldn't say with certainty she deserved one. She *hadn't* told her parents about them. Or Mandy. Or anyone. Further, she'd had no plans to do so. She had figured she would tell them at some point, but she understood why a vague someday was not good enough this time around.

She wished she was more like Spencer who showed up in all of her authenticity, bold and brave and unapologetic.

Not her—she apologized. She'd been taught not to rock the boat, to take care of the comfort of others, to be selfless and compassionate. The opposite of selflessness felt like selfishness, and she took pride in *not* being selfish. But she'd given of herself until she didn't know what was left. She'd spent so long living for others, she didn't feel like she belonged to herself anymore.

She had to find herself before she could fight for herself.

"Oh my God, do I ever need a drink today," Mandy said, taking the seat across from her, oblivious to her inner turmoil.

Faith managed to pull her practiced empathy into place, but for a brief moment she wondered why she was always so concerned about the feelings of others when those around her seemed so unaware and unconcerned about hers.

"What's going on?" she asked.

Mandy launched into her story. It was nothing out of the ordinary. She was putting in extra hours at the studio trying to get the students ready for competitions, and she was worried about the girls' performances.

"Kylie just isn't getting the height she needs on her leaps, and Summer is still rushing her turns."

"I'm sure they'll get the hang of it sooner or later," Faith said.

"We don't have the luxury of time," Mandy stressed. "The competition is in a month and I want to see them get the gold. These girls are all extremely talented and they've worked so hard. They *deserve* the gold. But right now? They're not there yet."

Faith struggled to connect with Mandy's concerns. Her students had worked hard and they would be better dancers at the end of the year. Winning the competition was nothing more than bragging rights, and if you asked Faith right then she'd have said that the bragging rights weren't worth it. She knew what it was like to be in those girls' shoes. They were all burning the candle at both ends to keep up with their academics and competitive dance. Their social circle was likely limited to the girls in their dance group because they didn't have time to socialize outside of the studio. They'd started dancing because they loved it, but now it was so wired into their identities they couldn't quit if they wanted to.

Did she want to?

"Anyway," Mandy said, "enough about me. How are you?"

That was the million-dollar question, wasn't it? She studied her friend and found genuine interest etched into Mandy's expression.

Perhaps she hadn't given her enough credit. They hadn't been friends their entire lives simply because of proximity. Mandy may have been a little self-focused lately, but that didn't mean she didn't care about Faith.

"I'm having a rough week," she admitted.

She hadn't shown up for drinks with the intention of telling Mandy, but, damn it, she didn't want Spencer to be right about her.

"What's wrong?" Mandy asked. Concern darkened her eyes and she leaned forward, her attention focused and genuine.

All of a sudden, the words seemed impossible to contain. She desperately wanted to not be afraid anymore. She wanted Spencer to be wrong. She wanted to finally stand up, not against anyone, but *for* herself.

"In high school, Spencer Adams and I were more than friends," she said, feeling the relief wash over her as she said the words. "I was in love with her."

Her heart hammered in her chest while she waited for a reply.

She had often imagined how the conversation might go with Mandy, and regardless of whether she was ultimately supportive or not, she'd always expected surprise. She expected questions. Instead, Mandy's face didn't change except for a slight tightening of the jaw, and she said, "I know."

Everything she had wanted to say collided with those two words, leaving scattered fragments of thoughts that she struggled to piece back together.

"What do you mean?" she asked—the only thing she could manage to say.

Mandy bit the inside of her cheek and looked out at the water before turning her focus back to Faith.

"Everyone knew Spencer was a lesbian and you started spending all of your free time with her. It wasn't hard to piece together. I figured something was probably going on. And then I saw the two of you one day, kissing in the music room."

They were sitting outside, but the conversation made Faith feel a sense of claustrophobia, as though there were walls closing around her and she couldn't breathe.

172

Mandy knew.

She thought back to the conversation they'd had that day of the dance competition. She'd thought about that moment many times over the years, and she'd often wondered how the outcome might have been different if she'd been honest with Mandy about her feelings for Spencer. She'd spent the years thinking that if Mandy had only known, she would have found a way to support her. She'd told herself Mandy had been scared, just like she'd been scared, but her friend would have found a way to love her if she'd known the truth.

She *had* known.

"You encouraged me to date Brett," she said, feeling the betrayal as she said the words.

"I don't know what happened between you and Brett," Mandy began, "but Spencer was bad news. Was I supposed to sit back and let my best friend throw her life away with some high school dropout? That's what she was going to be. She was always skipping school and when she was there, she had such an attitude problem."

"And she was a lesbian."

"Sure," Mandy agreed. "And that. But it was all of it together would have ruined your reputation, and mine by association."

Faith wanted the sick feeling in the pit of her stomach to be anger she could direct at Mandy, but it wasn't. The feeling was shame. Mandy had pushed her toward Brett out of fear, but she was the one who had *married* him out of that exact same fear.

"It turns out, Spencer became more than anyone ever gave her credit for," Faith said.

"She got lucky with her band," Mandy argued.

She could hear the continued disdain for Spencer in Mandy's voice.

She looked at her friend and the remaining words hung heavy and unspoken in the air between them.

It wasn't just high school. I'm in love with Spencer now.

She wanted to say those words, but she saw the way Mandy was steeling herself for them and she knew the minute she spoke her truth, their friendship would end. Maybe not immediately—she might *try* to be supportive—but she'd never be able to fully accept Faith.

And once she started telling people, who else would she lose? Would she be cast out of the dance studio? Would she be cast out of her parents' lives? Was she ready for that?

She took a sip of her sangria and every moment that went by while she said nothing further proved Spencer right about her.

She was a coward.

Chapter Twenty-One

Spencer had cranked her amplifier loud enough she could feel the reverberation of the power chords as she strummed her guitar with an angry fury. Anger was good. Over the past couple of weeks, she'd vacillated between anger and sadness, and while sadness left her feeling empty and useless, anger fueled her. She'd spent the entire day at the jam space, wearing her fingertips raw as she played through the new album—every song but one.

She threw her entire body into the heavy chords of the outro of the song that she was playing, the loudest and most aggressive one on their new album, and by the time she let the final chord ring out, she was sweaty and out of breath.

"I thought I'd find you here."

She quickly killed the amp with her foot pedal and spun to find Mari standing in the entryway.

"Hey," she managed.

"What are you doing, Spence?" she asked. "We don't have practice for another couple hours."

"I wanted to make sure the guitar parts are tight if we're going to record our demo to send to the label." She was amazed at how easily the lie rolled off her tongue.

Mari, however, didn't appear to buy it. She pulled the stool from her bass corner over so she sat directly in front of Spencer. The move made Spencer feel as though she was about to be interrogated.

"You've been burying yourself in music," Mari said. "Sienna, Wren, and I have all noticed the hours you've been pulling at the jam space.

You're here before we arrive. You don't pack up to leave when we finish our practices."

"I want to make sure the album is—"

"What happened with Faith?" Her words were gentle but their impact hit Spencer like a punch.

"Nothing."

"I know you well enough to know when you're hurting."

She couldn't meet Mari's eyes, and she began to play the opening riff to 'Bottle Rockets' on the quiet strings of the unamplified electric guitar. She played on muscle memory alone, her hands needing somewhere to put all of her discomfort.

A long moment of quiet stretched between them, and she made it to the second chorus of 'Bottle Rockets' before she said, "We broke up."

She really didn't think that Mari would be one to say *I told you so*, but she braced herself for the words anyway. She deserved to hear them. She'd been stupid to think that this time would be different. Foolish.

"I'm so sorry."

She heard no hint of judgment and she felt the dam that held back her emotions break at the genuine care and empathy in her friend's voice.

"Why would I have ever thought that this time could be different?" she asked, fighting back the wave of tears that threatened. "People don't change."

"What happened?" Mari's words were gentle, with no hint of the blame she'd expected.

"Faith hasn't changed." She began to strum a faster song, her hands trying to keep up and quell the fury of emotions. "And neither have I. I wasn't good enough for her before and I'm not good enough now."

She could feel Mari's anger at the statement. It radiated off of her. But Spencer didn't look up. The lump was thick and painful in her throat, and she tried to make her brain focus on the song her hands were playing.

"Did she say that?" Mari got up off her stool, as though she was ready to go after Faith herself.

Spencer shook her head. "She didn't have to."

"Well, what did she say?"

"She didn't have to say *anything*. She hasn't told anyone about me. That says enough, don't you think? She's ashamed of me, just like she was in high school. She's never going to tell anyone. She's never going to stand up for me. Nobody *ever* stands up for me."

She set her guitar down and got up off her stool. She wanted out of the jam space and away from the conversation.

Mari stopped her, putting her hands on Spencer's shoulders. "Look at me."

She couldn't bring herself to look up.

"Are we still talking about Faith?" Mari asked.

Her anger deflated and she swiped at the tears that leaked from her eyes. "She made me feel special and then she broke up with me for Brett Matheson. I thought, finally, here was somebody who would put me first, and she tossed me away."

Then the tears came harder. "And my mom—I was never enough for her. She kept taking my dad back, each and every time. I spent my whole life in fear because she wanted a boyfriend more than she wanted a safe home for me."

She *knew* it was more complicated than that, and intellectually didn't believe what she was saying, but what she knew in her head and what she felt in her heart were different.

"My dad called me worthless once, and he was right."

Mari moved her hands from Spencer's shoulders so that she could wrap her arms around Spencer, pulling her in tight in a hug.

"You're not worthless," Mari said.

She shook her head, the tears falling freely now. "I am, though. I'm worthless, and I was never going to come first. All I did was save Faith the trouble of having to tell me."

"Spence—"

"Don't." She straightened and wiped her eyes as she pulled her walls back into place. "I didn't make the wrong choice."

Her heart was broken, and she didn't need her best friend telling her it was broken for no reason. She'd made the right decision. It would have been too much to hear Faith reject her again.

"Come on," Mari said, her tone change indicating she was going to give Spencer a break for now. "Let's play through the album together."

Spencer gave a small smile of gratitude and picked up her guitar while Mari went to get her bass. She began rebuilding her protective wall, brick by brick, desperate to tamp down the guilt that threatened as the doubts surfaced. *What if I did make the wrong choice?*

No, she couldn't go there.

Ending things with Faith had been the *only* choice.

Chapter Twenty-Two

Faith stood in the middle of the small dance studio, staring numbly at her reflection in the mirror while the music played. Her students had left for the evening, so she'd shut the door and turned on the stereo, hoping to reconnect with what she loved about dance. She couldn't seem to bring herself to move, however, so she stood there, looking at her reflection, and hating herself.

On stage, off stage, her entire life had been a performance of sorts.

A couple of weeks had passed since she'd talked with Mandy about Spencer, and while they'd gone back to their routine—grabbing cocktails and catching up on Wednesday nights—she now found things to be shallow and unfulfilling.

She turned off the stereo, sat down on the floor, and began ripping at the ribbons of her pointe shoes, as though ripping them off meant ripping off at least one of the layers of inauthenticity in her life. She wanted out of the small studio and all of the expectations that had come along with it. She was tired of the empty conversations, the setups with various men, the pressure to look a certain way, to fit a certain mold...

She tossed her shoes on the floor, nearly hyperventilating as she did so.

She wanted Spencer.

She also wanted to not lose her friends and family.

She felt like she was on track to lose them *all*.

"Faith? Are you okay?"

She turned to find Callie standing in the doorway, concern etched into her delicate features.

She quickly nodded, but she could see in the mirror that her face was flushed, and her eyes were wild.

She tried to box herself back up—to regain her composure and put that polished exterior back into place— but she couldn't make herself fit in the box anymore.

"Do you ever *hate* it here?" she asked.

Callie shook her head, looking confused. "No. Never."

The quick answer made her feel worse, and her shoulders dropped forward as she tried to put her mess of thoughts into words. "Dance is supposed to be about passion, but it feels like there are so many expectations layered on top."

"Like what?" Callie asked, as if she genuinely had no idea what Faith was talking about.

Callie was young and bright-eyed, and she felt weird talking to the girl, but the need to get her thoughts off her chest won out.

"Like *everything*," she stressed. "We're all expected to look and act a certain way. We have a dress code, and hair guidelines, and makeup rules… Everything about how to *exist* is prescribed here."

Callie shrugged. "Those are just surface things, and then I get to express myself through dance."

Faith wished she felt the same.

"You come here often to dance on your own," Callie pointed out.

Yeah, she thought bitterly, *when nobody is watching.* "That's just for me."

"It should *all* be just for you," Callie said.

That was so much easier said.

"Dance is an art," Callie continued. "And art is meant to be authentic."

"You make it all sound so simple."

Callie stepped over to where she was still sitting and took a seat beside her. "Nobody has *ever* said that authenticity is easy."

Faith didn't have an answer, so she said nothing. It *seemed* easy for others—for those with accepting families and social circles, who never had to worry about disappointing their loved ones because their love wasn't conditional.

"Why don't you show me the dance you've been working on when you come here on your own?" Callie suggested.

"I just free dance," she said.

"Show me," Callie urged.

She turned her head to study Callie. The thought of free dancing with an audience, even if it was only an audience of one, felt terrifying and vulnerable, but there was no judgment waiting behind Callie's eyes, only encouragement.

She nodded and turned the stereo back on. She only took a second to consider the music that she wanted to put on, and then she cued up 'Bottle Rockets'. *That* was the song she danced to when she came in to dance on her own, and it was the song that captured all of the freedom and *life* she wanted to feel.

She walked to the center of the studio then closed her eyes and took a few steadying breaths while the opening riff played.

Her heart hammered in her chest, and her thoughts already spun with projections of what Callie must have been thinking.

This song? Really?

You dance ballet and this is a punk band.

Isn't this a lesbian band?

But the song was already playing so it felt too late to back out.

She began to dance, a few tentative movements at first, and then she let the music take over and she let herself go, letting the music carry her. As the song went on, she forgot that Callie was still sitting there. She let herself get lost in the music and her movements, pouring all of her regret and longing and hope into the dance. Each movement— every stretch and spin and leap—felt freeing.

Light it, ignite it, this spark you shouldn't fight it.

She felt a different kind of spark, and this time, she didn't *want* to fight it. She wanted to let that spark of bravery catch fire.

When the song came to an end, she was breathing heavily, but this time with exhaustion, not panic. She felt steady and grounded.

Callie clapped as she moved to the stereo to turn it off.

"I didn't know you were a Shattered Ceiling fan," Callie said.

She couldn't muster any embarrassment. "They're my favourite."

"Mine too," Callie said, and Faith froze with the shock of that statement.

"My girlfriend introduced me to them a few months ago," Callie continued, "and I've been obsessed with them ever since."

"Your girlfriend?" Faith asked. Her head spun. The dance world had felt like a heteronormative cage, and she struggled to process hearing Callie talk of a girlfriend.

If Callie registered her shock, she made no indication. Instead, she answered as casually as if Faith were clarifying the weather. "Yeah, have I not told you about her?"

She shook her head while Callie pulled out her phone and brought up a picture. She had her head resting on the shoulder of an athletic-looking girl in a soccer jersey, with short dark hair and a lip ring.

There was so much about the image that reminded Faith of her and Spencer when they were young. She almost felt as though she was looking at a photo of her own past, except an alternate past where she'd been open and proud of her relationship with Spencer.

"The two of you look so happy." Could she have had that same happiness if she'd stood up for what she and Spencer had? She pulled out her phone and found her skydiving photos. The only photo that she had of them together was the photo that had been taken of them after both surviving. They both had huge grins, and Spencer had an arm around her shoulder in a really carefree manner. She turned the phone to Callie.

"Wait a minute," Callie said, her eyes going wide as she turned to Faith. "That's you. And Spencer Adams."

She might have chuckled at Callie's disbelief if she didn't feel so heartbroken in that moment.

"It is," she said, with a small, sad nod.

"Are you two together?" Callie asked, turning to study Faith.

"Yes," she said, before correcting herself. "I mean, no. We *were*."

"I'm sorry," Callie said.

"So am I." Faith sighed, the hurt washing over her with a fresh wave of emotion. Everything had been so good, and then had gone sideways so quickly, and until this moment, she'd had no one to talk to about any of it. Still, despite the hurt that flooded back to the surface, her heart felt lighter having told *someone* who didn't judge the idea of her and Spencer being together. "Anyway, I should probably get home," she said. "But, Callie, thanks."

"I'm here," Callie said. "If you ever need to talk."

"I know," Faith said.

She quickly changed, then packed up her belongings and headed home for the night, her mind spinning as she tried to process everything that had unfolded in the conversation with Callie. She'd been so sure she was alone at the studio, and *nobody* would understand. Did it change anything, knowing that she *wasn't* alone? Mandy would still likely react the same, but she had an ally at least.

She hated that any of it even mattered. She hated herself for not giving her relationship with Spencer enough priority. Spencer should have been all that mattered. It was too late to save what she'd broken. But it *wasn't* too late to live out the rest of her life authentically.

It didn't matter if Spencer was in her life or not. She needed to be herself. Whatever the cost.

When she got home, she went to her little jewelry box and pulled out the emerald nose stud. She held it in her palm, turning it over with her fingers a few times. Spencer hadn't been wrong. It had *always* been more than just a piercing. She went to the mirror and carefully slipped it back in.

She was done hiding.

Chapter Twenty-Three

"After this next 5K race, my run club is talking about training for a 10K, and I actually think I might give it a go. I never would have thought I'd be a runner, but I've started to really enjoy it and the 5ks have stopped being enough of a challenge."

Faith nodded dutifully at her dad's words and poked at the shrimp on the plate, pushing them around instead of eating them. She didn't have any appetite. Her mom praised her dad's efforts, and the conversation about running faded into background noise, drowned out by the thundering of her heart in her chest.

Tonight was the night. It was time to tell them.

She cleared her throat, and her parents turned their attention her way. Immediately, the panic strangled her, but she was determined not to back out. She wasn't entirely sure what to expect, but she expected it would be similar to the reaction she'd received for the nose piercing. There would be the immediate protests, and her mom would scramble to set her up with every eligible bachelor she could think of, and then eventually they would simply stop talking about Faith's sexual orientation, as though not talking about her being a lesbian would somehow make it not true.

They wouldn't cast her out, but their relationship would never be the same. Still, Faith couldn't keep hiding who she was. Hiding would also irrevocably change their relationship.

"Um, Mom, Dad, there's something I want to tell you," she said, summoning every ounce of courage she could manage.

They both looked at her, expectant gazes on their faces.

She steeled herself for whatever reaction she was about to

184

encounter, sitting up a little straighter, and then after a deep breath she said the words as calmly and surely as she could manage. "I'm a lesbian."

The expressions on her parents' faces might have been comical had she not been so paralyzed with fear. Her mom froze, jaw somewhat agape, staring at her as though not able to comprehend what she'd just said. Her dad's brows knit together in confusion and he cocked his head slightly to the side as he visibly tried to make sense of the words.

"Say something," Faith said, after a long moment, unable to take the silence anymore.

"But you don't look like a lesbian," her mom blurted.

"What?" She was horrified and relieved by the response in equal measure. "What's that supposed to mean?"

Her mom shook her head, as if trying to shake the words into a different order that might make sense. "Nothing, I just... I never would have known. I had no idea."

Faith didn't know what to make of the reaction. Her parents hadn't criticized or argued with her, which was good, but still, their reaction didn't *feel* good. She wasn't quite able to put her finger on exactly what she was feeling in that moment.

"How long have you known?" her dad asked.

Too long. She thought of all the wasted years. She didn't need to get into all of the details about all of her doubts and uncertainty with her parents, instead needing to impress upon them that this was something long-standing and unwavering about herself. She might not have had a definite label for herself until recently, but even then, even if only deep down, she'd known for as long as Spencer had been in her life. She held her dad's gaze as she answered with confidence. "Since high school."

"But you married Brett," her mom said.

"So?" Marrying Brett had been one of the biggest mistakes of her life, and the last thing she needed was her parents using that relationship to discredit her now, when she had finally worked up the courage to tell them the truth about herself. "People get married for the wrong reasons all the time."

"Perhaps," her dad said, his voice stoic and unreadable, "but I like

185

to think we have raised you with more integrity than that. If you didn't love Brett, why did you feel the need to marry him?"

She wanted to scream at her parents to listen to her. The conversation was about her, not Brett, and now instead of talking about her identity and the important truth she needed to convey, they were dwelling on her marriage to Brett. Her marriage that had been a giant mistake. Her marriage that was long *over.*

"Everyone *expected* me to be with Brett." Her voice rose with exasperation. "I felt so much pressure. From friends, from relatives, from *you.* Being with Brett was the life I was *supposed* to lead."

"You're supposed to lead the life that makes you happy." Her dad said it like it was so obvious, like she should have known this entire time, and she hardened at the implications.

"How was I supposed to know that?"

"What do you mean?" her mom asked.

Faith had managed to barricade all her anger and hurt up until that point, but the barricade finally broke, and the words started bubbling up unfiltered. "You two have had an opinion about everything I've ever done in my entire life. You've had opinions about who I should be friends with, about what clothes I should wear, what hobbies I should take up. I couldn't even get a tiny piercing without each of you weighing in as though it were *your* body. But, I mean, it pretty much is, right? I'm just an extension of the two of you. I've always felt like I *belong* to you, like some trophy. You've never seen me as *me.*"

The look of pain on her mom's face brought her up short, and she wished she could take the words back, despite how overdue they were. For a long time, nobody spoke, and the only sound was her own heavy breathing and the ticking of the grandfather clock on the wall.

"You never let us," her mom said at last.

The anger turned to tears that burned behind Faith's eyes, but she refused to let them fall. "I know how you wanted a daughter more than *anything.* I was your dream. Everything you've ever wanted in life. I grew up hearing the story all the time, everything you went through to have a child, the perfect daughter to complete your perfect family. You wanted me *so* bad you had my entire life planned. I was supposed to go to law school so I could take over the firm. I was supposed to marry a nice boy from a good family and give you two perfect grandchildren. I was supposed to somehow do it all and fulfill all of those dreams of yours, but none of them ever fit me."

Her mom wiped at her eyes; her jaw set in indignation even as the tears fought their way past her pride.

"If we'd known you were a lesbian, we would have supported you wholeheartedly," her dad said.

Even that sentence didn't fill her with comfort. *If* we'd known, we *would* have. Somehow, still, the conversation was driven by what she had done wrong, the accusations simply lobbed in a different direction than she'd expected.

"You know *now*," she said. "Support me *now*."

She watched as the anger on her parents' faces shifted and softened.

"Are you seeing anyone?" her mom asked, breaking all the tension that had strung itself between them.

"Not right now." She hated the words. "But when I do date, I need you to know that anyone I bring home is someone I love and care about. You don't get to have an opinion. I get to decide who is right for me. I'm not going to end up in another relationship out of expectation."

"Of course," her dad said. "Whoever you love, we will welcome."

"Thank you." The anger and defensiveness dissipated, and a combination of regret and relief formed a lump in her throat. Had she judged them too harshly? Would they have actually supported her while she was growing up? She'd never know, but she *did* know what her fear of judgment had cost her. She wasn't even sure if she could fully trust her parents to support her now, but she'd stood up for herself, and she'd continue to do so. It was time to start living.

Chapter Twenty-Four

Spencer stopped at her mom's mailbox, finding it packed full. She sorted through the stack of mail, tossing the junk, until only a small handful of important items remained. Then she pocketed all the bills to take home and pay.

"Hey Mom," she called, as she let herself into her mom's small apartment. "I grabbed your mail. It's on the table."

"Thanks," her mom called back from the living room. "My show is just about done, and then we can visit."

She went into the living room and took a seat next to her mom on the old brown leather sofa. They'd picked the thing up from a local buy and sell page after they'd left Sunrise House for the last time. The colour was worn out in the seats, and it tended to sag a bit in the middle, but it was the most comfortable couch ever. Once the band had taken off and signed their big contract for their second album, she had helped her mom buy all new furniture, completely redecorating the place, but the couch, despite its condition, was the one item neither of them had any intention of parting with.

Running her fingers over the leather armrest, she remembered the apartment as it had been when they'd first moved in. Her mom had been full of optimism and excitement as she'd stood in the empty living room planning paint colours and furniture layouts. Spencer, though, had been determined not to get attached. Soon enough, she'd figured, it was bound to be one more place they would run from.

She looked around the living room, at the walls that had been purchased to represent safety and stability for her and her mom, and she wondered if she'd ever feel *truly* safe there. The thing was, she couldn't even put a finger on *why* she still had the feeling of unease. It had been ten years. She didn't *actually* think she'd come home to find her dad there again. Neither of them had heard from him since her parents' divorce had been finalized. It was like he finally realized he didn't own them, and backed down, disappearing to God-only-knew where. Spencer felt even less at ease this time than she usually did on visits, and it wasn't hard to pinpoint why. She hadn't been back to visit her mom since she'd called things off with Faith. That had been intentional. Everything with Faith opened all of her old wounds, and she'd felt too raw to step inside her mom's home. She'd known it would be painful, and she hadn't been wrong. Emotion constricted around her throat as the memories hit her.

The television flashed a flurry of images. Her mom was watching some medical drama, and the chaos of the scene—sirens, flashing ambulance lights, doctors working frantically and shouting orders at one another—amplified the tension that rose within Spencer.

She didn't think of the memories as much as she *felt* them. Her body tensed, as though readying for a fight, and she felt the ball of fear and rage and helplessness untwine itself in her chest and spread through her, as the memories flooded her, one after another, unrelenting.

Her dad yelling at her, the sweet smell of alcohol on his breath.

Her mom asking what colour she wanted to paint her room.

Faith kissing Brett Matheson by the lockers.

Her dad punching a hole in the wall.

Her mom telling her they were safe now.

Faith ending things, emotionless, like she'd never mattered.

Her dad, smiling at her in the living room of the apartment he was never supposed to know about.

Her mom promising things were different this time.

Faith promising *It's always been you.*

Her dad.

Her mom.

Faith.

Pain and promises and broken promises. An endless reel.

"Sorry, I had to know what happened. Show's over now. How has your week been?"

The words jarred her out of her memories, but she couldn't tamp down the tidal wave of emotion, and instead of answering, she turned to her mom and choked out, "Why did you ever take him back, even once?"

"What?" her mom asked, surprise and confusion registering across her face.

She pulled her knees up onto the couch and wrapped her arms around them. In that moment, she felt as small and scared as she'd been as a child, her years of experience and understanding crumbling beneath the heavy weight of the hurt.

"You always promised things would be different, and in the end, you always took him back."

"Where is this coming from?" her mom asked, and Spencer distantly registered the tension stiffening her mom's posture.

"I need to know—"

But she couldn't finish the sentence. *I need to know why I wasn't worth protecting.* It felt both too stupid to speak the words, and too important, all at once. The rational part of her felt silly for thinking the phrase, and the wounded part couldn't bear the answer.

"I left him in the end, didn't I?" her mom asked, her voice laden with defenses.

Spencer thought about all of the years of her childhood that had been ruined with fear. "But why did it take so many tries? We wasted so many years with him."

Hurt registered across her mom's face and she *knew* her blame was misplaced, but still, she needed answers.

"I didn't *choose* the abuse," her mom managed to bite out. "How it was in the end, was not how it started."

"But after the first time at the shelter… the second… We worked so hard to get out and we always ended up back there. Why did you always need him in your life? Why wasn't I enough?"

She hated the tears that clawed their way out from the depths of her memories. She'd buried all the hurt, she'd boxed it all up, but that last day with the music group, hearing Haley's story, had punctured the box, and the hurt had been escaping little by little until this moment when it was all right there, bursting out of her.

"You *were* enough," her mom said.

But Spencer shook her head, the words not reaching her.

She *wasn't* enough. Not for her mom. Not for Faith. Not for anyone.

"You were the only reason I ever got out. You're the reason we're sitting here right now."

She held her legs tight, shrouded in shame, her mom's voice distant.

"I should have left right away," her mom said.

She nodded. She and her mom had never talked about the abuse because Spencer had never wanted to blame her, but it wasn't until that moment that she had realized how much anger she carried.

"Try to understand," her mom begged. "I didn't *mean* for things to get as bad as they did. At first it was just put-downs, and I had no reason to believe what he was saying about me *wasn't* the truth. They were things I'd heard my entire life. That first time he hit me, he apologized *profusely*, but by that point I didn't even care about the apology because I believed I deserved it. Why wouldn't I? I was a frog in boiling water. By the time it got bad I had no friends or family, no job, and no sense of self-worth. I was completely dependent on him."

She knew it wasn't her mom's *fault*, and she wasn't trying to assign blame, but she was so damn tired of her life being determined by other people's hurts and fears and insecurities.

"You're the one good thing I've done in my life, Spencer," her mom said, speaking slowly to enunciate each word.

She traced her fingers over a small tear in the fabric of her jeans.

"I should have left sooner. If I could go back and do it all over again, I swear to God I would. But I never want you thinking you weren't enough. *You* were the only reason I ever made it out."

The words splintered through the thick shroud of shame, some of them finally reaching her.

"You don't have to forgive me," her mom said. "I'd understand if you don't. But at least forgive yourself. None of the blame was ever yours to carry."

"It's not about forgiveness," Spencer said. *Wasn't it, though?*
When somebody shows you who they are, believe them the first time.

191

She thought of the old refrain that often echoed in her mind. Forgiveness meant opening the door to more hurt. Look what happened when they'd forgiven her dad. Then again, hadn't her mom changed? That they were sitting there, just the two of them, safe now, said that she had.

Had Faith changed?

"What *is* it about?" her mom asked, gently.

She thought for a long time before answering. All of the fears thundered inside of her, a deafening roar that made it hard to hear the small voice of truth.

"I don't want to be the frog in boiling water," she said at last. "I'm tired of giving my heart away then finding out too late that I made a mistake—that I trusted when I shouldn't have. I can't be hurt anymore."

"And what exactly would make you a frog in boiling water?"

She shook her head and scoffed like it should have been obvious. "She broke up with me once already, and I'm supposed to believe she won't do the same this time? How can I trust her again? What if I let myself love her, and then it's too late to not get my heart broken?"

Her mom didn't ask who she was talking about, seeming to recognize the conversation was about more than surface details. Instead, she said, "Love wasn't the boiling water."

Spencer blinked at the sentence that made no sense to her.

"When I said I was like a frog in boiling water, and it became too late for me to get out, I was talking about the cruelty. *That's* what I wish I hadn't immersed myself in. You should *always* immerse yourself in love, even if it does mean you sometimes get hurt."

Spencer wiped her eyes and mulled over her mom's words. Faith had hurt her, deeply, but she'd never been cruel, and the hurt had never been intentional. She looked up at her mom. "I forgive you. In case you needed to hear it."

She hadn't thought she'd been holding onto anger, but when she said the words, she felt immediately lighter, the tightness in her chest releasing. She felt like she could truly breathe for the first time in forever.

"Thank you," her mom's eyes brimmed with tears. "I think I *did* need to hear that."

Spencer leaned her head against her, like a child seeking comfort. For as long as she could remember, she'd always been the one comforting her mom. She'd been the parent in so many regards, making sure she had enough food on the table, paying her bills, and making sure she remembered appointments. She hadn't realized how desperately she needed a parent.

Her mom stroked her back and gently said, "It sounds like there might be someone else you also need to forgive?"

Spencer's thoughts flashed back to Faith, and the hurt in her eyes when Spencer'd ended things.

She nodded.

She and Faith likely didn't have any future left, but regardless, it was time for her to let go of the past.

Chapter Twenty-Five

Faith watched the group of preschoolers free dance for the final song of their lesson, but she didn't feel the joy she'd previously experienced while seeing them express themselves without any fear of judgment. All she felt now was sad. She was *trying* to reclaim herself, to get some of that youthful confidence back, but it would be a process. She'd spent too many years not knowing who she was, living for everyone else.

She wasn't where she wanted to be, but she *was* making changes. She'd gone to dinner with her parents the night before. There had been some residual tension from the previous week palpable beneath the surface, but since coming out her parents had treated her more or less like they always had. They had gone on eating bland food and having bland conversation, as though nothing had changed. Coming out hadn't been a disaster, and had overall gone better than she'd hoped, but she was still left with the dissatisfaction of feeling kept in the same rut. Maybe her parents didn't yet recognize the full impact of the previous week's conversation, or maybe they were in denial, but try as they might, things *weren't* going to be the same anymore. She was ready to live out life on her own terms.

She still had to talk to Mandy, and she'd come to terms with the fact that it would mean the end of their friendship. She had skipped their past two cocktail nights, already beginning to grieve the loss. The two had been friends for nearly their entire lives, but Faith couldn't stay friends with somebody who wouldn't accept her. She didn't blame Mandy for pushing her away from Spencer and toward Brett; she was ultimately the one responsible for ending things, but that didn't lessen the anger she felt, that her friend had *known* about her relationship with Spencer the whole time, and pretended otherwise for over a decade.

Still, she wasn't sure what would happen after her conversation with Mandy. Could they both continue teaching dance at the same studio? Her confidence was bolstered knowing Callie was also gay and she had an ally there, but ultimately, she wasn't sure if she wanted to stay if there was going to be significant tension. She was tired of dance making her feel caged.

The song ended, and she called all her students up to give them a sticker and a high-five before they left to go meet their waiting parents. Then she turned to put the sticker package back in its drawer within the media center.

"Faith?"

She turned at the sound and froze at the sight of Spencer standing at the door. She couldn't find any words, and blinked, as though certain she was seeing an illusion that would disappear.

"I remembered that you teach on Saturday mornings, and I was hoping I might find you here."

Spencer had dressed up, Faith realized. She wore dark blue skinny jeans, a white collared shirt with sleeves rolled up above her elbows, and a plaid tie that disappeared beneath a gray vest. Her hands were shoved in her back pockets, and she shifted nervously, blue eyes pleading.

"Why are you here?" Hurt and fear and hope and hurt tumbled around inside of her, and she wasn't sure which emotion she would do best to grasp onto.

"Our band finished recording a quick demo of the new album to take to our producer," Spencer said, and it was then that she noticed Spencer had a thin CD case in her left hand, which she now held up in front of her. "I was hoping we could listen to part of it together."

The guarded part of her wanted to tell Spencer that it was best she leaves, but her heart had ached for weeks, and so she found herself nodding and motioning her over.

Spencer handed her a blank CD in a lime green jewel case, with only the word "DEMO" written on top. "Track three."

Faith took the disc and plugged it into the stereo.

She skipped to the third track and then sat down on the floor, motioning for Spencer to sit next to her. She did, sitting close enough that their shoulders nearly touched, and she had to refrain from scooting the inch closer that belonged to their old familiarity.

The opening notes began to fill the air. Faith recognized it immediately. It was the song Spencer had written for her when they were teenagers.

"You're putting this on your album?" she asked, feeling a sting of possessiveness. The song was *hers*. It had been written for her. She didn't want Shattered Ceiling playing it for all their fans while she and Spencer were no longer together. She didn't want to hear Sienna sing the lyrics Spencer had written for her.

"Tentatively," was all Spencer said in response.

The intro riff transitioned into the verse and the lyrics began.

She stilled, immediately realizing that it *wasn't* Sienna singing. She turned to Spencer. "That's your voice."

Spencer nodded and when she glanced over at Faith, her face was a shade paler than usual. She wasn't just a little nervous, she appeared full-on terrified.

Faith nudged her with a knee, despite her own anger and hurt, wanting to ease some of that fear.

She listened to the familiar song, feeling all of the same emotions it had inspired in her the first time she'd heard it. She felt honoured and loved and special.

A spark of light flickers between us. Let this spark become the sun. When I'm with you it feels like the endless night is done.

She listened to the chorus, knowing the darkness Spencer had gone through, and feeling an overwhelming wave of regret. She had wanted to be Spencer's safe place, but ultimately, she had broken her heart.

Her mind trailed away from the lyrics, and she thought about everything she wished she'd done differently over the years, and then the lyrics shifted, and her attention was grabbed once more as a new verse came over the stereo.

I thought I was unworthy, sure you'd leave me here alone, but you deserved to receive just as much love as I was shown. You shouldn't have to be the only one casting light across the sky. You be the sun, and I'll be the moon, and let's let our love shine.

She tried to process the words. The song ended and the next one on the album began to play, a heavy punk song that blasted the first few notes before Spencer hit the stop button.

"I was selfish," Spencer said. "And I was scared."

She didn't know what to say, so she waited for Spencer to continue, but hope blossomed in her chest.

"I wasn't there for you like I should have been," Spencer said. "It wasn't fair of me to leap to conclusions, pressure you to come out, or get upset that you didn't want to wear a piercing. That's not who I am, and that's not who I want to be. I don't care if you have a nose piercing or not, and I know how scary coming out is and that it's something you should do in your own time when you're ready. I should have supported you, but instead I expected you to be there for me and I gave you nothing in return."

"You've said, 'people don't change,'" Faith said, finding her voice finally. "But how could you not see how different I am now? I divorced Brett. I followed my own career path, despite the pressure to join my dad's law firm. I jumped out of a freaking airplane. I'm not the same scared kid I was in high school. I'm still scared sometimes, yes, but that's not all of who I am. I've grown and you didn't see that."

Spencer's head dropped a little, and Faith could see the weight of the shame on Spencer's shoulders. Maybe she hadn't heard Faith before, but she heard her now.

"The truth is," Spencer said, "I *have* seen how much you've grown and changed. It wasn't that I didn't believe you were capable of being different, it was that deep down, I didn't believe I was worthy of anything different. I had the message '*I'm not good enough*' stuck in my head, and that stemmed from more than just our high school breakup. I've felt it in every aspect of my life. I felt worthless."

"How can you say that?" Faith asked. "Look at you. You're talented and successful. Your band is the envy of every other band struggling to make it across the country right now. You're a role model to so many teens and youth, and not just the ones you've worked with directly. They listen to your music and idolize you."

"My life has turned around in the years since high school, but the belief was pretty deep-rooted. When Haley came in and played her song about wanting her mom's protection and not receiving it, my own sense of betrayal came flooding back. The thought *I wasn't worth protecting* became deafening. When you took out your piercing, it should have been inconsequential, but all I could think was *See? She thinks I'm not polished and professional. I'm not good enough. Just like before. She left me once and she'll leave me again.*"

Faith moved so she sat cross-legged in front of Spencer, and she rested her hands on Spencer's knees which were bent up toward her chest.

"I'm sorry I left you for Brett," she said. "It was the biggest mistake of my life. Not just because marrying Brett was an awful decision on its own, and not just because it cost me the chance to be with you, but because I was cowardly and insensitive in how I handled the situation."

Spencer met her eyes, and Faith choked up at the emotion she saw play across her face.

"I always wondered why you cared so much about what others thought, and tried so hard to protect their feelings, yet you didn't care enough to protect mine."

Faith shook her head, desperate for Spencer to understand. "I spent my entire life being the person I was *supposed* to be. I never had the chance to know who I was. Dating you in high school was the only thing I'd *ever* done for myself, and I didn't know how to stand up and say 'this is who I am.' All I knew was how to conform to expectations."

Spencer nodded and said softly, "I know that now, and I don't want to be one more person placing expectations on you. I love you, and I don't want shame to keep us apart anymore. I was scared and stupid. I want to be with you. I *love* you."

"Really?" The word bubbled up out of Faith's chest, hopeful and earnest.

"Faith, you're the most admirable woman I've ever met. I'm so in awe of you every day. You've used your own hurt to spend your life helping others. You give of yourself to everyone you meet. I love you, I respect you, and I want to be with you. Forever if you'll have me. I won't run again, I promise, even if I feel scared."

She swallowed the emotion that rose in her throat and said, "I came out to my parents."

Spencer's eyes widened.

"I want to be with you, too," she said. "You're the only person I've ever truly loved. And I want you to know that I love myself enough now to stand up for who I am. I want you, and I love you, and I'm not going to let the expectations of others dictate my life anymore. I won't repeat my mistake."

Spencer kissed her then, before she could say anything else, and Faith fell forward into her, all of the loss and longing melting away until there was nothing left between them but love.

"You're it for me, Spencer Adams," she said when she broke the kiss.

She didn't know what the future held, but she knew she wanted a life of love and adventure with Spencer.

The rest would figure itself out.

Epilogue

Spencer waited with bated breath as Mark Harmon, the producer for their new album, listened to *The Sun and the Moon*, the name the band had settled on for the track written for Faith. She was relatively confident about the rest of the album they were presenting, but *The Sun and the Moon* was a risk, both personally and professionally. In every sense, she was putting herself out on a limb, and she had no idea what kind of reaction to anticipate.

"You're singing," he stated, glancing over at her, with both his expression and tone completely unreadable.

"I am." She hoped her voice didn't sound as shaky and uncertain as she felt. "It's a song that's personal to me, and we decided I was the best person to do the vocals because of the emotion behind the lyrics."

He didn't reply, other than to hold up a hand to quiet her while he listened to the rest of the track.

Spencer could feel the same nerves radiating off the rest of the band. Sienna reached out and gave her hand a squeeze.

The four of them were all going into the meeting with Mark with equal parts excitement and abject terror. Their hearts and souls had been poured into the songs, and this was the day when they would finally find out if all their work was any good, or if they'd be back to the drawing board and behind schedule.

The song faded out and the next one began. Mark didn't offer any feedback, and while she had expected as much after the silence that had met the previous two tracks, she still had to suppress a groan at the realization she would have to wait until the entire album finished to get any word on whether or not their musical gamble had paid off.

The track list sat on the table in front of him, and he held a printout of the lyrics, which he read through as he listened. Everything was laid out, bare and vulnerable, for his judgment.

From start to finish, the album was just under an hour, but it felt like an eternity before the final track faded. He sat silent for a long, excruciating pause, visibly thinking over everything he had just listened to, and then he turned to them and said, "I *love* it."

The entire band let out a collective breath.

"It is a really solid punk album," Mark continued, "but you've also diversified. Your music has matured miles, and I think listeners will recognize and appreciate that. I say we launch *The Sun and the Moon* as your first single, and we should consider that for the album title. The song captures the dualities between two people, the need to give and not just take, and conquering darkness. Those themes are echoed in the messages about society on the rest of the tracks which mirror that expression of light and dark, heavy and happy, day and night."

"We were thinking *Riot Here* would make a good first single," Spencer said, not sure how to process the idea of launching *The Sun and the Moon* as *the* song.

Mark tipped his head from side to side a couple of times. "That would be a great single, I agree. It's fast-paced, has a memorable hook, and a good energy. It definitely has all the components for radio play."

Spencer sensed a *but* coming.

"If you four really want to launch *Riot Here* as your single, I would be in support of that, but I'm going to recommend it be the *second* single. It's the *safe* single. It's what everyone is expecting from you four. *The Sun and the Moon* is going to come out of left field and surprise listeners, and also, it's the more accessible song for those who would normally never pick up a punk album. Consider it."

Spencer looked to the rest of the band, feeling vulnerable and terrified, and needing to know their thoughts.

"Spence," Mari began, "this was what we wanted. A song to surprise people and engage a wider audience. I think we should do it."

"I agree," Wren said.

Spencer looked to Sienna, worried about overstepping by launching a track she wasn't lead vocalist on, but she appeared the most enthusiastic of all of them. "I've told you from the start, I love this song."

Spencer turned to Mark and nodded. "Well, okay then."

"Excellent!" Mark clapped his hands together. "We'll start recording in the fall, but in the meantime, we're going to get you into the studio to record *The Sun and the Moon* so we can get it on the radio and get people listening. You'll be playing the summer festivals and doing some small-scale touring over the next few months, and you can start to play that song at every show. Really get people invested in it. We want them chomping at the bit for the rest of the album to drop first thing in the new year. You've got it all written, now it's going to be a whirlwind. Are you four ready?"

Eager nods went around the room.

"We were born ready," Sienna said.

They left the studio and stepped outside into the bright Vancouver sun. Then they erupted with cheers and high-fives and enthusiastic chatter, all four of them, it seemed, talking at once. It wasn't until that moment that Spencer realized the full weight of what Mark's reaction to the presentation meant, and the full weight of the fear they'd carried going in.

"You'd better go tell Faith that she's going to be the subject of a famous song," Sienna said, nudging her playfully.

"Yeah," Mari agreed. "Get out of here and fill your girlfriend in. The two of you have a lot to discuss."

Her girlfriend.

Spencer had thought she was living her dream after their last album found success, but now she had the musical success *and* the girl of her dreams, and everything felt, quite simply, too good to be true.

This was the life she hadn't even dared hope for.

She said goodbye to her friends and headed off to meet Faith, who'd also had a really busy day. Spencer texted to ask where she was, and then met her outside of the empty commercial building she stood admiring alongside her friend, Callie.

"Hey you," Spencer said, getting out of her car and forcing herself to walk, not run, down the sidewalk toward Faith, trying to play it cool and keep her excitement under wraps.

"So," Faith urged, "how did it go?"

"Oh, you know . . ." she said half-heartedly, giving a single-shoulder shrug.

She watched the concern and confusion and anticipation all play across Faith's face for a moment.

Then, she couldn't contain the excitement any longer, and the grin broke through her cool facade. "He *loved* it!"

Faith gave a little shriek, pushed Spencer's shoulder in mock anger, and then pulled her in for a kiss.

"I *knew* it," Faith said, breaking the kiss. "I knew he'd love it."

She still held Faith; her arms wrapped around her waist. "Want to hear the really wild part?" She peered into Faith's eyes and bit her bottom lip nervously.

Faith nodded.

She braced herself for whatever reaction Faith might have. "He wants *The Sun and the Moon* to be the album's first single."

Faith's eyes widened. "Wow. Really?"

"If you're okay with that. We could insist on another song." She backpedaled as though they hadn't already agreed to launch the song.

"You're kidding, right? Of course, I'm okay with it."

"I wanted to be sure," Spencer said, still feeling apprehensive. "It's *our* song, and it's not just about the radio play. We'll have interviews about it after the release. I mean, I don't have to tell anyone *who* the song is about, if you don't want me to."

Faith held a finger to Spencer's lips to silence her. "I'm *in* this. I told you. No more hiding. I want to live my life with you, and I want that life to be lived out in the open. Play the song. Give the interviews. Tell the world it's about me, okay?"

Spencer thought the happiness might burst from her, and she pulled Faith close, holding her tight while she waited for all of the relief and joy to settle.

"How's the property search going?" she asked at last.

Faith stepped out of Spencer's embrace and pointed to the building they stood in front of. "We're really happy with this one."

After coming out to Mandy, their friendship had dissolved, and Faith had decided to step back from her work at the dance studio.

Spencer didn't want Faith to quit dance, but her concerns about Faith giving up her passion had been short-lived, because the next day Callie had approached Faith about opening their own studio.

Callie would be the primary owner, and her parents were helping with the financial cost of getting the studio up and running, but Faith had been asked to help select a property and provide input on the overall vision for the place. They wanted to create a dance studio focused on passion, not competition. One that built up dancers of all abilities and aspirations.

Since Callie had approached Faith about the new studio, Spencer heard the passion for dance return to Faith's voice.

"I'm glad you've found the perfect place," Spencer said.

Faith looked at her, her eyes warm with love, and said, "I've told Callie I'm only going to be teaching here on a casual basis."

"So, you'll join us when we go on tour?" Spencer asked. The band would be staying fairly close to home over the summer, touring British Columbia, Alberta, and Washington, but they were already starting to book European shows for a big world tour once they released their new album. She had put it out there that she hoped Faith would be able to join them, at least for part of the tour, but she expected Faith to list the reasons why she wouldn't be able to. Spencer had braced herself for the possibility of having to spend a couple months apart in the new year.

"I've told you," Faith said. "I want to see the world. I can't think of anyone I'd rather see it with than you. This really is the dream."

Spencer beamed. "Then, let's live it out."

Acknowledgments

This book began as a light-hearted homage to a pop-punk song that I hoped would provide me with some escapism while I was off work during the early days of the pandemic, and it grew in ways that I couldn't even imagine at the time.

I have to thank the wonderful team at Bywater Books, starting with my publisher, Salem West. When I first emailed Salem about this project, she replied with some potential titles, and I knew immediately that she really *got* what I was going for with this book.

Rachel Spangler, as always, I so appreciate you as an editor, but you had an extra level of patience throughout work on this book, especially when I emailed you in a panic to say that I'd broken my USB stick and needed to restart all of my edits. Thank you for always offering honest feedback to strengthen my book, while simultaneously building me up and making me feel like the book has value even while I'm was in the weeds with it.

Thank you to Elizabeth Andersen and Nancy Squires for your attention to detail that makes my mess of words look good on the page; and thank you, Ann McMan, for always taking my words and wrapping them in the most perfect packaging.

Sandra, thank you always, both for your support as a partner and for your sharp insight as a beta reader. This book, and its characters, are stronger because of you.

Thank you to my mom, for always offering to help babysit my children so that I can carve out time for writing. You are the best mom and grandma that we could have asked for.

Thank you to my girls, Addie and Eloise, for your patience with me when I take time to write, and for forcing me to slow down and notice the little things in life. Addie you have a love of adventure that I hope never fades. Eloise, you were the best part of 2021.

I also want to thank my writing friends for making this career less isolating. Anna and Samara, I admire you both as writers, and our group chats help keep me motivated and on track (somewhat); Josh, thank you for your endless positivity and encouragement; and Bryan, thank you for opening your home and giving me a little writing retreat while I was stuck on a difficult draft.

And finally, to my readers, thank you for reading this book, and for all of the kind words you've left for me. I am infinitely grateful that I get to put books out into the world and will forever be in awe that there are people out there reading them.

About the Author

Jenn Alexander is an award-winning author from Edmonton, Canada, where she also works in community mental health. She has been writing for as long as she can remember, but her first novel, *Song of the Sea*, was released in 2019, and she is forever grateful to have the opportunity to put her words out into the world. Her spare time is typically spent playing drums, traveling, and seeking outdoor adventures with her family. She lives with her partner, Sandra, and their two daughters, Addison and Eloise. *Live It Out* is her third novel, and she is already hard at work on her fourth (and fifth).

At Bywater, we love good books by and about women, just like you do. And we're committed to bringing the best of contemporary literature to an expanding community of readers. Our editorial team is dedicated to finding and developing outstanding writers who create books you won't want to put down.

For more information about Bywater Books, our authors, and our titles, please visit our website.

www.bywaterbooks.com

CPSIA information can be obtained
at www.ICGtesting.com
Printed in the USA
JSHW081242090223
37449JS00005B/5